Shallow Soil

Shallow Soil

by Knut Hamsun

Copyright © 6/25/2015
Jefferson Publication

ISBN-13: 978-1514711408

Printed in the United States of America

All rights reserved. No part of this book may be reprinted or reproduced or utilized in any form or by any electronic, mechanical, or other means, now known or hereafter invented, including photocopying and recording, or in any form of storage or retrieval system, without prior permission in writing from the publisher.'

Contents

PREFACE 4
PROLOGUE 6
I 6
II 7
III 11
IV 16
V 18
VI 28
GERMINATION 30
I 30
II 34
III 38
IV 42
V 46
VI 53
RIPENING 56
I 56
II 59
III 65
IV 67
V 70
VI 75
SIXTYFOLD 78
I 78
II 83
III 88
IV 91
V 95
VI 99
FINALE 101
I 101
II 102

III	107
IV	110
V	112
VI	115
VII	116
VIII	118
IX	121
X	124

PREFACE

In the autumn of 1888 a Danish magazine published a few chapters of an autobiographical novel which instantly created the greatest stir in literary circles throughout Europe. At that time Ibsen, Björnson, Brandes, Strindberg, and other Scandinavian writers were at the height of their cosmopolitan fame, and it was only natural that the reading world should keep in close touch with the literary production of the North. But even the professional star-gazers, who maintained a vigilant watch on northern skies, had never come across the name of Knut Hamsun. He was unknown; whatever slight attention his earlier struggles for recognition may have attracted was long ago forgotten. And now he blazed forth overnight, with meteoric suddenness, with a strange, fantastic, intense brilliance which could only emanate from a star of the first magnitude.

Sudden as was Hamsun's recognition, however, it has proved lasting. The story of his rise from obscurity to fame is one of absorbing interest. Behind that hour of triumph lay a long and bitter struggle, weary years of striving, of constant and courageous battle with a destiny that strewed his path with disappointments and defeats, overwhelming him with adversities that would have swamped a genius of less energy and real power.

Knut Hamsun began life in one of the deep Norwegian valleys familiar to English readers through Björnson's earlier stories. He was born in August, 1860. When he was four years old his poverty-stricken parents sent him to an uncle, a stern, unlovely man who made his home on one of the Lofoten Islands—that "Drama in Granite" which Norway's rugged coast-line flings far into the Arctic night. Here he grew up, a taciturn, peculiar lad, inured to hardship and danger, in close communion with nature; dreaming through the endless northern twilight, revelling through the brief intense summer, surrounded by influences and by an atmosphere which later were to give to his production its strange, mystical colouring, its pendulum-swings from extreme to extreme.

At seventeen he was apprenticed to a cobbler, and while working at his trade he wrote and, at the cost of no one knows what sacrifices, saved enough money to have his first literary efforts printed and published. They consisted of a long, fantastic poem and a novel, "Björger"—the latter a grotesque conglomeration of intense self-analytical studies. These attracted far less attention than they really deserved. However, the cobbler's bench saw no more of Knut Hamsun.

During the next twelve years he led the life of a rover, but a rover with a fixed purpose from which he never swerved. First he turned his face toward Christiania, the capital and the intellectual centre of the country; and in order to get there he worked at anything that offered itself. He was a longshoreman on Bodö's docks, a road-labourer, a lumberjack in the mountains; a private tutor and court messenger. Finally he reached the metropolis and enrolled as a student at the university. But the gaunt, raw-boned youth, unpractical and improvident, overbearing of manner, passionately independent in thought and conduct, failed utterly in his attempts to realise whatever ambitions he had cherished. So it was hardly strange that this the first chapter of his Odyssey should end in the steerage of an American-bound emigrant steamer.

In America, where he landed penniless, he turned his strong and capable hands to whatever labour he could find. He had intended to become a Unitarian minister. Instead of doing so he had to work as a farm-hand on the prairie, street-car conductor in Chicago, dairyman in Dakota; and he varied these pursuits by giving a series of lectures on French literature in Minneapolis. By that time he probably imagined that he was equipped for a more successful attack on the literary strongholds of his own country, and returned to Christiania. Disappointments and privations followed more bitter than any he had ever known. He starved and studied and dreamed; vainly he made the most desperate attempts to gain recognition. In despair he once more abandoned the battle-field and fled to America again, with the avowed purpose of gaining a reputation on the lecture platform.

Once more he failed; his countrymen resident in the Northwest would have none of him. Beaten back in every attempt, discouraged, perhaps feeling the need of solitude and the opportunities for introspective thought which he could not find in the larger cities, he exiled himself to that most desolate of existences, a life on a Newfoundland fishing-smack. Three long years he spent as one of a rude crew with whom he could have nothing in common save the daily death-struggle with the elements. But these years finished the preparatory stage of Hamsun's education. During the solitary watches he matured as an artist and as a man. In his very first effort upon his return to civilisation he proved that the days of aimless fumblings were over: in "Hunger" he stands suddenly revealed as a master of style and description, a bold and independent thinker, a penetrating, keen psychologist, a realist of marked virility.

Since "Hunger" was written Hamsun has published over thirty large works— novels, dramas, travel descriptions, essays, and poems. Every one of them is of a high order. Each is unlike the rest; but through them all flash in vivid gleams a dazzling witchery of style, a bewildering originality, a passionate nature-worship, and an imagination which at times takes away the breath.

"Shallow Soil," in some respects the most contained of Hamsun's works, is perhaps best suited as a medium for his introduction to Anglo-Saxon readers. In a very complete analysis of Hamsun's authorship the German literary critic, Professor Carl Morburger, thus refers to "Shallow Soil":

"Not only is this book Knut Hamsun's most significant work, but it gives the very best description available of life in Christiania toward the close of the century. A book of exquisite lyric beauty, of masterly psychology, and finished artistic form, it is so rich in idea and life that one must refrain from touching on the contents in order to keep within the narrow limits of this essay. A most superbly delicate delineation of the feminine soul is here given in the drawing of Hanka and Aagot; nowhere else is woman's love in its dawn and growth described with such mastery, with a deftness and sureness of touch which reminds one of the very greatest passages in that Danish classic, 'Niels Lyhne.'"

Hamsun is now in his fifty-fourth year. The expectations aroused by his first book have been more than fulfilled; the star that was born overnight still shines with undimmed brilliance—nay, with a purer, warmer, steadier flame. The volcanic violence of earlier days has been mellowed and subdued; the "red eruptions of flame-tongued, primeval power" have all but ceased. In one of his latest works Hamsun himself notes this change in saying: "When a wanderer reaches fifty years he plays with muted strings." But with or without the sordine Hamsun's production is equally seductive, equally entrancing and compelling. All over the continent of Europe he is known and his writings treasured; in Russia his popularity exceeds that of many of its own inimitable writers. It is to be expected that the English-speaking world will accord him that appreciation which is the natural tribute to genius, irrespective of language or clime.

CARL CHR. HYLLESTED.
NEW YORK, December, 1913.

PROLOGUE

I

A faint, golden, metallic rim appears in the east where the sun is rising. The city is beginning to stir; already can be heard an occasional distant rumble of trucks rolling into the streets from the country, large farm-wagons heavily loaded with supplies for the markets—with hay and meat and cordwood. And these wagons make more noise than usual because the pavements are still brittle from nightly frosts. It is the latter part of March.

Everything is quiet around the harbour. Here and there a sleepy sailor tumbles out of a forecastle; smoke is curling from the galleys. A skipper puts his head out of a companionway and sniffs toward the weather; the sea stretches in undisturbed calm; all the winches are at rest.

The first wharf gate is thrown open. Through it one catches a glimpse of sacks and cases piled high, of cans and barrels; men with ropes and wheelbarrows are moving around, still half asleep, yawning openly with angular, bearded jaws. And barges are warped in alongside the docks; another army begins the hoisting and stowing of goods, the loading of wagons, and the moving of freight.

In the streets one door after another is opened; blinds are raised, office-boys are sweeping floors and dusting counters. In the H. Henriksen office the son is sitting at a desk, all alone; he is sorting mail. A young gentleman is strolling, tired and sleepy, toward the railway square; he comes from a late party given in some comrade's den and is taking the morning air. At Fire Headquarters he runs across an acquaintance who has also been celebrating.

"Abroad so early, Ojen?" asks the first stroller.

"Yes—that is to say, I haven't been in bed yet!"

"Neither have I," laughs the first. "Good night!"

And he wanders on, smiling in amusement over that good night on a bright and sunny morning. He is a young and promising man; his name had suddenly become famous two years ago when he published a lyric drama. His name is Irgens; everybody knows him. He wears patent-leather shoes and is good-looking, with his curled moustache and his sleek, dark hair.

He drifts from one market square to another; it amuses him, sleepy as he is, to watch the farmers who are invading the public squares with their trucks. The spring sun has browned their faces; they wear heavy mufflers around their necks, and their hands are sinewy and dirty. They are in such a hurry to sell their wares that they even hail him, a youth of twenty-four without a family, a lyric writer who is simply loitering at random in order to divert himself.

The sun climbs higher. Now people begin to swarm in all directions; shrill whistles are heard, now from the factories in the city suburbs, now from the railway stations and docks; the traffic increases. Busy workers dart hither and thither—some munching their breakfast from newspaper parcels. A man pushes an enormous load of bundles on a push-cart, he is delivering groceries; he strains like a horse and reads addresses from a note-book as he hurries along. A child is distributing morning papers; she is a little girl who has Saint Vitus's dance; she jerks her angular body in all directions, twitches her shoulders, blinks, hustles from door to door, climbs the stairs in the high-storied houses, presses bells, and hurries on, leaving papers on every doorstep. A dog follows her and makes every trip with her.

Traffic and noise increase and spread; beginning at the factories, the wharves, the shipyards, and the sawmills, they mingle with wagon rumblings and human voices; the air is rent by steam-whistles whose agonising wails rise skyward, meeting and blending above the large squares in a booming diapason, a deep-throated, throbbing roar that enwraps the entire city. Telegraph messengers dart hither and yon, scattering orders and quotations from distant markets. The powerful, vitalising chant of commerce booms through the air; the wheat in India, the coffee in Java promise well; the Spanish markets are crying for fish—enormous quantities of fish during Lent.

It is eight o'clock; Irgens starts for home. He passes H. Henriksen's establishment and decides to drop in a moment. The son of the house, a young man in a business suit of cheviot, is still busy at his desk. His eyes are large and blue, although his complexion is rather dark otherwise; a stray wisp of hair sags untidily over his forehead. The tall, somewhat gaunt and taciturn fellow looks about thirty years old. His comrades value him highly because he helps them a good deal with money and articles of commerce from the firm's cellars.

"Good morning!" calls Irgens.

The other looks up in surprise.

"What—you? Are you abroad so early?"

"Yes. That is to say, I haven't been to bed yet."

"Oh—that's different. I have been at my desk since five; I have cabled to three countries already."

"Good Lord—you know I am not the least interested in your trading! There is only one thing I want to discuss with you, Ole Henriksen; have you got a drink of brandy?"

The two men leave the office and pass through the store down into the cellar. Ole Henriksen pulls a cork hurriedly; his father is expected any moment, and for this reason he is in haste. The father is old, but that is no reason why he should be ignored.

Irgens drinks and says: "Can I take the bottle along?" And Ole Henriksen nods.

On their way back through the store he pulls out a drawer from the counter, and Irgens, who understands the hint, takes something from the drawer which he puts in his mouth. It is coffee, roasted coffee; good for the breath.

II

At two o'clock people swarm up and down the promenade. They chat and laugh in all manner of voices, greet each other, smile, nod, turn around, shout. Cigar smoke and ladies' veils flutter in the air; a kaleidoscopic confusion of light gloves and handkerchiefs, of bobbing hats and swinging canes, glides down the street along which carriages drive with ladies and gentlemen in stylish attire.

Several young gentlemen have taken their accustomed stand at "The Corner." They form a circle of acquaintances—a couple of artists, a couple of authors, a business man, an undefinable—comrades all. They are dressed variously: some have already dispensed with their overcoats, others wear long ulsters with turned-up collars as in midwinter. Everybody knows "the clique."

Some join it while others depart; there remain a young, corpulent artist by the name of Milde, and an actor with a snub nose and a creamy voice; also Irgens, and Attorney Grande of the prominent Grande family. The most important, however, is Paulsberg, Lars Paulsberg, the author of half a dozen novels and a scientific work on the Atonement. He is loudly referred to as the Poet, even though both Irgens and Ojen are present.

The Actor buttons his ulster tightly and shivers.

"No—spring-time is a little too chilly to suit me," he says.

"The contrary here!" exclaims the Attorney. "I could shout all the time; I am neighing inwardly; my blood sings a hunting chorus!" And the little stooping youth straightens his shoulders and glances secretly at Paulsberg.

"Listen to that!" says the Actor sarcastically. "A man is a man, as the eunuch said."

"What does that remark signify?"

"Nothing, God bless you! But you in your patent leathers and your silk hat hunting wolves—the idea appealed to my sense of humour."

"Ha, ha! I note the fact that Norem has a sense of humour! Let us duly appreciate it."

They spoke with practised ease about everything, had perfect control over their words, made quick sallies, and were skilled in repartee.

A number of cadets were passing.

"Did you ever see anything as flabby as these military youths!" said Irgens. "Look at them; they do not walk past like other mortals, they *stalk* past!"

Both Irgens and the Artist laughed at this, but the Attorney glanced quickly at Paulsberg, whose face remained immovable. Paulsberg made a few remarks about the Art Exhibition and was silent.

The conversation drifted to yesterday's performance in Tivoli, and from there to political subjects. Of course, they could refuse to pass all financial bills, but—And perhaps there was not even a sufficient majority to defeat the government budget. It certainly looked dubious— rotten—They cited quotations from leading parliamentarians, they proposed to put the torch to the Castle and proclaim the republic without delay. The Artist threatened a general revolt of the labouring classes. "Do you know what the Speaker told me in confidence? That he never, *never* would agree to a compromise—rather let the Union sink or swim! 'Sink or swim,' these were his very words. And when one knows the Speaker—"

Still Paulsberg did not say anything, and as the comrades were eager to hear his opinion, the Attorney finally ventured to address him:

"And you, Paulsberg, you don't say a word?"

Paulsberg very seldom spoke; he had kept to himself and to his studies and his literary tasks, and lacked the verbal facility of his comrades. He smiled good-naturedly and answered:

"'Let your communication be Yea, yea, and Nay, nay,' you know!" At this they all laughed loudly. "But otherwise," he added, "apart from that I am seriously considering going home to my wife."

And Paulsberg went. It was his wont to go when he said he would.

But after Paulsberg's departure it seemed as if they might as well all go; there was no reason to remain now. The Actor saluted and disappeared; he hurried off in order to catch up with Paulsberg. The Painter threw his ulster around himself without buttoning it, drew up his shoulders, and said:

"I feel rotten! If a fellow could only afford a little dinner!"

"You must try and strike a huckster," said Irgens. "I struck one for a brandy this morning."

"I am wondering what Paulsberg really meant by that remark," said the Attorney. "'Your communication shall be Yea, yea, and Nay, nay'; it is evident it had a deeper meaning."

"Yes, very evident," said Milde. "Did you notice, he laughed when he said it; something must have amused him."

Pause.

A crowd of promenaders were sauntering continually up and down the street, back and forth, laughing and talking.

Milde continued:

"I have often wished that we had just one more head like Paulsberg's here in Norway."

"And why, pray?" asked Irgens stiffly.

Milde stared at him, stared at the Attorney, and burst into a surprised laugh.

"Listen to that, Grande! He asks why we need another head like Paulsberg's in this country!"

"I do," said Irgens.

But Grande did not laugh either, and Milde was unable to understand why his words failed to provoke mirth. He decided to pass it off; he began to speak about other things.

"You said you struck a huckster for brandy; you have got brandy, then?"

"As for me, I place Paulsberg so high that I consider him *alone* able to do what is needed," said Irgens with thinly veiled sarcasm.

This took Milde by surprise; he was not prepared to contradict Irgens; he nodded and said:

"Certainly—exactly. I only thought it might accelerate matters to have a little assistance, so to speak—a brother in arms. But of course I agree with you."

Outside the Grand Hotel they were fortunate enough to run across Tidemand, a huckster also, a wholesaler, a big business man, head of a large and well-known business house.

"Have you dined?" called the Artist to him.

"Lots of times!" countered Tidemand.

"Now, no nonsense! Are you going to take me to dinner?"

"May I be permitted to shake hands first?"

It was finally arranged that they should take a run up to Irgens's rooms to sample the brandy, after which they were to return to the Grand for dinner. Tidemand and the Attorney walked ahead.

"It is a good thing that we have these peddlers to fall back on," said Milde to Irgens. "They are useful after all."

Irgens replied with a shrug of the shoulders which might mean anything.

"And they never consider that they are being imposed upon," continued Milde. "On the contrary, they think they are highly favoured; it flatters them. Treat them familiarly, drink their health, that is sufficient. Ha, ha, ha! Isn't it true?"

The Attorney had stopped; he was waiting.

"While we remember it, we have got to make definite arrangements about that farewell celebration for Ojen," he said.

Of course, they had almost forgotten about that. Certainly, Ojen was going away; something had to be done.

The situation was this: Ojen had written two novels which had been translated into German; now his nerves were bothering him; he could not be allowed to kill himself with work—something had to be done to procure him a highly needed rest. He had applied for a government subsidy and had every expectation of receiving it; Paulsberg himself had recommended him, even if a little tepidly. The comrades had therefore united in an effort to get him to Torahus, to a little mountain resort where the air was splendid for neurasthenics. Ojen was to go in about a week; the money had been raised; both Ole Henriksen and Tidemand had been exceedingly generous. It now only remained to arrange a little celebration to speed the parting comrade.

"But where shall we find a battle-ground?" asked Milde. "At your house, Grande? You have plenty of room?"

Grande was not unwilling; it might be arranged; he would speak to his wife about it. For Grande was married to Mrs. Liberia, and Mrs. Liberia simply had to be consulted. It was agreed to invite Paulsberg and his wife; as contributors Mr. and Mrs. Tidemand and Ole Henriksen were coming as a matter of course. That was settled.

"Ask whom you like, but I refuse to open my doors to that fellow Norem," said the Attorney. "He always gets drunk and sentimental; he is an awful bore. My wife wouldn't stand for him."

Then the affair could not be held at Grande's house. It would never do to slight Norem. In the perplexity Milde offered his studio.

The friends considered. It was not a bad idea; a better place would be hard to find. The studio was big and roomy as a barn, with two cosy adjoining rooms. Milde's studio, then—settled.

The affair was coming off in a few days.

The four gentlemen stopped at Irgens's place, drank his brandy, and went out again. The Attorney was going home; this decision about the studio did not suit him; he felt slighted. He might decide to stay away altogether. At any rate, he said good-bye now and went his own way.

"What about you, Irgens—I hope you will join us?"

Irgens did not say no; he did not at all refuse this invitation. To tell the truth, he was not unduly eager to return to the Grand; this fat artist vexed him considerably with his familiar manners. However, he might be able to get away immediately after the dinner was over.

In this desire Tidemand himself unconsciously assisted him; he left as soon as he had paid the check. He was going somewhere.

III

Tidemand made his way to H. Henriksen's large warehouse on the wharf where he knew that Ole could be found at this time.

Tidemand had passed thirty and was already getting a little grey around the temples. He, too, was dark of hair and beard, but his eyes were brown and had a listless expression. When he was sitting still and silent, blinking slowly, these heavy lids of his would rise and sink almost as if they were exhausted by much watching. He was beginning to get a little bit stout. He was considered an exceedingly able business man.

He was married and had two children; he had been married four years. His marriage had begun auspiciously and was still in force, although people were at a loss to understand how it could possibly last. Tidemand himself did not conceal his astonishment over the fact that his wife had managed to tolerate him so long. He had been a bachelor too long, had travelled too much, lived too much in hotels; he admitted it himself. He liked to ring whenever he wanted anything; he preferred his meals served at all hours, whenever he took a notion, no matter if it happened to be meal-time or not. And Tidemand went into details: he could not bear to have his wife serve him his soup, for instance—was it possible for a woman, even with the best intention in the world, to divine how much soup he might want?

And, on the other side, there was Mrs. Hanka, an artistic nature, two and twenty, fond of life and audacious as a boy. Mrs. Hanka was greatly gifted and warmly interested in many things; she was a welcome guest wherever the youthful assembled, whether in homes or bachelor dens; nobody could resist her. No, she did not greatly care for home life or house drudgery. She could not help that; unfortunately she had not inherited these tastes. And this unbearable blessing, of a child every year two years running, drove her almost to distraction. Good Lord! she was only a child herself, full of life and frivolity; her youth was ahead of her. But pursuant to the arrangement the couple had made last year, Mrs. Hanka now found it unnecessary to place any restraint upon herself....

Tidemand entered the warehouse. A cool and tart smell of tropical products, of coffee and oils and wines, filled the atmosphere. Tall piles of tea-boxes, bundles of cinnamon sewn in bast, fruits, rice, spices, mountains of flour-sacks—everything had its designated place, from floor to roof. In one of the corners a stairway led to the cellar, where venerable hogsheads of wine with copper bands could be glimpsed in the half-light and where enormous metal tanks rested in massive repose.

Tidemand nodded to the busy warehousemen, walked across the floor, and peeped through the pane into the little office. Ole was there. He was revising an account on a slate.

Ole put the slate down immediately and rose to meet his friend.

These two men had known each other since childhood, had gone through the business college together, and shared with each other their happiest moments. Even now, when they were competitors, they continued to visit each other as often as their work would permit. They did not envy each other; the business spirit had made them broad-minded and generous; they toyed with ship-loads, dealt in large amounts, had daily before their eyes enormous successes or imposing ruin.

Once Tidemand had expressed admiration for a little yacht which Ole Henriksen owned. It was two years ago, when it was known that the Tidemand firm had suffered heavy losses in a fish exportation. The yacht lay anchored just outside the Henriksen warehouse and attracted much attention because of its beautiful lines. The masthead was gilded.

Tidemand said:

"This is the most beautiful little dream I have ever seen, upon my word!"

Ole Henriksen answered modestly:

"I do not suppose I could get a thousand for her if I were to sell her."

"I'll give you a thousand," offered Tidemand.

Pause. Ole smiled.

"Cash?" he asked.

"Yes; I happen to have it with me."

And Tidemand took out his pocketbook and paid over the money.

This occurred in the warehouse. The clerks laughed, whispered, and wondered.

A few days later Ole went over to Tidemand's office and said:

"I don't suppose you would take two thousand for the yacht?"

"Have you got the money with you?"

"Yes; it just happens that I have."

"All right," said Tidemand.

And the yacht was Ole's once more....

Tidemand had called on Ole now in order to pass away an hour or so. The two friends were no longer children; they treated each other with the greatest courtesy and were sincerely fond of each other.

Ole got hold of Tidemand's hat and cane, which he put away, at the same time pointing his friend to a seat on the little sofa.

"What may I offer you?" he asked.

"Thanks—nothing," said Tidemand. "I have just had my dinner at the Grand."

Ole placed the flat box with Havanas before him and asked again:

"A little glass? An 1812?"

"Well, thank you, yes. But never mind; it is too much trouble; you have to go downstairs for it."

"Nonsense; no trouble at all!"

Ole brought the bottle from the cellar; it was impossible to tell what it was; the bottle appeared to be made of some coarse cloth, so deeply covered with dust was it. The wine was chilled and sparkling, it beaded in the glass, and Ole said:

"Here you are; drink hearty, Andreas!"

They drank. A pause ensued.

"I have really come to congratulate you," said Tidemand. "I have never yet made a stroke like that last one of yours!"

It was true that Ole had turned a trick lately. But he insisted that there really was nothing in it that entitled him to any credit; it was just a bit of luck. And if there was any credit to bestow, then it belonged to the firm, not to him. The operations in London had succeeded because of the cleverness of his agent.

The affair was as follows:

An English freight-steamer, the *Concordia*, had left Rio with half a cargo of coffee; she touched at Bathurst for a deck-load of hides, ran into the December gales on the north coast of Normandy, and sprung a leak; then she was towed into Plymouth. The cargo was water-soaked; half of it was coffee.

This cargo of damaged coffee was washed out and brought to London; it was put on the market, but could not be sold; the combination of sea-water and hides had spoiled it. The owner tried all sorts of doctorings: he used colouring matter—indigo, kurkuma, chrome, copper vitriol—he had it rolled in hogsheads with leaden bullets. Nothing availed; he had to sell it at auction. Henriksen's agent bid it in for a song.

Ole went to London; he made tests with this coffee, washed out the colouring matter, flushed it thoroughly, and dried it again. Finally he had the entire cargo roasted and packed in hermetically sealed zinc boxes. These boxes were brought to Norway after a month of storing; they were unloaded, taken to the warehouse, opened, and sold. The coffee was as good as ever. The firm made a barrel of money out of this enterprise.

Tidemand said:

"I only learned the particulars a couple of days ago; I must confess that I was proud of you!"

"My part of the business was simply the idea of roasting the coffee— making it sweat out the damage, so to speak. But otherwise, really—"

"I suppose you were a little anxious until you knew the result?"

"Yes; I must admit I was a little anxious."

"But what did your father say?"

"Oh, he did not know anything until it was all over. I was afraid to tell him; he might have disinherited me, cast me off, you know. Ha, ha!"

Tidemand looked at him.

"Hm. This is all very well, Ole. But if you want to give your father, the firm, half the credit, then you should not at the same time tell me that your father knew nothing until it was all over. I have you there!"

A clerk entered with another account on a slate; he bowed, placed the slate on the desk, and retired. The telephone rang.

"One moment, Andreas; it is probably only an order. Hello!"

Ole took down the order, rang for a clerk, and gave it to him..

"I am detaining you," said Tidemand. "Let me take one of the slates; there is one for each now!"

"Not much!" said Ole; "do you think I will let you work when you come to see me?"

But Tidemand was already busy. He was thoroughly familiar with these strange marks and figures in the many columns, and made out the account on a sheet of paper. They stood at the desk opposite each other and worked, with an occasional bantering remark.

"Don't let us forget the glasses altogether!"

"No; you are right!"

"This is the most enjoyable day I have had in a long time," said Ole.

"Do you think so? I was just going to say the same. I have just left the Grand—By the way, I have an invitation for you; we are both going to the farewell celebration for Ojen—quite a number will be there."

"Is that so? Where is it going to be?"

"In Milde's studio. You are going, I hope?"

"Yes; I will be there."

They went back to their accounts.

"Lord! do you remember the old times when we sat on the school bench together?" said Tidemand. "None of us sported a beard then. It seems as if it were only a couple of months ago, I remember it so distinctly."

Ole put down his pen. The accounts were finished.

"I should like to speak to you about something—you mustn't be offended, Andreas—No; take another glass, old fellow, do! I'll get another bottle; this wine is really not fit for company."

And he hurried out; he looked quite confused.

"What is the matter with him?" thought Tidemand.

Ole returned with another bottle, downy as velvet, with trailing cobwebs; he pulled the cork.

"I don't know how you'll like this," he said, and sniffed the glass. "Try it, anyhow; it is really—I am sure you'll like it; I have forgotten the vintage, but it is ancient."

Tidemand sniffed, sipped, put down his glass, and looked at Ole.

"It isn't half bad, is it?"

"No," said Tidemand, "it is not. You should not have done this, Ole."

"Ho! don't be silly—a bottle of wine!"

Pause.

"I thought you wanted to speak to me about something," asked Tidemand.

"Yes, well—I don't know that I do, exactly." Ole went over and locked the door. "I thought that, as you cannot possibly know anything about it, I had perhaps better tell you that people are talking about you, calumniating you, blackening your reputation, so to speak. And you hear nothing, of course."

"Are they blackening me? What are they saying?"

"Oh, you can feel above anything they say. Never mind what they say. The gossip is that you neglect your wife; that you frequent restaurants although you have a home of your own; that you leave her to herself while you enjoy life single-handed. You are above such insinuations, of course. But, anyway, why do you eat away from home and live so much in restaurants? Not that I have any business to—Say, this wine is not half bad, believe me! Take another glass; do me the favour—"

Tidemand's eyes had suddenly become clear and sharp. He got up, made a few turns across the floor, and went back to the sofa.

"I am not at all surprised that people are talking," he said. "I myself have done what I could to start the gossip; I know that only too well. But I have ceased to care about anything any more." Tidemand shrugged his shoulders and got up again. Drifting back and forth across the floor, staring fixedly straight ahead, he murmured again that he had ceased to care about anything.

"But listen, old friend, I told you you need not pay the slightest attention to such contemptible gossip," objected Ole.

"It is not true that I neglect Hanka, as people think," said Tidemand; "the fact is that I don't want to bother her. You understand, she must be allowed to do as she pleases; it is an agreement, otherwise she will leave me." During the following sentences Tidemand got up and sat down again; he was in a state of deep emotion. "I want to tell you this, Ole; it is the first time I have ever mentioned it to anybody, and no one will ever hear me repeat it. But I want you to know that I do not go to restaurants because I like to. Where else can I go? Hanka is never at home; there is no dinner, not a soul in the whole house. We have had a friendly understanding; we have ceased to keep house. Do you understand now why I am often seen in restaurants? I am not wanted; I keep to my office and go to the Grand, I meet friends of whom she is one, we sit at a table and have a good time. What should I do at home? Hanka is more likely to be at the Grand; we sit at the same table, perhaps opposite each other; we hand each other a glass, a carafe. 'Andreas,' she says, 'please order a glass for Milde, too.' And, of course, I order a glass for Milde. I like to do it; don't believe anything else! 'I have hardly seen you to-day,' she sometimes says; 'you left very early this morning. Oh, he is a fine husband!' she tells the others and laughs. I am delighted that she is in good spirits; I help her along and say: 'Who in the world could wait until you have finished your toilet; I have business to attend to!' But the truth is that perhaps I haven't seen her for a couple of days. Do you understand why I go to restaurants? I go in order to meet her after not having seen her for a couple of days; I go to spend a few moments with her and with my friends, who all are exceedingly nice to me. But, of course, everything has been arranged in the friendliest manner possible; don't think otherwise. I am sure it is all for the best; I think the arrangement excellent. It is all a matter of habit."

Ole Henriksen sat with open mouth. He said in surprise:

"Is that how matters stand? I had no idea it was that way with you two— that it was that bad."

"Why not? Do you find it strange that she prefers the clique? All of them are famous men, artists and poets, people who count for something. When you come to look at it they are not like you and me, Ole; we like to be with them ourselves. Bad, you say? No, understand me rightly, it is not at all bad. It is a good arrangement. I couldn't always get home on time from the office, and so I went to a restaurant, naturally. Hanka could not make herself ridiculous and preside at table in solitary state, and so she went to a restaurant. We do not go to the same place always; sometimes we miss each other. But that is all right."

There was a pause. Tidemand leaned his head in his hands. Ole asked:

"But who started this? Who proposed it?"

"Ha, do you think for a moment it was I? Would I be likely to say to my wife: 'You will have to go to a restaurant, Hanka, so I can find the house empty when I get home to dinner!' Hardly. But all the same, things are not so bad as you might think—What would you say if I were to tell you that she does not even regard herself as being married? Of course, you cannot realise that. I reasoned with her, said this and that, a married woman, house and home, and she answered: 'Married, did you say? That is rather an exaggeration, don't you think?' How does *that* strike you? For this reason I am careful not to say anything to her; she isn't married; that is her affair. She lives occasionally where I live, we visit the children, go in and out, and part again. It is all right as long as she is satisfied."

"But this is ridiculous!" exclaimed Ole suddenly. "I can't imagine—Does she think you are an old glove she can throw away when she is through with it? Why haven't you put your foot down?"

"Of course, I have said something like that. Then she wanted a divorce. Twice. What could I do then? I am not made so that I can tear everything up all at once; I need a little time; it will come later. She is right about the divorce; it is I who am against it; she is justified in blaming me for that. Why haven't I played the part of a man, showed her her place, made her behave? But, my dear man, she would have left me! She said so plainly; there was no misunderstanding possible; it has happened twice. What could I do?"

The two men sat awhile in silence. Ole asked quietly:

"But has your wife, then—I mean, do you think she is in love with somebody else?"

"Of course," answered Tidemand. "Such things are bound to happen; not intentionally, of course, but—"

"And you do not know who it is?"

"Don't you think I know? That is, I don't know really; how could I know for sure? I am almost certain she is not really in love with anybody; it is hard to say. Do you think that I am jealous, perhaps? Don't for a moment imagine anything, Ole; I am glad to say that I have a little sense left; not much, perhaps, but a little. In short, she is not in love with anybody else, as people suspect; it is simply a whim, a fancy. In a little while she will probably come and propose that we shall begin housekeeping again and live together; it is not at all impossible, I tell you, for I know her thoroughly. She is, at any rate, very fond of the children; I have never seen anybody so fond of children as she has been lately. You ought to come and see us some time—Do you remember when we were married?"

"I certainly do."

"She was a somewhat passable bride, what? Not at all one to be ashamed of, don't you think? Ha, ha, ha, not at all, Ole! But you ought to see her now, I mean at home, now that she is so very fond of the children again. I cannot describe her. She wears a black velvet gown—Be sure and come over some time. Sometimes she is in red, a dark red velvet— This reminds me— perhaps she is at home now; I am going to drop in; I might be able to do something for her."

The two friends emptied their glasses and stood facing each other.

"I hope everything will come out all right," said Ole.

"Oh, yes, it will," said Tidemand. "I am grateful to you, Ole; you have been a good friend to me. I haven't had such a pleasant hour as long as I can remember."

"Listen!" Tidemand turned in the doorway and said: "What we have discussed here remains between us, eh? Not a hint on Thursday; everything is as it should be as far as we are concerned, what? We are no mopes, I hope!"

And Tidemand departed.

IV

Evening falls over the town. Business rests, stores are closed, and lights are lowered. But old, grey-haired business men shut themselves in their offices, light their lamps, take out papers, open heavy ledgers, note some figures, a sum, and think. They hear the noise from the docks where steamers load and unload all night long.

It gets to be ten, eleven; the cafés are crowded and the traffic is great. All sorts of people roam the streets in their best attire; they follow each other, whistle after girls, and dart in and out from gateways and basement stairs. Cabbies stand at attention on the squares, on the lookout for the least sign from the passers-by; they gossip between themselves about their horses and smoke idly their vile pipes.

A woman hurries past—a child of night whom everybody knows; after her a sailor and a gentleman in silk hat, both eagerly stepping out to reach her first. Then two youths with cigars at an impertinent angle, hands in pockets, speaking loudly. Behind them another woman; finally, a couple of men hurrying to catch up with her.

But now one tower-clock after another booms forth the twelve solemn strokes all over the city; the cafés empty themselves, and from the music-halls crowds of people swarm into the streets. The winches are still groaning along the docks; cabs roll through the streets. But inside the hidden offices one old business chief after another has finished his accounts and his planning; the grey-headed gentlemen close their ledgers, take their hats from the rack, put out the lights, and go home.

And the last guests depart from the Grand, a crowd that has stuck to the end, young fellows, joyful souls. They saunter down the street with coats wide open, canes held jauntily under the arms, and hats slightly askew. They talk loudly, hum the latest popular air, call jestingly to a lonely, forgotten girl in a boa and white veil.

The company wanders toward the university. The conversation is about literature and politics, and, although nobody contradicts them, they are loud and eager: Was Norway a sovereign state or not? Was Norway perhaps not entitled to the rights and privileges of a sovereign state? Just wait a moment, the Speaker had promised to attend to things; besides, there were the elections.... All were agreed, the elections would decide.

Three of the gentlemen part from the group when the university is reached; the remaining two take another turn down the street, stop outside the Grand, and exchange opinions. It is Milde and Ojen. Milde is highly indignant.

"I repeat: If Parliament yields this time, it is me for Australia. In that case it will be unbearable here."

Ojen is young and nervous; his little, round, girlish face is pale and void of expression; he squints as if he were near-sighted, although his eyes are good, and his voice is soft and babyish.

"I am unable to understand that all this can interest you so greatly. It is all one to me." And Ojen shrugs his shoulders; he is tired of politics. His shoulders slope effeminately.

"Oh well, I won't detain you," says Milde. "By the way, have you written anything lately?"

"A couple of prose poems," replies Ojen, brightening at once. "I am waiting to get off to Torahus so I can start in in earnest. You are right —this town is unbearable!"

"Well—I had the whole country in mind, though—Say, don't forget next Thursday evening in my studio. By the way, old fellow, have you got a crown or so you could spare?"

Ojen unbuttons his coat and finds the crown.

"Thanks, old man. Thursday evening, then. Come early so that you can help me a little with the arrangements—Good Lord, silk lining! And I who asked you for a miserable crown! I hope I did not offend you."

Ojen smiles and pooh-poohs the joke.

"As if one sees anything nowadays but silk-lined clothes!"

"By Jove! What do they soak you for a coat like that?" And Milde feels the goods appraisingly.

"Oh, I don't remember; I never can remember figures; that is out of my line. I put all my tailor bills away; I come across them whenever I move."

"Ha, ha, ha! that is certainly a rational system, most practical. For I do not suppose you ever pay them!"

"In God's own time, as the Bible says—Of course, if I ever get rich, then—But I want you to go now. I must be alone."

"All right, good night. But listen, seriously speaking: if you have another crown to spare—"

And once more Ojen unbuttons his coat.

"A thousand thanks! Oh, you poets, you poets! Where, for instance, may you be going now?"

"I think I'll walk here awhile, and look at houses. I can't sleep, so I count the windows; it is not such a bad occupation at times. I take an exquisite pleasure in satiating my vision with squares and rectangles, with pure lines. Of course, you cannot understand such things."

"I should say I did understand—no one better! But I prefer human beings. Don't you at times—flesh and blood, humans, eh—they have their attraction, don't you think?"

"I am ashamed to say it, but people weary me. No; take for instance the sweep of a solitary, deserted street—have you never noticed the charm of such a view?"

"Haven't I? I am not blind, not entirely. A desolate street, of course, has its own beauty, its own charm, in its kind the highest charm imaginable. But everything in its place—Well, I must not detain you! *Au revoir*—Thursday!"

Milde saluted with his cane, turned, and strolled up the street. Ojen continued alone. He proved a few moments afterward that he had not lost all his interest in human beings; he had calumniated himself. To the very first hussy who hailed him he gave, absent-mindedly, every penny he had left, and continued his way in silence. He had not spoken a word; his slender, nervous figure disappeared in the darkness before the girl could even manage to thank him—

And at last everything is still; the winches fall to rest along the wharves; the town has turned in. From afar, nobody knows from where, comes the sound of a single footfall; the gas flames flicker in the street lamps; two policemen talk to each other, occasionally stamping their feet to keep warm.

Thus the night passes. Human footsteps here and there; now and then a policeman who stamps his feet to keep warm.

V

A barnlike room with blue walls and sliding windows, a sort of drying-loft with a stove in the middle, and with stovepipes hanging in wires along the ceiling. The walls are decorated with a number of sketches, painted fans, and palettes; several framed pictures lean against the wainscoting. Smell of paints and tobacco smoke; brushes, tubes, overcoats which the guests had thrown aside; an old rubber shoe filled with nails and junk; on the easel in the corner a large, half-finished portrait of Paulsberg.

This was Milde's studio.

When Ole Henriksen entered about nine o'clock all the guests were assembled, also Tidemand and his wife. There were altogether ten or twelve people. The three lamps were covered with opaque shades, and the heavy tobacco smoke did not make the room any lighter. This obscurity was evidently Mrs. Hanka's idea. A couple of very young gentlemen, beardless students with bachelor degrees, were of the party; they were poets who had put aside their studies last year. Their heads were so closely cropped as to be almost entirely naked. One of them carried a small compass on his watch-chain. They were Ojen's comrades, his admirers and pupils; both wrote verses.

Besides these, one noticed a man from the *Gazette*, Journalist Gregersen, the literary member of the staff. He was a man who did his friends many a favour and published in his paper many an item concerning them. Paulsberg showed him the greatest deference, and conversed with him about his series, "New Literature," which he found admirable; and the Journalist was happy and proud because of this approbation. He had a peculiar habit of twisting words so that they sounded odd and absurd, and nobody could turn this trick as smartly as he.

"It is rather difficult to write such a series within reasonable limits," he says. "There are so many authors that have to be included—a veritable choas!"

He makes Paulsberg smile over this "choas," and they talk on in the best of harmony.

Attorney Grande and his wife were absent.

"So the Attorney is not coming," says Mrs. Hanka Tidemand, without referring to his wife. Mrs. Liberia never came, anyway.

"He sulks," said Milde, and drank with Norem, the Actor. "He did not want to come because Norem was invited."

Nobody felt the least constraint; they chatted about everything, drank, and made plenty of noise. It was a splendid place, Milde's studio; as soon as one got inside the door one felt free to do or say anything one's inclination prompted.

Mrs. Hanka is seated on the sofa; Ojen sits beside her. On the other side of the table sits Irgens; the light falls across his narrow chest. Mrs. Hanka hardly glances at him.

She is in her red velvet gown; her eyes have a greenish sheen. Her upper lip is slightly raised. One glimpses her teeth and marvels at their whiteness. The face is fresh and the complexion clear. Her beautiful forehead is not hidden beneath her hair; she carries it sweetly and candidly, like a nun. A couple of rings flash on her fingers. She breathes deeply and says to Irgens, across the table:

"How hot it is here, Irgens!"

Irgens gets up and goes over to open a window, but a voice is raised in protest; it is Mrs. Paulsberg's. "For Heaven's sake, no open windows. Come away from the sofa; it is cooler further back!"

And Mrs. Hanka gets up. Her movements are undulating. When she stands up she is like a young girl, with bold shoulders. She does not glance into the large, cracked mirror as she passes; she exhales no odours of perfumes; she takes, accidentally, her husband's arm and walks up and down with him while the conversation and the refreshments keep the other guests at the table.

Tidemand is talking, with somewhat forced liveliness, about a cargo of grain, a certain Fürst in Riga, a raise in customs duties somewhere. Suddenly he says, bending toward her:

"Yes; I am very happy to-day. But, pardon me, you are hardly interested in these things—Did you see Ida before you left? Wasn't she sweet in her white dress? We'll get her a carriage when spring comes!"

"Yes; in the country! I am beginning to long for it already!" Mrs. Hanka herself is animated. "You must get the garden and the grove fixed up. It will be fine."

And Tidemand, who already has arranged to have the country-house put in order, although it is not April yet, is delighted because of his wife's sudden interest. His sombre eyes brighten and he presses her arm.

"I want you to know, Hanka, I am very happy to-day," he exclaims.
"Everything will be all right soon, I am sure."

"Are you—What will be all right, by the way?"

"Oh, nothing," he says quickly. He turns the subject, looks down, and continues: "Business is booming; I have given Fürst orders to buy!"

Fool that he was! There he had once more made a mistake and bothered his wife with his shop talk. But Mrs. Hanka was good enough to overlook it; nobody could have answered more patiently and sweetly than did she:

"I am very glad to hear it!"

These gentle words embolden him; he is grateful and wants to show it as best he can; he smiles with dewy eyes and says in a low voice:

"I should like to give you a little present if you care—a sort of souvenir of this occasion. If there is anything you would like—"

Mrs. Hanka glances at him.

"No, my dear. What are you thinking of? Though, perhaps—you might let me have a couple of hundred crowns. Thanks, very much!" Suddenly she spies the old rubber shoe with nails and junk, and she cries, full of curiosity: "Whatever is this?" She lets go her husband's arm and brings the rubber over to the table. "Whatever have you got here, Milde?" She rummages in the rubbish with her white fingers, calls Irgens over, finds one strange thing after another, and asks questions concerning them. "Will somebody please tell me what this is good for?"

She has fished out an umbrella-handle which she throws aside at once; then a lock of hair enclosed in paper. "Look—a lock of somebody's hair! Come and see!"

Milde joined her.

"Leave that alone!" he said and took his cigar out of his mouth. "However did that get in there? Did you ever—hair from my last love, so to speak!"

This was sufficient to make everybody laugh. The Journalist shouted:

"But have you seen Milde's collection of corsets? Out with the corsets, Milde!"

And Milde did not refuse; he went into one of the side rooms and brought forth his package. There were both white and brown ones; the white ones were a little grey, and Mrs. Paulsberg asked in surprise:

"But—have they been used?"

"Of course; why do you think Milde collects them? Where would be their sentimental value otherwise?" And the Journalist laughed heartily, happy to be able to twist even this word around.

But the corpulent Milde wrapped his corsets together and said:

"This is a little specialty of mine, a talent—But what the dickens are you all gaping at? It is my own corsets; I have used them myself—don't you understand? I used them when I began to grow stout; I laced and thought it would help. But it helped like fun!"

Paulsberg shook his head and said to Norem:

"Your health, Norem! What nonsense is this I hear, that Grande objects to your company?"

"God only knows," says Norem, already half drunk. "Can you imagine why? I have never offended him in my life!"

"No; he is beginning to get a little chesty lately."

Norem shouted happily:

"You hear that? Paulsberg himself says that Grande is getting chesty lately."

They all agreed. Paulsberg very seldom said that much; usually he sat, distant and unfathomable, and listened without speaking; he was respected by all. Only Irgens thought he could defy him; he was always ready with his objections.

"I cannot see that this is something Paulsberg can decide," he said.

They looked at him in surprise. Was that so? So Paulsberg could not decide that? He! he! so that was beyond him? But who, then, could decide it?

"Irgens," answered Paulsberg caustically.

Irgens looked at him; they gazed fixedly at each other. Mrs. Hanka stepped between them, sat down on a chair, and began to speak to Ojen.

"Listen a moment!" she called after a while. "Ojen wants to read his latest—a prose poem."

And they settled down to listen.

Ojen brought forth his prose poem from an inside pocket; his hands trembled.

"I must ask your indulgence," said he.

But at this the two young students, the close-cropped poets, laughed loudly, and the one with the compass in his fob said admiringly:

"And *you* ask for *our* indulgence? What about us, then?"

"Quiet!"

"The title of this is 'Sentenced to Death,'" said Ojen, and began:

> For a long time I have wondered: What if my secret guilt were known?...

Sh....

Yes, sh....

For then I should be sentenced to death.

And I would sit in my prison and know that I should be calm and indifferent when the supreme moment should arrive.

I would ascend the steps of the scaffold, I would smile and humbly beg permission to say a word.

> And then I would speak. I would implore everybody to learn something good from my death. A speech from my inmost heart, and my last farewell should be like a breath of flame....

Now my secret guilt is known.

Yes!

And I am sentenced to death. And I have languished in prison so long that my spirit is broken.

I ascend the steps to the scaffold; but to-day the sun is shining and my eyes fill with tears.

> For I have languished so long in prison that I am weak. And then the sun is shining so—I haven't seen it for nine months, and I haven't heard the birds sing for nine months—until to-day.

> I smile in order to hide my tears and I ask humbly if my guards will permit me to speak a word.

But they will not permit me.

> Still I want to speak—not to show my courage, but really I want to say a few words from my heart so as not to die mutely—innocent words that will harm nobody, a couple of hurried sentences before they clap their hands across my lips: Friends, see how God's sun is shining....

And I open my lips, but I cannot speak.

> Am I afraid? Does my courage fail? Alas, no, I am not afraid. But I am weak, that I am, and I cannot speak because I look upon God's sun and the trees for the last time....

What now? A horseman with a white flag?

Peace, my heart, do not tremble so!

No, it is a woman with a white veil, a handsome woman of my own age. Her neck is bare like my own.

> And I do not understand it, but I weep because of this white veil, too, because I am weak and the white veil flutters beautifully against the green background of the forest. But in a little while I shall see it no more....

Perhaps, though, after my head has fallen I may still be able to see the blessed sky for a few moments with my eyes. It is not impossible, if I only open my eyes widely when the axe falls. Then the sky will be the last I see.

But don't they tie a bandage across my eyes? Or won't they blindfold me because I am so weak and tearful? But then everything will be dark, and I shall lie blindly, unable even to count the threads in the cloth before my eyes.

    How stupidly mistaken I was when I hoped to be able to turn my eyes upward and behold the blessed vault of heaven. They will turn me over, on my stomach, with my neck in a clamp. And I shall be able to see nothing because of my bandaged eyes.

    Probably there will be a small box suspended below me; and I cannot even see the little box which I know will catch my severed head.

    Only night—a seething darkness around me. I blink my eyes and believe myself still alive—I have life in my fingers, even—I cling stubbornly to life. If they would only take off the bandage so I could see something—I might enjoy looking at the dust grains in the bottom of the box and see how tiny they were....

Silence and Darkness. Mute exhalations from the crowds....

    Merciful God! Grant me one supplication—take off the bandage!
Merciful God! I am *Thy* creature—take off the bandage!

Everybody was silent when he was through. Ojen drank; Milde was busy with a spot on his vest, and did not understand a word of what he had heard; he lifted his glass to the Journalist and whispered:

"Your health!"

Mrs. Hanka spoke first; she smiled to Ojen and said, out of the goodness of her heart:

"Oh, you Ojen, you Ojen! How everything you write seems evanescent, ethereal! 'Mute exhalations from the crowds'—I can hear it; I can feel it! It is thrilling!"

Everybody thought so, too, and Ojen was happy. Happiness was very becoming to his girlish face.

"Oh, it is only a little thing, a mood," he said. He would have liked to hear Paulsberg's opinion, but Paulsberg remained sphinxlike and silent.

"How *do* you think of such things? These prose poems are really exquisite!"

"It is my temperament, I suppose. I have no taste for fiction. In me everything turns to poetry, with or without rhymes; but verses always. I have entirely ceased to use rhymes lately."

"But tell me—in what manner does your nervousness really affect you?" asked Mrs. Hanka in her gentle voice. "It is so very sad; you must really try to get well again."

"Yes, I'll try. It is hard to explain; at times I will suddenly become excited without the slightest reason. I shudder; I simply tear myself to pieces. Then I cannot bear to walk on carpets; if I should lose anything I should never find it again. I should not hear it drop, and consequently I should never think of looking for it. Can you imagine anything more distracting than to have something you have lost lying there without your knowing it? It tortures me, therefore, to walk on carpets; I am in constant fear and I keep my hands over my pockets; I look at my vest buttons to be sure of them. I turn around again and again to make sure that I haven't by chance lost something or other—And there are other annoyances: I have the strangest ideas, the most peculiar hallucinations. I place a glass on the very edge of the table and imagine I have made a bet with some one—a bet involving enormous amounts. Then I blow on the glass; if it falls I lose—lose an amount large enough to ruin me for life; if it remains I have won and can build myself a castle on the Mediterranean. It is the same whenever I go up a strange stairway: should there be sixteen steps I win, but if there are eighteen I lose. Into this, though, there enter other intricate possibilities: Suppose there should be twenty steps, have I lost or won? I do not yield; I insist on my rights in the matter; I go to law and lose my case—Well, you mustn't laugh; it is really annoying. Of course these are only minor matters. I can give other examples: Let somebody sit in a room next to yours and sing a single verse of a certain song, sing it endlessly, without ceasing, sing it through and begin again; tell me—would this not drive you crazy? Where I live there is such a person, a tailor; he sits and sings and sews, and his singing is unceasing. You cannot stand it; you get up in a fury and go out. Then you run into another torture. You meet a man, an acquaintance, with whom you enter into a conversation. But during this conversation you suddenly happen to think of something pleasant, something good that is in store for you, perhaps—something you wish to return to later and thoroughly enjoy. But while you stand there talking you forget that pleasant thought, forget it cleanly and cannot recall it at any cost! Then comes the pain, the suffering; you are racked on the wheel because you have lost this exquisite, secret enjoyment to which you could have treated yourself at no cost or trouble."

"It *must* be strange! But you are going to the country, to the pine woods now; you will get well again," says Mrs. Hanka, and feels like a mother.

Milde chimes in:

"Of course you will. And think of us when you are in your kingdom."

Ole Henriksen had remained quietly in his chair; he said little and smoked his cigar. He knew Torahus; he gave Ojen a hint about visiting the house of the county judge, which was a mile away. He had only to row across a lake; pine woods all around—the house looked like a little white marble palace in the green surroundings.

"How do you know all this?" asked Irgens, quite surprised to hear Ole speak.

"I went through there on a walking trip," answered Ole, embarrassed. "We were a couple of boys from the college. We stopped at the house and had a glass of milk."

"Your health, Mr. College Man!" called the Journalist sarcastically.

"Be sure and row over," said Ole. "County Judge Lynum's family is charming. There is even a young girl in the house if you care to fall in love," he added smilingly.

"He, he! No; whatever else one can accuse Ojen of, the ladies he leaves severely alone!" said Norem, good-natured and tipsy.

"Your health, Mr. College Man!" shouted Gregersen again.

Ole Henriksen looked at him.

"Do you mean me?" he asked.

"Of course, I mean you, certainly I do! Haven't you attended college? Well, aren't you a college man, then?"

The Journalist, too, was a little tipsy.

"It was only a business college," said Ole quietly.

"Of course, you are a peddler, yes. But there is no reason why you should be ashamed of that. Is there, Tidemand? I say there is no reason whatever! Does anybody feel called upon to object?"

Tidemand did not answer. The Journalist kept obstinately to the question; he frowned and thought of nothing else, afraid to forget what he had asked about. He began to lose his temper; he demanded a reply in a loud voice.

Mrs. Hanka said suddenly:

"Silence, now. Ojen is going to read another poem."

Both Paulsberg and Irgens made secretly a wry face, but they said nothing; on the contrary, Paulsberg nodded encouragingly. When the noise had subsided a little Ojen got up, stepped back, and said:

"I know this by heart. It is called 'The Power of Love.'"

> We rode in a railway carriage through a strange landscape—strange to me, strange to her. We were also strangers to each other; we had never met before. Why is she sitting so quietly? I wondered. And I bent toward her and said, while my heart hammered:
>
> "Are you grieving for somebody, madam? Have you left a friend where you come from—a very dear friend?"

"Yes," she answered, "a very dear friend."

"And now you sit here unable to forget this friend?" I asked.

And she answered and shook her head sadly:

"No, no—I can never forget him."

She was silent. She had not looked at me while she spoke.

> "May I lift your braid?" I asked her. "What a lovely braid—how very beautiful it is!"

"My friend has kissed it," she said, and pushed back my hand.

> "Forgive me," I said then, and my heart pounded more and more. "May I not look at your ring—it shines so golden and is also so very beautiful. I should like to look at it and admire it for your sake."

But to this she also said no and added:

"My friend has given it to me."

Then she moved still further away from me.

"Please forgive me," I said....

> Time passes, the train rolls on, the journey is so long, so long and wearisome, there is nothing we can do except listen to the rumbling of the wheels. An engine flares past, it sounds like iron striking iron, and I start, but she does not; she is probably entirely absorbed in thoughts about her friend. And the train rolls on.
>
> Then, for the first time, she glances at me, and her eyes are strangely blue.

"It grows darker?" she says.

"We are approaching a tunnel," I answer.

And we rode through the tunnel.

Some time passes. She glances at me, a trifle impatiently, and says:

"It seems to me it grows dark again?"

"We are drawing near the second tunnel, there are three altogether," I answer. "Here is a map—do you want to see?"

"It frightens me," she says and moves closer to me. I say nothing. She asks me smilingly:

"Did you say three tunnels? Is there one more besides this one?"

"Yes—one more."

> We enter the tunnel; I feel that she is very close to me, her hand touches mine. Then it grows light again and we are once more in the open.

We ride for a quarter of an hour. She is now so close to me that I feel the warmth from her.

"You are welcome to lift my braid if you wish to," she says, "and if you care to look at my ring—why, here it is!"

I held her braid and did not take her ring because her friend had given it to her. She smiled and did not offer it to me again.

> "Your eyes are so bright, and how white your teeth!" she said and grew confused. "I am afraid of that last tunnel—please hold my hand when we get to it. No—don't hold my hand; I didn't mean that, I was jesting; but talk to me."

I promised to do what she asked me to.

A few moments later she laughed and said:

"I was not afraid of the other tunnels; only this one frightens me."

She glanced at my face to see how I might answer, and I said:

"This is the longest, too; it is exceedingly long."

Her confusion was now at its highest.

> "But we are not near any tunnel," she cried. "You are deceiving me; there is no tunnel!"

"Yes, there is, the last one—look!"

And I pointed to my map. But she would see nothing and listen to nothing.

"No, no,—there is no tunnel, I tell you there is none! But speak to me if there be one!" she added.

She leaned back against the cushions, and smiled through half-closed lids.

> The engine whistled; I looked out; we were approaching the black opening. I remembered that I had promised to speak to her; I bent towards her, and in the darkness I felt her arms around my neck.

"Speak to me, please do! I am so frightened!" she whispered with beating heart. "Why don't you speak to me?"

I felt plainly how her heart was beating, and I placed my lips close to her ears and whispered:

"But now you are forgetting your friend!"

> She heard me, she trembled and let me go quickly; she pushed me away with both hands, and threw herself down in the seat. I sat there alone. I heard her sobs through the darkness.

"This was The Power of Love," Ojen said.

Everybody listened attentively; Milde sat with open mouth.

"Well—what more?" he asked, evidently thinking there must be a climax yet to come. "Is that all? But Heaven preserve us, man, what is it all about? No; the so-called poetry you young writers are dishing out nowadays—I call it arrant rot!"

They all laughed loudly. The effect was spoiled; the poet with the compass in his fob arose, pointed straight at Milde, and said furiously:

"This gentleman evidently lacks all understanding of modern poetry."

"Modern poetry! This sniffing at the moon and the sun, these filigree phrases and unintelligible fancies—There must, at least, be a point, a climax, to everything!"

Ojen was pale and furious.

"You have then not the slightest understanding of my new intentions," said the poor fellow, trembling with excitement. "But, then, you are a brute, Milde; one could not expect intelligent appreciation from you."

Only now did the fat painter realise how much he had offended; he had hardly expected this when he spoke.

"A brute?" he answered good-naturedly. "It seems we are beginning to express ourselves very plainly. I did not mean to insult you, anyway. Don't you think I enjoyed the poem? I did, I tell you; enjoyed it immensely. I only thought it a little disembodied, so to speak, somewhat ethereal. Understand me correctly: it is very beautiful, exceedingly artistic, one of the best things you have produced yet. Can't you take a joke any more?"

But it was of no avail that Milde tried to smooth things over; the seriousness of the moment had gone, they laughed and shouted more than ever, and cut loose in earnest. Norem opened one of the windows and sang to the street below.

To mend matters a little and make Ojen feel better, Mrs. Hanka placed her hand on his shoulder and promised to come and see him off when he started on his trip. Not she alone—they would all come. When was he going?

She turned to Ole Henriksen: "You'll come, won't you, and see Ojen off when he goes?"

Ole Henriksen then gave an unexpected reply which surprised even Mrs. Hanka: He would not only go with Ojen to the station, he would go with him all the way to Torahus. Yes, he had suddenly made up his mind, he would make this little trip; he had, in fact, a sort of reason for going—And he was so much in earnest that he buttonholed Ojen at once and arranged the day for the departure.

The Journalist drank with Mrs. Paulsberg, who held her glass in a peculiar masculine fashion. They moved over to the sofa on account of the draught, and told each other amusing anecdotes. Mrs. Paulsberg knew a story concerning Grande and one of Pastor B.'s daughters. She had reached the climax when she paused.

"Well—go on!" the Journalist exclaimed eagerly.

"Wait a moment!" answered Mrs. Paulsberg smilingly, "you must at least give me time to blush a little!"

And she recounted merrily the climax.

Norem had retired to a corner and was fast asleep.

"Does anybody know the time?" asked Mrs. Paulsberg.

"Don't ask me," said Gregersen, and fumbled at his vest pocket. "It is many a day since I carried a watch!"

It turned out that it was one o'clock.

About half-past one Mrs. Hanka and Irgens had disappeared. Irgens had asked Milde for roasted coffee, and since then had not been seen. Nobody seemed to think it strange that the two had sneaked away, and no questions were asked; Tidemand was talking to Ole Henriksen about his trip to Torahus.

"But have you time to run off like this?" he asked.

"I'll take time," answered Ole. "By the way, I want to tell you something by and by."

Around Paulsberg's table the political situation was being discussed. Milde once more threatened to banish himself to Australia. But, thank

Heaven, it now looked as if Parliament would do something before it was dissolved, would refuse to yield.

"It is a matter of indifference to me what it does," said Gregersen of the *Gazette*. "As things have been going, Norway has assumed the character of a beaten country. We are decidedly poverty-stricken, in every respect; we lack power, both in politics and in our civic life. How sad to contemplate the general decline! What miserable remnants are left of the intellectual life that once flamed up so brightly, that called loudly to Heaven in the seventies! The aged go the way of the flesh; who is there to take their places? I am sick of this decadence; I cannot thrive in low intellectual altitudes!"

Everybody looked at the Journalist; what was the matter with the ever-merry chap? He was not so very drunk now; he spoke passably clearly, and did not twist any words. What did he mean? But when the witty dog reached the declaration that he could only thrive in a high spiritual altitude, then the guests broke into peals of merriment and understood that it was a capital hoax. The merry blade—hadn't he almost fooled them all! "Poor remnants of the intellectual life of the seventies!" Didn't we have Paulsberg and Irgens, and Ojen and Milde, and the two close-cropped poets, and an entire army of first-class, sprouting talents besides!

The Journalist himself laughed and wiped his forehead and laughed again. It was generally believed that this fellow was possessed of a literary talent which had not entirely stagnated in his newspaper. A book might be expected from him some day, a remarkable work.

Paulsberg forced a smile. In reality he was offended because nobody had alluded to his novels or to his work on the Atonement during the entire evening. When therefore the Journalist asked him his opinion concerning the intellectual life of the nation, his reply was brief:

"It seems to me I have had occasion to express an opinion somewhere in my works."

Of course, of course; when they came to think of it they certainly remembered it. It was true; a speech somewhere or other. Mrs. Paulsberg quoted from book and page.

But Paulsberg made up his mind to leave now.

"I'll come and sit for you to-morrow," he said to Milde, with a glance at the easel. He got up, emptied his glass, and found his overcoat. His wife pressed everybody's hand vigorously. They met Mrs. Hanka and Irgens in the door.

From now on the merriment knew no bounds; they drank like sponges; even the two young poets kept up as well as they could, and talked with bloodshot eyes about Baudelaire. Milde demanded to know why Irgens had asked him for coffee. Why did he need coffee? He hoped he had not been making preparations to kiss Mrs. Hanka? Damn him, he would hate to trust him.... Tidemand hears this and he laughs with the others, louder than the others, and he says: "You are right, he is not to be trusted, the sly dog!" Tidemand was sober as always.

They did not restrain themselves; the conversation was free and they swore liberally. When all was said and done, it was prudery that was Norway's curse and Norway's bane; people preferred to let their young girls go to the dogs in ignorance rather than enlighten them while there was time. Prudery was the nourishing vice of the moment. So help me, there ought to be public men appointed for the sole purpose of shouting obscenity on the streets just to make young girls acquainted with certain things while there was still time. What, do you object, Tidemand?

No, Tidemand did not object, and Ole Henriksen did not object. The idea was original, to say the least. Ha, ha!

Milde got Tidemand over in a corner.

"It is like this," he said, "I wonder if you have got a couple of crowns?"

Yes; Tidemand was not entirely stripped. How much? A ten-spot?

"Thanks, old man, I'll give it back to you shortly," said Milde in all seriousness. "Very soon, now. You are a brick! It is not more than a couple of days since I said that you hucksters were great fellows. That is exactly what I said. Here is my hand!"

Mrs. Hanka got up at last; she wanted to leave. It was beginning to grow light outside. Her husband kept close by her.

"Yes, Hanka, that is right—let us be going," he said. He was on the point of offering her his arm.

"Thank you, my friend, but I have an escort," she said with an indifferent glance.

It took him a moment to recover himself.

"Oh, I see," he said with a forced smile. "It is all right; I only thought—"

He walked over to the window and remained standing there.

Mrs. Hanka said good night to everybody. When she came to Irgens she whispered eagerly, breathlessly: "To-morrow, then, at three." She kept Ojen's hand in hers and asked him when he was going. Had he remembered to make reservations at Torahus? No; she might have known it; these poets were always forgetting the most essential. He would have to telegraph at once. Good-bye! And get well soon.... She was maternal to the last.

The Journalist accompanied her.

VI

"You said there was something you wanted to tell me," said Tidemand.

"Yes; so there is—You were surprised that I wanted to go along to Torahus. Of course, I said that I had business there. That is not so; I just said that. I know nobody there except Lynums; that is all there is to it. I did really visit their house once. You never heard anything so ridiculous; we came there, two thirsty tourists, and they gave us milk; since then I have met the family when they came to town last fall and this winter. It is quite a family—seven altogether, including the tutor. The oldest daughter's name is Aagot. I'll tell you more about them later. Aagot was eighteen the 7th of December; ha, ha! she is in her nineteenth year; I happen to remember that she told me. In short, we are not exactly engaged; I don't mean to say that; we have only written to each other once in a while. But there is no telling what may happen—What do you say to that?"

Tidemand was more than surprised; he stopped.

"But I had not the slightest idea; you haven't said a word to me about it!"

"No; I was hardly in a position to say anything yet. There is nothing definite; she is very young, you know. Suppose she had changed her mind? She may tell me she has other intentions when I get there. In that case nothing can be said against her; the execution will take place without witnesses; her reputation will have suffered nothing—I want you to see her, Andreas; I have a picture of her. I won't say that she gave it to me; I almost took it forcibly; but—"

They stopped a moment and looked at the photograph.

"Charming!" said Tidemand.

"Isn't she? I am glad you think so. I am sure you will like her."

They walked on.

"I want to congratulate you!" said Tidemand and stopped again.

"Thanks!" Ole added a moment afterward: "Yes, I thank you. I may as well tell you that it *is* really decided, practically, that is. I am going up to bring her to town with me."

They had almost reached the Railway Square when Tidemand suddenly stared straight ahead and whispered:

"But isn't that my wife there ahead of us?"

"Yes; so it is," whispered Ole. "I have noticed this lady ahead of us a long while; it is only now I see who it is."

Mrs. Hanka walked home alone; the Journalist had not accompanied her at all.

"Thank God!" exclaimed Tidemand involuntarily. "She told me she had an escort, and now she goes home all alone. Isn't she a darling? She is going straight home. But tell me—why did she say she had an escort?"

"Oh, you mustn't take such things too literally," answered Ole. "She probably did not want anybody to go with her, neither you nor I nor anybody else. Couldn't she feel that way inclined, perhaps? Young ladies have their moods, just like you or me."

"Of course, that is perfectly true." Tidemand accepted this explanation. He was happy because his wife was alone and was making straight for home. He said, nervously glad: "Do you know, to judge by a few words I had with her this evening it seems as if things were coming around more and more. She even asked about the business, about the Russian customs duty; honest, she wanted to know everything about Fürst. You should have seen how delighted she was because business is looking up again. We spoke about our summer vacation, our country house. Yes, it is getting a little better every day."

"There you are—didn't I tell you? It certainly would be a pity otherwise."

Pause.

"There is something I am at a loss to explain, though," continued Tidemand, worried again. "Here lately she has been talking about what a woman like herself should do with her life. She must have a career, something to do and accomplish. I must confess it astonished me a little, a woman with two children and a large household—She has also begun to use her former name again, Hanka Lange Tidemand, just as if her name still were Lange."

Mrs. Hanka had stopped outside her own entrance; she was evidently waiting for her husband. She called to him jestingly that he had better hurry—she was almost freezing to death. And she lifted her finger banteringly and asked:

"What plots and conspiracies are you two wholesalers now hatching? Where is the price of wheat now, and what are you going to put it up to? God have mercy on you on the day of judgment!"

Tidemand answered in kind: What in the world had she done with the Journalist? So she had not wanted company, not even her own husband's; she had been in a sentimental mood? But how could she be so cruel as to let this poor fellow Gregersen ramble home all alone, drunk as he was? It was simply heartless—

* * * * *

In about a week Ole Henriksen had returned from Torahus. Ojen had remained, but Ole had brought back a young lady, his fiancée, Aagot Lynum. With them had come a third person, a somewhat peculiar fellow.

GERMINATION

I

Ole returned from Torahus the 5th of April. He introduced his fiancée at once to the clique, presented her to his friends, and spent all day in her company. He had not as yet introduced her to Irgens and Attorney Grande because he had failed to run across them.

She was young and fair, with high bosom and a straight carriage. Her blond hair and her frequent laughter gave an impression of extreme youthfulness. She had a dimple in her left cheek and none in her right, and this solitary dimple made her peculiar, characteristic. Wasn't it strange to have one side of the face different from the other? She was of average height.

She had been so carried away with everything she had seen in the city that she wandered around in a state of joyful excitement all day. The clique had capitulated to her charm and shown her much amiability; Mrs. Hanka had simply embraced her and kissed her the moment she saw her.

She followed Ole around in the establishment, peeped into all the wonderful drawers and boxes in the store, tasted old, strong wines in the cellars, and opened in fun the heavy ledgers in the office. But she was especially fond of the warehouse, the little stall of an office down there that was filled with tart and peculiar odours from all kinds of tropical products. From the window she could see the docks, the harbour, the tugs that brought cargoes in and out and puffed stertorously, shaking the very air with their efforts. Just outside floated the little yacht with the golden masthead; it was hers; it had been conveyed to her and belonged to her legally. Ole had even been in *Veritas* [Footnote: The Maritime Insurance and Registry Office in Christiania.] and had its name changed to *Aagot*. She had all the documents.

And slate after slate is brought into the office; the accounts grow a little every day, they fill many columns, swell into larger and larger amounts; the spring season has commenced, the active period just before summer; all the pulses of trade the world over leap and quiver with passionate energy.

While Ole counts and makes notes, Aagot busies herself with something or other on the other side of the desk. She was often unable to understand how Ole managed to keep all these accounts straight without getting the amounts mixed; she had tried it herself, but in vain. The only thing she can be trusted with is the entering of endless orders in the books, and this she does carefully and conscientiously.

Ole looks at her and says suddenly:

"Lord, what tiny hands you have, Aagot! He, he! they are next to nothing. I can't understand how you can get along with them."

That is enough. Aagot throws down her pen and runs over to him. And they are happy and silly until the next slate arrives.

"Little Mistress!" he says smilingly, and looks down into her eyes, "Little Mistress!"

Time passes. At last the work is done, the accounts finished, and Ole says, while he slams the ledger shut:

"Well, I have got to go and send some wires. Are you coming along?"

"Yes, dear, if you'll let me!" she answers. And she trips along, greatly pleased.

On the way Ole remembers that he has not as yet presented his sweetheart to Irgens. "You ought to meet this fellow Irgens," he says; "he is a great man, one of the deep talents; everybody says so." Suppose they went as far as the Grand; he might be there.

They entered the Grand, passed by the tables where people sat drinking and smoking, and found Irgens far back in the room. Milde and Norem were with him.

"So here you are!" called Ole.

Irgens gave him his left hand and did not get up. He glanced through half-closed lids at Aagot.

"This, Aagot, is the poet Irgens." Ole presented him, somewhat proud of his intimate acquaintance with the great man. "My fiancée, Miss Lynum."

Irgens got up and bowed deeply. Once more he looked at Aagot, looked persistently, even, and she looked back at him; she was evidently surprised to find the poet different from what she had thought. It was over two years since she had read his book, the lyric drama which had brought him so much fame. She had thought the master to be an elderly man.

"May I congratulate?" said Irgens finally, and gave Ole his hand.

They all sat down; each got a seidel and began a conversation. The spirits around the little table rose; even Irgens grew communicative and joined in. He addressed Aagot across the table, asked if she had been in the city before, in the theatre, in Tivoli, read this book or that, visited the Exhibition of paintings? "But, Miss Lynum, you must really see the Exhibition! I should be delighted to show it to you if you cannot find a better guide—" They conversed for about ten minutes across the table, and Aagot replied rapidly to every question, sometimes laughing, now and then forgetting herself and asking questions with her head tilted sideways; her eyes were wide open and sparkling; she was not the least bit embarrassed.

Ole called the waiter. He had to leave; he was going to the telegraph office. Aagot, too, got up.

"But there is no reason why you should go, Miss Lynum," said Milde. "You can come back for Miss Lynum when you have telegraphed, Ole."

"Yes, I am going," said Aagot.

"But if you want to stay I'll call for you in a few moments," said Ole and took his hat.

She looked at him and answered almost in a whisper:

"Won't you let me come with you?"

"Certainly, if you want to."

Ole paid his check.

"Say," said Milde, "be good enough to settle this check, too. None of us is very flush to-day." And he smiled and glanced at Aagot.

Ole settled, said good-bye, and walked out with Aagot on his arm.

The three gentlemen looked after her.

"The devil!" murmured Irgens in sincere admiration. "Did you notice her."

"Did we! How the dickens did that groceryman get hold of such a beauty?"

Milde agreed with the Actor; it was simply incomprehensible. What in the world could she be thinking of!

"Don't talk so loud; they have stopped over by the entrance," said Irgens.

They had run across the Attorney. The same introduction followed; a little talk could not be avoided. They did not remove their hats and gloves and were ready to go at a moment's notice. At last they left.

That very moment a man got up from one of the farthest tables and approached the entrance.... He was a man in the forties, with greyish beard and dark eyes; his clothes were a little shabby; he was partly bald.

He walked straight over to the Attorney, bowed, and said:

"Do you mind if I sit down here? I noticed that Mr. Henriksen spoke to you; you must know him, then. As for me, I am acquainted with Miss Lynum, who was introduced to you. I am the tutor in her home; my name is Coldevin."

Something about the stranger appealed to the little Attorney's curiosity; he made room for him at once and even offered him a cigar. The waiter brought his glass over.

"I visit the city only very seldom," said Coldevin. "I live in the country. During the last ten years I have hardly been anywhere with the exception of a trip to Copenhagen during the Exhibition. So I run around all day and look things over. There are many changes; the city grows bigger and bigger."

"It is a pleasure to walk around down by the docks and watch the traffic."

His voice was well modulated; he spoke simply and quietly, although his eyes at times glowed with a smouldering fire.

The Attorney listened and answered cordially. Yes, one had to admit that the city was making progress; an electric car line was being built; several more streets were going to be asphalted; the last census showed an enormous increase.... Wasn't it strange to live in the country always? No? But in the winter—in the darkness and the snow?

No; it was glorious! Dazzling snow everywhere; silent, wild woods, ptarmigan, hares, and foxes. White, glittering white snow! But summer, of course, was more beautiful. It would be high summer when he returned; his intention was to stay a couple of months, perhaps even longer. That ought to suffice to see and hear most of what went on. What was happening, anyway? What was the situation?

"Well," answered the Attorney, "the situation is serious. But we place our faith in Parliament. Several of the leaders have given their ultimatum; if all signs do not fail, they surely will make short shrift this time."

"Yes, if the signs do not fail—"

"You appear to have your doubts?" asked the Attorney smilingly.

"No; only there seems to be too much confidence placed in the leaders and in their promises. I come from the country; we have our suspicions; it is hard to get rid of them. The leaders might fail us now as heretofore. Indeed, they might."

Coldevin drank from his glass.

"I cannot say that I remember their failing us heretofore," said the Attorney. "Do you refer to any particular occasion when the leaders have betrayed us?"

"Well, yes. Promises have been broken, promises have been interpreted, promises have been openly and dispassionately denied. We should not forget these things. One should not rely too much on the leaders; the country's youth should be our hope. No; a leader is apt to prove a broken reed. It is an old law that whenever a leader reaches a certain age he pauses—yes, he even turns right about face and pushes the other way. Then it is up to the young to march on, to drive him ahead or trample him down."

The door opened and Lars Paulsberg entered. He nodded to the Attorney, who returned his greeting. The Attorney pointed to a chair at his table, but Paulsberg shook his head and said:

"No, I am looking for Milde. He has not done a stroke on my picture to-day."

"Milde is over in the corner," said the Attorney. And he turned to Coldevin and whispered: "This is one of the most prominent of our young men—their leader, so to speak, Lars Paulsberg. Do you know him? If only the rest were like him."

Yes, Coldevin knew his name. So this was Paulsberg? He could plainly see that he was an important personality; people craned their necks, looked after him and whispered. Yes, indeed, we had quite a number of writers, it could not be denied—"There came to Torahus, for instance, one of them before I left; his name was Stefan Ojen. I have read two of his books. He was nervous, he told me; he spoke a good deal about a new school, a new intention within the realm of literature. His clothes were silk lined, but he did not put himself forward much. Of course, people were curious and wanted to see him, but he appeared very modest. I met him one evening; his entire shirt-front was covered with writing, with verses—long and short lines, a poem in prose. He said that he had waked up in the morning and found himself in the throes of an inspiration, and, as he had no paper handy, he simply wrote on his shirt-front. He asked us not to mind it; he had two more shirts with him, but as they were unlaundered he had to use that one for his verses. He read something for us, things full of sentiment. He gave us the impression that he was very clever."

The Attorney did not know if this were irony or not, for Coldevin smiled one of his rare smiles. But he was probably serious.

"Yes, Ojen is one of our most significant ones," he said. "He is beginning to create a school in Germany. There can be no doubt that his poetry is unique."

"Exactly. I, too, got that impression. A little childish, perhaps; a little immature, but— He, he! as we were sitting there that evening he suddenly exclaimed: 'Do you know, gentlemen, why I use a capital R in God?' 'A capital R in God!' we wondered and looked at each other blankly; no; we did not know why. But Ojen burst into a peal of laughter and left— It was a good joke; it wasn't at all bad, he, he!"

And Coldevin smiled.

The Attorney laughed with him. "Oh, that fellow Ojen could surprise you with far better inventions; that was nothing for him. But his writing was euphonious, his diction pure—Do you know Irgens?"

Yes, Coldevin knew his name. He hadn't written very much?

"He does not write for the masses, no," answered the Attorney. "He writes for the chosen few. But his friends know that he has many beautiful things unpublished. Good God, what a master! It is impossible to place one's finger on a single thing he has done and say that it is below par. He is sitting in the corner now. Do you wish to meet him? I can arrange it for you. I know him well; no preliminaries are necessary."

But Coldevin asked to be excused. Some other time; then he could meet Paulsberg and the others also—"So that is Paulsberg!" he repeated. "One could tell it when he passed by; people were whispering about him. Nobody whispered when Ole Henriksen passed by. By the way, I suppose Mr. Henriksen is going to get married now?"

"I suppose so—Tell me—is it at all interesting to be a tutor? Isn't it a somewhat tedious occupation at times?"

"Oh, no," answered Coldevin smilingly. "Of course, it depends a good deal on both parents and children. It is all right if one happens to get among good people. It is, of course, only a poor and modest situation, but—I would not change even if I could."

"Are you a college man?"

"Theology, yes. Unfortunately, a rather antiquated student now." And Coldevin smiled once more.

They continued the conversation for some time, told a couple of anecdotes about a university professor, and drifted back to the situation. Finally they discussed the grain prices. It looked bad; there was some talk of crop failures in Russia.

Coldevin was absolutely normal in his talk; he evidently was well informed and spoke quietly and thoughtfully. When he got up to leave he asked casually:

"By the way, do you happen to know where Mr. Henriksen went?"

"To the telegraph office. He told me he had some wires to send."

"Thank you. I trust you will pardon me for descending upon you so informally. It is kind of you to allow me to make your acquaintance."

"If you are going to stay awhile I trust we shall meet again," said the Attorney amiably. Coldevin took his leave.

He walked straight to the telegraph office. He remained outside awhile; then he ascended the stairs and peeped through the glass doors. Then he turned, went back to the street, and made for the harbour. He sauntered back and forth outside the Henriksen warehouse and glanced furtively toward the little office window. He did not take his eyes from the window for a long time. One would have thought he was anxious to find Ole Henriksen but did not know whether he was in the warehouse or not.

II

Irgens was sitting in his room, Thranes Road, No. 5. He was in fine spirits. The elegant man whom nobody suspected of doing anything sat there in all secret and corrected proofs and slaved like a farmer. Who would have believed it? He was the one in the clique who talked least about his work; nobody could understand how he managed to live. It was more than two years since his drama had been published, and he had apparently not done a stroke of work since. Of course, he might be working quietly, but nobody knew anything about it, nothing definitely. He owed a lot of money.

Irgens had locked his door so as not to be disturbed; he was very secretive. When he had finished his proof-reading he got up and looked out of the window. The weather was bright and sunny, a glorious day. He was going to take Miss Lynum to the Art Exhibition at three. He looked forward to this pleasure; it was really enjoyable to listen to this unsophisticated girl's chatter. She had burst upon him like a revelation; she reminded him of the first bird notes in spring.

There was a knock at the door. His first thought was to throw the proofs beneath the table-cloth, but he refrained. He opened. He knew this knock; it was Mrs. Hanka's finger which knocked twice so resolutely. She entered, closed the door, and glided over to him. She smiled, bent toward him, and looked into his eyes.

"It isn't me at all!" she said, and laughed quietly. "I want you to know that!" She could not hide her embarrassment entirely and flushed deeply.

She wore a grey woollen gown, and looked very young with her low lace collar and her bare neck.

He said:

"So it isn't you? Well, it doesn't matter who you are—you are equally lovely! And what glorious weather you are bringing!"

They sat down. He placed before her the proof-sheet, and she clapped her hands and cried: "Didn't I tell you? I knew it! No; but you are wonderful!" And she did not get tired of marvelling at him—that he was that far already! Oh, but wouldn't it come like a thunderclap; not a soul suspected anything! They all went around thinking that he did not work any more. Oh, Heavens! but nobody in the wide world was half as happy as she. She smuggled an envelope with something in it under the proof-sheet and pulled him away from the table. She talked all the time.

They sat down on the sofa. Her happiness, her violent joy, communicated itself to him, carried him away, and made him tender with gratitude. How she loved him, how she sacrificed herself for him and did for him what she could! He embraced her passionately, kissed her time and again, and held her close to his breast.

"I am so happy," she whispered. "I knew something was going to make me glad; as I walked upstairs it seemed as if I were going into an embrace! Dearest boy, no—the door—!"

The sun rose higher, the thrushes twittered passionately outside. The first bird notes of spring, he thought again, how unsophisticated these little creatures were in their chatter!

"How bright it is here!" she said; "it is much brighter here than elsewhere."

"Do you think so?" he answered smilingly. He walked over to the window and began to pluck from his clothes the fine, grey woolly fuzz her dress had left there. She sat still on the sofa, her eyes on the floor, blushing, arranging her hair a little. A ring flashed on each of her hands.

He could not remain there at the window so indifferently. She was beginning to notice it; she looked up; and besides, she was remarkably beautiful as she sat there fixing her hair. He stepped over to her and kissed her as warmly as he could.

"Don't kiss me, darling," she said; "be careful! Look here—it is the spring air."

She showed him a little red spot on her under lip. He asked her if it hurt, and she answered that it was not that, but she was afraid he might catch it from her. Suddenly she asked:

"Listen, can you come to Tivoli to-night? There is an operatic performance. Couldn't we meet there? Otherwise I'll die of loneliness."

He remembered that he was going to the Art Exhibition. What might happen afterward was hard to tell; he had better not promise anything. No, he said, he was afraid it would be impossible; he had made certain arrangements with Ole Henriksen.

"Oh, please—do come! I would be so proud and grateful!"

"But why in the world do you want to go to Tivoli?"

"But there is opera to-night!"

"Well, what of it? That means nothing to me. Well, if you like—"

"No, not if I like," she said sadly. "You seem so indifferent, Irgens! Yes, I admit I should like to go to the opera, but—Where are you going this evening? I am just like a compass-needle now: I oscillate, I may even swing all the way round, but I hark constantly back to one point—I point continually in one direction. It is you I am thinking of always."

Her little bewildered heart trembled. He looked at her. He knew it only too well—there was nothing he could reproach her with; she had been more than good to him. However, all he could promise was that he would come if at all possible.

* * * * *

Mrs. Hanka had left. Irgens was ready to go out; he put his proof-sheets in his pocket and took his hat. Had he forgotten anything? He had the proofs; that was the most important thing at present—the beginning of a book which was to startle the community with the suddenness of an explosion. He was going to see if his quiet industry would be denied appreciation. He, too, was going to send in an application for the government subsidy; he would delay until the very last day in order to avoid having his name paraded in the daily press alongside all those nonentities who already were licking their chops in anticipation of this modest emolument. His application should be brief and to the point, without recommendations, simply accompanied by his book. He would tell nobody, not even Mrs. Hanka. They should not be able to say that he had moved heaven and earth in order to secure this well-earned encouragement. But he was curious to see if they would ignore him. He knew all his fellow applicants, from Milde to Ojen; he did not fear any of them. He would have preferred to stand back and yield his right to this charity, but he could not afford it; he was obliged to accept it.

He brushed his clothes carefully all the way down the street; a little of the grey wool still clung to him—what a provoking dress! He dropped into a printing-office with his proofs. The foreman called his attention to a letter, an envelope with something enclosed, which he found between the sheets. Irgens turned in the door. A letter? Oh, yes; he had forgotten it. He knew this envelope and he opened it at once. When he had seen what was in it he lifted his brows, greatly pleased. The envelope he put in his pocket without further ado.

Ole and Aagot were in the warehouse. She was sewing on some red plush cushions for the cabin of the *Aagot*—doll cushions, one would almost think, they were so small. Irgens put his cheek to one of them, closed his eyes, and said, "Good night, good night."

"So you are going to the Art Exhibition!" said Ole smilingly. "Aagot has hardly spoken about anything else all day."

"Couldn't you come, too?" she asked.

But Ole had no time; just now he was very busy. "Be off—don't disturb me any more; out with you! Have a good time!"

It was the promenade-hour. Irgens proposed that they take the way through the park; they could then hear a little music at the same time. Did she like music?

Aagot was in a dark suit and wore a cape with red silk lining. The snug-fitting garment clung to her body without a wrinkle; around her neck she simply wore a bit of lace. The cape fluttered at times with scarlet silken flashes. She was sorry to say that she was not very musical. She liked to hear music, of course, but she lacked a thorough understanding of it.

"Exactly like myself," answered Irgens. "That is funny; are you like that, too? To tell the truth, I understand music unpardonably poorly, but I show up in the park every day; it would never do to stay away." Much depended upon that; if one did not show oneself and keep abreast of the procession, one would soon be lost, submerged, forgotten.

"Can one be forgotten so easily?" she asked. "But that does not apply to you, surely."

"Oh, yes, to me as well as to the rest," he replied. "Why shouldn't I be forgotten?"

She answered quite simply:

"I thought you were too well known."

"Known? Oh, as to that, Lord help us! I may not be so entirely unknown, of course, but—You must not think it is an easy matter to keep one's head above water here; one friend is envious, another hateful and malicious, a third simply despicable. No; as far as *that* is concerned—"

"It seems to me, however, that you are known, and well known, too," she said. "We cannot walk two steps that somebody isn't whispering about you; I have noticed it all along." She stopped.

"No, it is unbearable; I just heard another remark! Rather let us go up to the Exhibition at once!"

He laughed heartily, greatly flattered. How charming she was in her naive and unspoiled way! He said: Never mind; keep on! Pay no attention whatever. One got used to this whispering; if it amused people, what of it? He himself never noticed it any more; honestly, it did not affect him in the least. Besides, he wanted to let her know that to-day *he* was not the only subject of conversation—what about her? She could believe him or not; she was being thoroughly discussed. One could not come to a city like this one and look as she did without attracting attention; she could be very sure of that.

It was not his intention to flatter her; he was sincere in what he said. Still she did not seem to believe him.

They walked toward the park, where the band thundered Cherubini's "Overture to the Water-Carrier" across the place.

"It seems to me this is an altogether unnecessary noise," he said smilingly.

She laughed; she laughed often and heartily over his remarks. This laughter from her fresh lips, the dimple in her left cheek, her many cute and childlike ways, drove his spirits still higher; even her nose, which was somewhat irregular in profile and a little too large, made him almost feel as if he were in love. Greek or Roman noses were not always the most beautiful—not at all; it depended on the rest of the face. There was no such a thing as an authorised standard for noses.

He chatted about one thing after another and made time fly; he proved himself the poet who could interest those he addressed himself to, the highly cultured man, the genius of scintillating words. Aagot listened attentively; he tried to amuse her and came back to the subject of music again, to operatic music, which he simply abominated. He had, for instance, never been to the opera that he didn't happen to get a seat right behind a lady with a sharply bulging corset line, and he was condemned to stare at this ghastly back during three, four long intermissions. Then there was the performance itself, the brass instruments close to the ear, and then the singers who tried with all their might to drown their blatant blare in a roar of noise. At first one would appear who made strange contortions and meanwhile produced song; then another would stalk forth who did not want to take a back seat either, and who likewise did his utmost; then a third, a fourth, men and women, long processions, an army; and all sang their questions and sang their answers and beat their arms in the air and rolled their eyes, exercising their vocal chords without a moment's pause. Wasn't it true? They wept to music, sobbed to music, gritted teeth, sneezed, and fainted to music, and the conductor urged them on frantically with an ivory hammer-handle. She might laugh, but it was just that way. Then all of a sudden the conductor appears to become terror-stricken because of that infernal noise he has inspired; he swings his hammer-handle as a sign that there must be a change. Now the chorus starts in. This is not so bad; the chorus can pass muster; at least, it does not use such heartrending gestures. But in the midst of the singing another person strides forth, and he spoils the whole thing again; ah! it is the Prince; he has a solo— and when a prince has a solo of course everybody else has to keep still. But imagine this more or less corpulent masculine person standing there, bellowing, with legs wide apart! One gets furious; one experiences a well-nigh irrepressible desire to yell to this fellow to get out, to stop spoiling the evening for those who wanted to hear some music—hear the chorus sing!

Irgens was not displeased with himself—he attained his object. Aagot laughed incessantly and was hugely amused. How he did make things interesting and give life and colour to the most commonplace!

They finally got to the Exhibition, looked at what there was to see, and talked about the pictures as they went along. Aagot's questions were fully answered; Irgens knew everything and even told her anecdotes about the exhibiting painters. Here, too, they met curious people, who put their heads together and looked after them when they passed; but Irgens hardly glanced to the left or right; he seemed entirely indifferent to the attention accorded him. He only bowed a couple of times.

When, after an hour or so, they started to leave, they did not notice in an obscure corner a greyish-bearded, somewhat bald person, nor did they perceive two fathomless, burning eyes that followed them as they departed.

On the street Irgens said:

"I wonder—You are not going home at once, I hope?"

"Yes," she said, "I am going right back."

He asked her several times to stay a little longer, but Aagot thanked him and said that she wanted to get home. There was nothing to be done; she could not be persuaded, and he had to let her have her way. But they could make up for it some other time? There were both museums and galleries she ought to see; he would gladly act as her guide. She smiled and thanked him.

"I am admiring your walk," he said. "It is the most perfect walk I have ever seen."

She flushed and looked at him quickly.

"You cannot mean that," she said. "I who have lived in the backwoods all my life."

"Well, you may believe me or not, just as you please—You are altogether unusual, Miss Lynum, gloriously uncommon; in vain I seek words that would describe you. Do you know what you remind me of? I have carried this impression around all day. You remind me of the first bird note, the earliest warm spring tones—you know what I mean—that surge through the heart when the snow is gone and the sun and the birds of passage are here! But that isn't all about you. God help me, I cannot find the words I want, poet though I am supposed to be!"

"But I have never heard anything like it!" she cried, and laughed vivaciously. "I am supposed to be like all that? I should like to be, that much is certain. If only it were true!"

"You have come in here from the blue mountains; you are full of smiles," he said. "For this reason the description should call to mind the wild things—should have a flavour of venison, so to speak. I am not sure, though."

They were at the warehouse. They stopped and shook hands.

"I am ever so much obliged," she said. "Aren't you coming up? Ole must be in the office now."

"No, thanks—But listen, Miss Lynum, I would like to come soon and drag you with me to some museum; may I?"

"Yes," she answered hesitatingly. "That is very kind of you. I'll see—But I thank you for your company to-day."

She went in.

III

Irgens walked up the street. Where should he go now? He might go to Tivoli; there was plenty of time; in fact, it was much too early; he would have to kill an hour or so first. He felt in his pocket for the envelope; he had money; he might as well go to the Grand.

As he entered the door he was hailed by Journalist Gregersen, the literary member of the *Gazette* staff. Irgens did not like this fellow; he did not care to cultivate his friendship in order to get an item published in the paper now and then. Paulsberg had now two days running had a paragraph concerning his excursion to Honefos: the first day about his going, the second about his return; Gregersen had in his usual accommodating manner concocted two very excellent little items about this excursion. That such a man could descend to such coarse work! It was said that the fellow was capable of greater things; he would surely blossom forth some day; all right, time enough then. Irgens did not care for him very much nowadays.

Unwillingly, he walked over to the Journalist's table. Milde was there, also the Attorney and Coldevin, the grey tutor from the country. They were waiting for Paulsberg. They had been discussing the situation again; it commenced to look a little dubious now when several of the leading parliamentarians had shown symptoms of vacillation. "Just as I have told you," said Milde, "it is beginning to be unbearable here!"

Mrs. Grande was not present. Mrs. Liberia stayed at home.

The Journalist reported that the talk about crop failures in Russia evidently had something in it. It could not be concealed much longer in spite of the fact that the correspondent of the London *Times* had been sharply contradicted by the Russian press.

"I had a letter from Ojen," said Milde. "It looks as if he were coming back soon; he does not appear to enjoy himself out in the woods."

All these matters did not interest Irgens in the least. He made up his mind to get away as soon as he could. Coldevin said nothing, but glanced from one to another with his sombre eyes. When he had been presented to Irgens he had murmured a few words, sat down again and remained silent. Irgens looked at him languidly and was silent too. When he had finished his seidel he got up to go.

"Are you leaving us so soon?"

"Yes; I have got to go home and dress. I am going to Tivoli. See you later."

Irgens left.

"There you see the famous Irgens," said the Attorney to Coldevin.

"Yes, indeed," answered Coldevin with a smile. "I see so much greatness here that I am getting altogether bewildered. I saw the Art Exhibition to-day—It seems to me that our poets are beginning to pay considerable attention to their personal appearance; I have seen a couple of them; they are so groomed and patent-leathered—one can hardly say they come thundering along with foam-flecked bridles."

"Why should they? The fashions have changed, you know."

"I suppose so."

Coldevin was again silent.

"The fire-and-sword period has passed by, my good man," said the Journalist patronisingly, yawning across the table. "What the devil can be keeping Paulsberg?"

When Paulsberg at last showed up they made room for him with alacrity; the Journalist sat close by him and wanted to hear his opinion concerning the situation. What did these events portend—what could be done now?

Paulsberg, reserved and taciturn as always, gave a half reply, a fragmentary opinion: What could be done? Oh, one had to try to live even if a couple of parliamentarians were to fail the cause. All the same, he was going to publish an article soon; it would be worth while observing what effect that would have. He was going to give it to the traitors good and proper.

Goodness! Was he going to publish an article? That certainly would put matters right. "Not too gentle, now, Paulsberg; don't show them any consideration."

"I imagine Paulsberg knows exactly how gentle he is going to be," said Milde reprovingly. "You can safely leave that to him."

"Of course," answered the Journalist, "that goes without saying. I had no idea of offering any suggestions."

He was a little offended, but Paulsberg smoothed matters over by saying:

"I thank you for the two notices, Gregersen. It is fortunate for us that you keep an eye on us; otherwise people would entirely forget that we writers existed."

The Attorney ordered another round.

"I am waiting for my wife," said Paulsberg.

"She stopped in to borrow a hundred from Ole Henriksen. I see there is talk about famine in Russia—Well, I can't say that I have starved as yet."

Milde turned to Coldevin and remarked pompously:

"That is something it wouldn't hurt you to know out in the country: so shabbily does Norway treat her great men!"

Coldevin glanced from one to another.

"Indeed," he said, "it is sad." A moment later he added: "Well, one cannot say things are much better out in the country. The struggle to live is bitter there, too."

"But, so help me, there is a difference between poets and peasants, I should think!"

"In the country people adjust themselves to the law that the weak must perish," said Coldevin quietly. "For instance, people who cannot support a wife do not marry. If they do, and if they later on have to rely on others to discharge their obligations, then they are disgraced, branded with shame."

Everybody looked at the bald fellow; even Paulsberg snatched his glasses that were hanging on a cord across his breast, looked at him a moment, and asked in a stage whisper:

"What in the world—what kind of a phenomenon is that?"

This happy word made the friends smile; Paulsberg was asking what kind of a phenomenon this was, a phenomenon—he, he! It was not often Paulsberg said that much. Coldevin looked unconcerned; he did not smile. A pause ensued.

Paulsberg looked out of the window, shivered a little, and murmured:

"Drat it, I cannot get anything accomplished these days; this eternal sunshine has played me the scurvy trick of paralysing my imagination. I am in the middle of a descriptive passage about a rainy season, a raw and chilly milieu, and I cannot get anywhere with it." He mumbled maledictions about the weather.

The Attorney was incautious enough to remark:

"Why don't you write about the sunshine, then?"

It was not many days since Paulsberg himself, in Milde's studio, had bluntly expressed an opinion to the effect that Attorney Grande had showed symptoms of a certain arrogance lately. He was right, the Attorney was becoming a little impertinent; it might be well to put him in his place once and for all.

"You talk according to your lights!" said the Journalist oracularly.

This reproach was received in silence; but shortly afterward Grande got up and buttoned his coat.

"I don't suppose any of you are going my way?" he asked in order not to show any ill feeling. And as nobody answered he paid his check, said goodbye and left.

More drinks were ordered. Mrs. Paulsberg arrived in the company of Ole and his fiancée. Coldevin moved as far back as he could until he found himself almost at another table.

"We had to accompany Mrs. Paulsberg," said Ole good-naturedly; "we couldn't let her go alone." And he slapped Paulsberg on the shoulder.

Miss Aagot had let a joyous exclamation escape her and had walked straight over to Coldevin, to whom she gave her hand. But what in the world had become of him? Hadn't she kept a continuous lookout for him on the streets and asked Ole about him every day? She was at a loss to understand why she saw him so rarely. She had had another letter from home, and everybody sent him their kindest regards. Why did he keep so entirely to himself?

Coldevin stuttered many brief replies: there was no end of things to see and do, exhibitions and museums, Tivoli and Parliament; there were newspapers to read, lectures to attend; he also had to look up a few old friends. Furthermore, it was best not to disturb a newly engaged couple too much.

Coldevin smiled archly; his lips trembled a little and he spoke with bowed head.

Ole came over, overwhelmed him with the same reproaches, and received the same excuses. Coldevin was going to call on them to-morrow, though, they could rely on it; he had made up his mind before he met them. Provided he would not disturb them, of course.

Disturb? He? What was he thinking of?

Beer was served and everybody talked. Mrs. Paulsberg crossed her legs and gripped the glass in her masculine fashion. The Journalist monopolised her immediately. Ole continued his conversation with Coldevin.

"I hope you are enjoying yourself here? Interesting people, these! There is Lars Paulsberg; have you met him?"

"Yes, I have met him. He is the third one of our authors I have met. No doubt it is my fault; but, to tell the truth, none of them have made an overwhelming impression on me."

"No? That is because you do not know them well enough."

"But I know what they have written. It seems to me they do not exactly soar to the solitary heights. It is probably my own fault, though—Lars Paulsberg uses perfumes."

"Does he? A little peculiarity. One must pardon such men a few oddities."

"But I notice that they treat each other with the greatest respect," Coldevin continued. "They talk about everything; they make excellent speeches on every subject imaginable."

"Don't they, though? It is wonderful to listen to them, I must say."

"But how are you getting on—in the business, I mean?"

"Oh, we take one day at a time. We have just turned a little trick in Brazil which I hope will prove satisfactory. I remember, you are interested in business matters. When you come down tomorrow I will take you around and show you how we do it. We will all go—you and Aagot and myself—we three old friends."

"I thought I heard my name?" said Aagot merrily and joined them. "Yes, I did; don't try to fool me, Ole. It seems to me it is my turn to speak a little with Coldevin; you have had him to yourself long enough, Ole."

And she took Ole's chair and sat down.

"The letters from home are full of questions about you. Mamma asked me to see that you were comfortable at your hotel."

Coldevin's lips quivered again, and he said, with his eyes on the floor:

"How can you bother with such things now? Don't worry about me; I am very comfortable. I hope you are enjoying yourself? Though I hardly need to ask you that."

"But, do you know, there are times when I am longing for home, too. Can you understand that?"

"That is only the first few days—It will be a little hard never to see you again, Miss Aagot—I mean a little—that is—"

"You talk so strangely to-night," she said. "You almost make me want to cry; honestly you do."

"But, dear Miss Aagot—"

"To get married isn't the same as to die, I'm sure."

Coldevin's manner instantly changed; he became jocular.

"Die! Well, I like that! But you are right in saying that I have been sitting here and depressing you with my talk. It was mostly your mother I was thinking of. It was nobody else—Tell me, have you finished the cushions for the yacht?"

"Yes," answered Aagot absently.

"But you have not been in Parliament yet? I imagine you have hardly had time for that as yet. I have been there every day; but then I haven't anything else to do."

"Listen," she said suddenly; "I may not have an opportunity to bid you good night later, so I will do it now." She gave him her hand. "And remember, you have promised to call to-morrow! I—You will make me very happy if you come."

She dropped his hand and got up.

He sat there a moment as in a trance. He heard somebody say: "What can Miss Aagot and Coldevin be so deeply absorbed in?" He heard that Aagot was on the point of answering, and he exclaimed hurriedly:

"I shake hands with Miss Aagot on a promise to call on her to-morrow."

"Be sure and keep your promise, now," he heard Ole say. "Well, Aagot, I suppose we ought to be getting home."

Ole put his hand in his pocket to pay the waiter; the Journalist did the same, but Milde seized his arm and said:

"Leave that to Ole Henriksen. Kindly pay for us, too, Ole."

"With pleasure."

At the door Lars Paulsberg caught up with him and said:

"Don't go away without giving me the opportunity of shaking hands with you. I hear you could lend me these rotten crowns."

Ole and Aagot went. A little later Coldevin got up, too; he bowed to each of the clique and departed. He heard laughter behind his back and the word "phenomenon" several times. He hurried into the first gateway he passed and took out from his pocketbook a little silken bow, in the Norwegian colours, carefully wrapped in paper. He kissed the bow, looked at it a long time, and kissed it again, trembling in the grip of a silent, deep emotion.

IV

It was Ole Henriksen's habit to make his rounds through the business establishment immediately after his early morning coffee. He was an early riser and had usually accomplished a great deal before breakfast, inspected store and cellars, read and answered mail, telegraphed, given instructions to his clerks; everything devolved upon him. Aagot kept him company nowadays; she insisted on getting up as early as he, and her little hands lightened many a task for him. Ole Henriksen worked more enthusiastically than ever. The old man did nothing nowadays but make out an occasional bill and balance up the cash-book; he kept to himself up-stairs most of the time, and spent many an hour in the company of some old crony, some visiting ship's captain or business acquaintance. But before retiring old Henriksen always lit a lamp, shambled down-stairs to the office, and took a last survey of the books. He took his time; and when he came up about midnight he retired immediately.

Ole did the work for both of them; it was like play to him to direct all these threads which he knew from the days of childhood. Aagot did not disturb him much; it was only down in the little warehouse office that she was apt to delay him at times. Her youth and gaiety filled the little room, glorified everything, and brightened the world.

She was so cheerful that she carried away even the phlegmatic Ole. He was lost in her; he played little tricks on her and trembled with the tenderest affection for this hoydenish girl who wasn't even full grown. When in the company of others he appeared vastly superior—she was his little sweetheart; she was so young, much younger than he, it was up to him to display his knowledge and experience. But when they were alone, alas! then he could not keep up this pretence; he lost his seriousness and was a child with her. He stole many a glance from his books and papers, gazed at her secretly, lost in contemplation of her radiant figure and worshipping to distraction her dimpling smile. How she could make his heart pound when she would glance archly at him and then come over to him and whisper: "So you are *my* boy, are you?" She had so many adorable ways. At times she could sit and gaze at the floor, gaze fixedly at something which made her eyes dewy—memories, perhaps—some old memory—

Ole asked her at last when she thought they ought to get married, and when he saw her blush deeply, even to her neck, he regretted that he had been too abrupt. There was no hurry; she must decide that herself; no need to answer now, not at all.

But she answered:

"I am ready when you are."

There was a knock at the door and Irgens entered. He came in order to propose a visit to the sculpture-gallery. Ole said jestingly:

"I see! You have chosen this hour because you knew I couldn't come along!"

"What nonsense! We have to go when the galleries are open, naturally."

Ole laughed loudly.

"Look, he is getting mad, furious, ha, ha, ha! I fooled you that time, Irgens!"

Aagot got her hat and coat and went with Irgens. Ole called after her:

"Don't stay too late, Aagot! Remember, we have promised to go with Tidemand to Tivoli."

On the street Irgens glanced at his watch and said:

"I see it is a little too early yet. If you have no objections we might take a walk up toward the Castle."

And they walked toward the Castle. The band played; people strolled up and down. Irgens talked again interestingly and facetiously about different matters, and Aagot replied and laughed, listening curiously to his words; at times she would make some admiring little exclamation when he made a specially striking remark. She could not refrain from looking at his face—a handsome face, rich, curly moustache, a somewhat broad, voluptuous mouth. He was in an entirely new suit to-day; she noticed it was bluish like her own. He wore a silk shirt and grey gloves.

As they passed Our Saviour's Church he asked her if she liked to go to church. She said yes—didn't he?

"Oh, no, not very often."

That was not nice of him.

He bowed smilingly. If she said so, of course. The fact of the matter was that he had received a rude shock once; it sounded silly, it was only a bagatelle, but it proved of far-reaching effect. He was sitting in this very church on an occasion; a high mass was being celebrated. The minister was all right; he was doing splendidly. He was even eloquent; he spoke convincingly, with feeling and pathos. But in the middle of a most stirring peroration in which he, carried away in an outburst of spiritual fervour, had meant to shout: "Jews and Gentiles!" his tongue had tripped and he had said: "Gents and Jewtiles! *Gents and Jewtiles!*—Imagine these silly words hurled over the heads of the congregation in a loud, sonorous voice! And the poor fellow stood there in full daylight and could not get away from his miserable blunder. I assure you, it shocked me like a cold shower!"

It sounded genuine as he spoke, not at all like an episode invented for the occasion. Was it not possible that a particularly sensitive soul could be seriously shaken by such a grotesque and silly mishap? Aagot could very well understand it; and at the same time she had to laugh over that miserable "Gents and Jewtiles," which she repeated over and over.

When they passed the Parliament buildings, Irgens pointed to the greystone colossus and said:

"There we have Parliament; have you been there yet?"

"No, not yet."

Well, it wasn't a very cheerful place just now—wavering and treason all along the line! The doughty parliamentarians lolled in their chairs and chewed tobacco and grew fat and lazy; they used sonorous phrases and challenged Sweden to a fight with bare knuckles, but when time for action came—where were they then? She had no idea how he and others were boiling with indignation over this display of loathsome cowardice. And what was the mighty adversary like? Sweden! That invincible world power full of doddering senility! He must compare Sweden to an octogenarian who sat, dead drunk and feeble, and boasted of his warlike temper: "I'll never yield—never!" And when Parliament heard that quavering voice it grew palsied with fear. No, he, Irgens, should have been in Parliament!

How manly and proudly he spoke! She looked at him and said: "How zealous you are now!"

"You must pardon me; I always grow impatient when our sovereignty is discussed," he replied. "I trust I haven't unwittingly offended you by trespassing on your personal opinions? I am glad to hear that."

They reached the Castle, turned aside, and entered the park; they forgot that time was passing. He had started in to tell her a story from the day's news, a scene from one of the courts: A man was being tried for murder and had confessed. The question of mitigating circumstances arose, and it was decided that there were mitigating circumstances. All right; penitentiary for life. "Next case!" Suddenly a voice is heard from among the spectators; it is the murderer's sweetheart, who shouts: "His confession is untrue; he has not committed murder! How could he possibly have done it; no one who knows him will believe it! And there are mitigating circumstances; you cannot sentence him, for it wasn't premeditated murder! No, Henry is innocent! Won't any of you who know him say that he is innocent? Why are you all silent?" And the lady was led out of the courtroom. That was love!

Aagot, the little goose, was moved. How beautiful—sad and beautiful! And they carried her out? What a tragedy!

"Well, probably the story is a little exaggerated," he said. "Love as strong as that does not grow on the bushes nowadays."

"But it does exist!"

"Perhaps, somewhere—on the Isle of the Blest—" But this expression awoke the poet in him, and he rhapsodised. "And the place was called Evenrest, because it was green and silent when the two arrived. A boy and a girl; she fair, bright, shining like a white pinion against him who was dark— two souls who gazed smilingly into each other, who voicelessly implored each other, who closed rapturously around each other. And blue mountains looked at them—"

He paused abruptly.

"I am making myself ridiculous," he said. "Let us sit down awhile."

They sat down. The sun sank, sank deeper; a tower-clock in the city somewhere boomed forth the hour. Irgens continued to speak, impressively, dreamily, warmly. He might go into the solitudes this summer, he said; settle down in a cabin by the water and row around at night. Imagine, wonderful nights in a rowboat!... But he had a feeling now that Aagot was beginning to be uneasy because of the lateness of the hour, and in order to keep her mind occupied he said:

"You must not believe, Miss Lynum, that I go around and prate about blue mountains always; if I do it now it is only because of you. You impress me deeply; you enrapture me when you are near me. I know what I am saying. It is the loveliness and brightness of your face, and when you tilt your head sideways—Of course, this is meant aesthetically, impersonally!"

Aagot had given him a quick glance, and this made him add the last words. She did not understand him, perhaps; the reason for this last remark was not quite clear to her, and she was on the point of saying something when he resumed laughingly:

"I sincerely trust I haven't bored you too much with my nonsense? If I have I'll go right down to the harbour and drown myself. Yes, you laugh, but—I want to tell you, though, that your displeasure was charmingly becoming to you, really. I saw that you were provoked. If I may be allowed to express myself aesthetically once more, I would say that for a moment you looked as the slender, wild fawn must look when she lifts her head and snorts."

"But now I want to tell *you* something," she said and got up. "What time is it? But you must be crazy! Let us be off at once! If it is my fault that you have talked too much, it is certainly yours that I have listened to you and forgotten the time entirely. This is awful!"

And they hurried away down the park slope.

As they were going to turn toward the museum he wondered if there would be time for a visit to-day. Perhaps they had better wait until some other time? What did she think?

She stopped and reflected a moment; then she laughed merrily and exclaimed:

"But we will have to go, if only for a moment! We must be able to say that we have been there. No, this is simply terrible!"

And they hurried along.

The fact that she was conspiring with him to hide this peccadillo, that from now on they would have a sort of secret together, filled him with a warm pleasure. He wanted to keep on talking, to continue to keep her interested; but she did not listen; she hurried along in order to get to the museum before it should close. She skipped quickly up the many stairs, ran past people going out, glanced quickly right and left in order to identify the chief works of art, and asked breathlessly: "Where is the Laocoön Group? Quick! I must see that!" They ran off in a wild search for the Laocoön Group. It turned out that they had at least ten minutes before closing time, and they took things a little easier.

Suddenly she imagined seeing Coldevin's dark eyes peering out from a corner; but as she took a step forward to look closer the eyes disappeared and she forgot all about it.

"What a pity we are in such a hurry!" she said several times.

When they had rushed through the first floor their time was up and they had to leave. She talked with Irgens on the way back and seemed as pleased as before; she gave him her hand at the door and thanked him, thanked him twice. He begged her forgiveness because he had been responsible for her failure to view the sculptures thoroughly, and she smiled amiably and said that she had had a good time.

"I shall see you later at Tivoli," said Irgens.

"Are you going there?" she asked in surprise.

"I have been asked to come; I am going with some friends."

Aagot did not know that Irgens had received a pressing invitation from Mrs. Hanka; she said all right, nodded, and went in.

Ole was waiting for her; she threw herself on his neck and cried eagerly:

"It was glorious—the Laocoön Group—everything! We did not have time to see everything, that is, to see everything carefully; but you will take me there some time, won't you? Promise! For I want you to take me."

* * * * *

When later on Ole and Aagot were going to Tidemand's house on their way to Tivoli, Aagot remarked casually:

"It is a pity that you are not a poet, Ole."

He looked at her in surprise. "Do you think so?" he asked.

Then suddenly it dawned on her what a tactless thing she had said. As a matter of fact, she had not meant it at all; it was just a thoughtless word, a thoughtless, thoughtless word. She repented it bitterly and would have given anything to have it unsaid. She stopped, threw her arms around Ole's neck right in the middle of the street, and said in agitation:

"And you believe it? It is easy to fool you, Ole! Listen—you don't for a moment think—I swear I didn't mean it, Ole. It was so stupid of me to say it, but I didn't for a moment think you would take it seriously. I want to know if you think I meant it; tell me if you do?"

"Of course I don't," he said and patted her cheek; "not at all, dearest. That you can make so much of a little thing like that, you foolish child! He, he!"

They continued their interrupted walk. She was so grateful to him because he had taken it so nicely. Oh, he was so good and considerate, she loved him; Heavens! how she adored him....

But this little scene had its influence over her conduct all during the evening.

V

When the performance was over they all gathered in the restaurant. The entire clique was there, even Mr. and Mrs. Paulsberg; later on Attorney Grande appeared, dragging with him Coldevin, who followed unwillingly and protestingly; he wanted to be excused. The Attorney had met him outside and had thought it would be fun to bring him along.

Everything under the sun had been discussed: literature and art, man and God; they had settled the suffrage question, taken a fall out of Malthus, strayed onto the political preserves. It had unfortunately turned out that Paulsberg's article in the *Gazette* failed to have the desired effect on Parliament. With sixty-five votes to forty-four it had decided to postpone matters indefinitely; five representatives had suddenly been taken ill and could not participate in the voting. Milde declared that he was going to Australia.

"But you are painting Paulsberg?" objected Norem, the Actor.

"Well, what of it? I can finish that picture in a couple of days."

It was, however, a secret arrangement that the picture was not to be finished until after the close of the Exhibition. Paulsberg had expressly demanded it. He did not want to be exhibited in mixed company; he desired solitude, veneration, a large window all to himself on the promenade. This was just like Paulsberg.

When, therefore, Milde said that he could finish the picture in a couple of days, Paulsberg answered curtly:

"I shall be unable to sit for you at present; I am working."

That settled it.

Mrs. Hanka had placed Aagot next to her. She had called to her: "Come here, you with the dimple, here by me!" And she had turned to Irgens and whispered: "Isn't she sweet?"

Mrs. Hanka was again in her grey woollen dress with low lace collar; her neck was bare. Spring seemed to affect her; she looked a little played out. Her lips were cracked, and when she laughed her features were distorted into wry grimaces because of these cracked lips.

She told Aagot that they were going to the country shortly and hoped to see her there. They were going to eat currants and rake hay and loll in the grass. Suddenly she turned to her husband across the table and said:

"While I remember it, can you let me have a hundred?"

"I wish you hadn't remembered it," said Tidemand good-naturedly. He winked, jested happily, and was delighted. "Don't marry, my friends; it is an expensive luxury! Another hundred!"

And he handed the bill to his wife, who thanked him.

"But what is it for?" he asked her banteringly.

"I refuse to tell you," she said, and turned to Aagot in order to avoid further references to the matter.

Attorney Grande and Coldevin entered just then.

"Of course you are coming," said the Attorney. "I never heard anything like it! I want you to join me in a little drink. Come and help me, you fellows; I can't get the man inside!"

But when Coldevin saw who were present he wrenched himself free quickly and disappeared.

He had visited Ole Henriksen one morning according to his promise, but he had vanished since then and nobody had seen him until now.

The Attorney said:

"I discovered him outside; I had pity on the poor man, he seemed so altogether alone, and I—"

Aagot had jumped up quickly and hurried outside; she caught up with Coldevin on the stairs. They talked together a few moments; finally they both returned.

"I beg your pardon," he said. "Attorney Grande was kind enough to ask me to come with him, but I did not know that there were others here—that there was a party here," he corrected himself.

The Attorney laughed.

"Sit down, drink, and be merry," he said.

And Coldevin made himself at home. This tutor from the country, bald and grey, generally taciturn and restrained, talked now with and like the rest. He seemed somewhat changed since his arrival; he answered boldly when he was addressed, and was not backward in expressing his opinions. Journalist Gregersen spoke again about the political situation. He had not heard Paulsberg say anything about it. What was going to happen? What were they going to do?

"What can one do about an accomplished fact?" asked Paulsberg. "Simply take it like men; that is all I can say."

The Attorney now asked Coldevin:

"I suppose you have been in Parliament to-day, also?"

"Yes."

"You know, then, what took place. What do you think of it?"

"That is not easy to say on the spur of the moment."

"Perhaps you haven't followed matters very closely; you have just arrived, I understand," said Mrs. Paulsberg amiably.

"Followed matters closely! I should say he has; don't you worry about that!" cried the Attorney. "I have talked with him before."

The discussion grew violent. Milde and the Journalist simultaneously demanded the dismissal of the cabinet; others expressed their opinion about the Swedish opera they had just attended; it appeared that not one among them understood music in the least, and they strayed back to politics.

"So you were not seriously shaken by what occurred to-day, Mr. Coldevin?" asked Paulsberg in order to be friendly, too. "I am ashamed to confess that I have sat at home and cursed all afternoon!"

"Indeed!" answered Coldevin.

"Don't you hear that Paulsberg asked if you were shaken?" said the Journalist sharply across the table.

Coldevin murmured:

"Shaken? One can, of course, not avoid feeling disappointed when such things happen. But the climax to-day was hardly unexpected by me. As I see it, it was only a last rite."

"Oh, you are a pessimist."

"Indeed, no, you are mistaken. I am not that."

Beer and sandwiches were served, afterward coffee. Coldevin glanced at those present; he met Aagot's eyes looking at him very gently, and this agitated him so that he suddenly spoke out loudly what was on his mind:

"Did this decision to-day surprise you so very much, then?" And when he received a qualified affirmation he continued, in order to make himself understood: "To me it appears to be entirely in harmony with conditions otherwise prevailing.—People are saying to themselves: 'We have our liberty; the constitution guarantees it, and now we want to enjoy it for a while!' Behold—the sons of Norway have become freemen and the peers of anybody."

Everybody agreed with him. Paulsberg nodded; this phenomenon from the country might not be entirely impossible, after all. But he would say no more; he preserved an obstinate silence. At last the Attorney got him started again; he asked:

"When I met you at the Grand recently you insisted that it was wrong ever to forget, ever to forgive. Is that a principle, or how—"

"Yes, you who are young should remember, should always remember, the disappointment you have suffered to-day. You have put your faith in a man, and the man has betrayed your confidence; this you should never forget. One should never forgive, never; such wrongs should be avenged. Once I saw two truck-horses maltreated; it was in a Catholic country, in France. The driver sat high in his seat and swung his enormous whip; it was of no use, the horses slipped and could not budge the heavy load, even though they, so to speak, dug their hoofs into the asphalt. The driver got down; he turned his whip around and used the handle; he beat the horses across their backs; they tried again, stumbled and fell, got up and made another effort. The driver became more and more enraged as people gathered around and witnessed his dilemma; he went forward and beat the horses across the eyes; he went back and struck them on the tender spots beneath the flanks, and the horses squirmed and stumbled, and fell to their knees again, as if they begged for mercy—Three times I tried to get at that brute, and every time I was pushed back by the railing mob who wanted no interference. I had no gun; I was helpless; I stood there with a penknife in my hands and cursed and swore to high Heaven at that barbaric beast. Then somebody next to me—a woman, a nun who carried on her breast the cross of Christ—said mildly and reproachfully: 'You are committing an awful sin, sir; the Lord is good; he forgives everything!' I turned to that unspeakably brutal creature and said nothing, but glared at her and happened to spit in her face—"

This delighted the clique.

"In the face? How did it turn out? The devil you say! Did you get away with it?"

"No; I was arrested—But what I wanted to say is this: Never forgive; it is brutal; it turns justice into a farce. A kind act should be repaid with a still kinder act, but a wicked wrong should be avenged. If one is struck on one cheek and turns the other in forgiveness and submission, then goodness and justice lose all value. I wish to point out that the result in Parliament to-day is not altogether an illogical consequence of the conditions that have developed among us. We forgive and forget treason in our leaders and excuse their vacillation and weakness in every crisis. Now the youthful element should step forward, the young Norway, invincible in its indignation and irresistible in its strength. But the young Norway does not step forward; indeed no, we have mollycoddled it with hymns and rot about peace eternal; we have taught it to admire gentleness and submissiveness; above all, to emulate those who have reached the highest degree of neutral toothlessness. Behold the country's youth, strapping and full-grown, six foot tall, sucking its bottle and growing fat and harmless. If some one smites it on one cheek it turns the other accommodatingly, and keeps its fists in its pockets with admirable self-control."

Coldevin's speech attracted not a little attention; they all looked closely at him. He sat there as usual and spoke quietly, without excitement. But his eyes blazed, and his hands trembled as he awkwardly bent back his fingers until they cracked. He did not lift his voice above the normal. Otherwise he did not look well; he wore a loose shirt-front, and this had become disarranged and hung lopsidedly so that one could glimpse a blue cotton shirt beneath. His beard straggled down his breast.

The Journalist nodded and remarked to his neighbour:

"Not at all bad! He is almost one of us."

Lars Paulsberg said jestingly, and still amiably:

"As I said before, I have done nothing but curse all day, so I guess I have contributed considerably to the indignation of our youth."

Attorney Grande, who enjoyed himself immensely, was quite proud over his idea of getting Coldevin to come. He told Milde once more how it had happened: "I thought it would not be very lively here, and just then I ran across this fellow outside, standing there all by himself looking in. It kind of moved me, you know—"

Milde spoke up.

"You mentioned the conditions now prevailing. If by that you mean that we are entirely surrounded by weakness and submissiveness, let me inform you that you are much mistaken—"

"In that case I do not mean it, of course."

"But what do you mean, then? You cannot say that youth like ours, teeming with talent and genius, is weak and of no account. Good God, man! there never was a time when our youth was as rich in talent as at present."

"If there was, then I never heard of it," said even Norem, who had been sitting quietly at a corner of the table emptying glass upon glass.

"Talent? Now that is an entirely different question, you know," said Coldevin quietly. "But do you really think that the talents within our youth are so sweepingly great?"

"He—he asks if—So our talents at present do not amount to so very much, Mr. Coldevin?" Milde laughed contemptuously and turned to Irgens, who had kept aloof from the conversation. "It looks bad for us, Irgens; the phenomenon does not approve of us."

Mrs. Hanka now spoke; she wanted to smooth matters over. It could only be a misunderstanding; Mr. Coldevin would surely explain himself satisfactorily. Couldn't they listen to a man without losing their temper? "You ought to be ashamed of yourself, Milde—"

"You are not much impressed with us who are supposed to have a little talent, then?" asked Paulsberg, still indulgent.

"Impressed? I must admit that in my humble opinion things are a little on the down grade with us," answered Coldevin. "I confess that that is my opinion. And it is especially the country's youth I am thinking of. We have begun a slow retrogression; in plain words, we are lowering our standards, we are tapering down to a general zero. The young do not demand much from themselves or from others any more; they accept the diminutive and call it great; there is not much, not very much, needed to create a stir nowadays. That is what I meant when I referred to the general conditions."

"But, good Lord! what do you think of our younger writers, then?" cried Journalist Gregersen, flushed and angry. "Our poets, yes! Have you read any of them? Have you, for instance, ever come across the name of Paulsberg, the name of Irgens?"

Aagot could not refrain from observing her old tutor. She was surprised to note that this man, who invariably used to yield when he was contradicted, now sat there with a ready reply to every remark and did not look very timid either.

"You must not take offence at what I say," he begged. "I admit that I have no business to express such opinions here; I ought to leave that to others who understand these matters better than I; but if you want to know what I think, then I must say that, according to my lights, our younger writers do not seem to improve the conditions greatly. Of course, there can be no fixed standard; everything depends on the point of view, and yours is not mine; we are bound to differ. But, anyway, our younger writers do not lift the level greatly; hardly, according to my understanding. It would seem they lack the ability. Of course, that is no fault of theirs; but then they have no right to pose as being greater than they are. It is a pity that we lose sight of the greater and make mediocrity take its place. Look at our youth; look at our authors; they are very clever, but—Yes, they are both clever and industrious; they labour and toil, *but they lack the spark*. Good God, how far they are from squandering their treasures! They are saving and calculating and prudent. They write a few verses and they print these few verses. They squeeze out a book now and then; they delve into their inmost recesses and conscientiously scrape the bottom until they arrive at a satisfactory result. They do not scatter values broadcast; no, they do not fling gold along the highways. In former days our poets could afford to be extravagant; there was wealth untold; they towered rich and care-free and squandered their treasures with glorious unconcern. Why not? There was plenty left. Oh, no, our present-day authors are clever and sensible; they do not show us, as did the old, a flood, a tempest, a red eruption of flame-tongued, primeval power!"

Aagot's eyes were on him; he caught her glance of rapt attention, and she made him understand with a warm smile that she had listened to his every word. She wanted to show Ole how little she had meant her thoughtless regret that he was no poet. She nodded to Coldevin and wished the poets all they got. Coldevin was grateful for her smile; she was the only one who smiled at him, and he did not mind the violent interruptions, the shouts and rude questions: What kind of a phenomenon was he who could assume this superior pose? What world-subduing exploits had he performed? He should not remain incognito any longer; what was his real name? They wanted to acclaim him!

Irgens was least affected of them all; he twirled his moustache and looked at his watch to make everybody understand how this bored him. Glancing at Coldevin, he whispered to Mrs. Hanka with an expression of disgust:

"It seems to me that this man is a little too untidy. Look at his collar, or bib, or whatever one may call it. I noticed that he put his cigar-holder in his vest-pocket a moment ago without first putting it in a case. Who knows, there might be an old comb in the same pocket."

But with his air of undisturbed serenity, with his eyes fixed on a point in the table, quietly indifferent, Coldevin listened to the exclamations from the gentlemen of the party. The Journalist asked him pointblank if he were not ashamed of himself.

"Leave him alone!" said Paulsberg. "I don't see why you want to annoy him."

"It certainly looks bad for our poor country!" sneered the Journalist. "No talents, no youth, nothing only a 'general condition.' He, he! God only knows how it will all end! And we who have innocently assumed that a people should honour and respect its young writers!"

Coldevin seized on this.

"Yes, but that is exactly what people are doing; nobody can justly complain on that score! People respect most highly a man who has written a book or two; he is admired far more, for instance, than the ablest business man or the most talented professional! To our people an author means a great deal; he is the essence of all that is distinguished and admirable. There are probably very few countries in which the intellectual life is dominated by authors to the degree it is here. As you probably will admit, we have no statesmen; but our authors direct our politics, and they do it well. It may have struck you that there are barren spots in our scientific attainments; however, with true intuition, our authors are not afraid to assume the burden and pose as scientists. It has surely not escaped your attention that in all our history we have never produced a thinker; never mind, our authors dabble in philosophy, and everybody thinks they do it splendidly. It seems highly unjust to complain because of a lack of appreciation of and admiration for our authors."

Paulsberg, who in his works had repeatedly proven himself a thinker and philosopher of rank, sat and toyed with his eye-glass and smiled superciliously. But when Coldevin added a few words and ended up with saying that he had the greatest hope and faith in the country's practical youth, in its young commercial talents, then a loud laugh greeted him, and both the Journalist and Paulsberg shouted simultaneously that this was great, by all the saints the best ever, so help me! Commercial talents— whatever could that be? Talents for trading—what? Glory be!

"In my opinion you will find really great talents within the ranks of our business youth," Coldevin continued undisturbed. "And I would advise you to pay a little attention to them. They are building ships, opening new markets, carrying on involved business enterprises on a hitherto undreamed of scale—"

Coldevin could not be heard; they laughed and shouted, although out of respect for their good friends the business men present they endeavoured to change the subject. Ole Henriksen and Tidemand had listened in silence; they were embarrassed and did not know how to take it, but began to speak together in low voices. Suddenly Tidemand whispered:

"Can I come over and see you to-morrow about a business matter? I would like to come early, about ten, if you have time then? All right; thanks!"

At Milde's corner of the table the discussion had swung to wines—old wines, Johannisberger, Cabinet, Musigny. Milde understood the subject thoroughly and contradicted the Attorney violently, although Grande, of the well-known Grande family, was supposed to have drunk such wines since he was a child.

"There is no end to your assertiveness lately," said Milde.

The Attorney glanced at him and muttered:

"Such a bit of an oil-painter will also presume to understand wines!"

Conversation strayed to the government art subsidies. Irgens listened without changing a feature when Milde asserted that Ojen was the worthiest applicant. It was exceedingly generous in Milde to express such views; he himself had applied and needed the money as much as anybody. Irgens could hardly understand it.

Interest in the preposterous tutor had entirely waned. Nobody spoke to him any more; he had got hold of his hat, which he sat and twirled. Mrs. Hanka addressed a couple of questions to him in order to be polite, but after answering them he was entirely silent. It was strange that the man did not notice how his shirt-front sagged; the slightest movement would correct it. But he did not adjust it.

Paulsberg got up to take his leave. Before he went he manoeuvred the Journalist into a corner and whispered:

"You might do me the favour to mention that I have about half completed my new book. It might interest people to know I am at it."

Milde and the Attorney got up next; they awoke Norem, who was dozing after all the many glasses he had emptied, and they got him on his legs with difficulty. He began to speak; he had not quite heard the last, the very last of the discussion; how had the poets fared? Oh, there was Mrs. Hanka; so pleased to see her. But why had she arrived so late?

He was finally led outside.

"This means a general departure, I suppose?" asked Irgens, displeased. He had tried to approach Miss Lynum once during the evening but without success. She had plainly avoided him. He had noticed later on that Coldevin's foolish remarks about the poets and the youth of the country had amused her inordinately; what could that mean? Altogether it had been an unpleasant evening. Mrs. Hanka had sat there with her cracked lips unable to smile decently, and Mrs. Paulsberg was impossible. The evening was simply wasted.

And now the company was breaking up; no prospects for livening up one's spirits with a little intimate half-hour.

Irgens promised to take his revenge on the clique because of the indifference it seemed to show him. Perhaps next week....

Outside Tivoli the company parted. Mrs. Hanka and Aagot walked together down the street.

VI

Tidemand came to H. Henriksen's office at ten the next morning. Ole was standing at his desk.

Tidemand's errand was, as he had said, a matter of business only; he spoke in a low voice and placed before Ole a telegram couched in mysterious words. Where it said "Rising One," it really meant "Ten," and where it said "Baisse U. S.," it meant an exportation prohibition on the Black Sea and along the Danube, and a rise in America. The telegram was from Tidemand's agent in Archangel.

Ole Henriksen immediately grasped the situation: on account of the Russian crop failure, in connection with the already low supplies, Russia was preparing to prohibit all grain exports. Hard times were coming. Norway, too, would feel the pressure, and grain would soar to incredible prices. It was necessary to get hold of as much as possible at no matter what figure. In spite of official Russian denials of the rumours in English newspapers, it seemed as if America already had scented the danger, for American wheat was rising daily. From eighty-seven and eighty-eight it had risen until it now fluctuated between one hundred and ten and one hundred and fifteen. Nobody could predict to what heights it would climb.

Tidemand's business with Ole was a proposition that the two friends and colleagues join in a speculation in American rye while there still was time. They were to join forces and import a mass of rye that should materially assist in keeping the country fed during the coming year. But it was a matter of urgency; rye, too, was soaring; in Russia it was almost unpurchasable.

Ole left his desk and began to walk up and down. His mind was working; he had intended to offer Tidemand some refreshment, but forgot it entirely. He was greatly tempted, but he was up to his neck in other pressing engagements—that Brazilian affair had almost paralysed him for the moment, and he did not expect to be able to take his profits until early summer.

"There ought to be money in it," said Tidemand.

No doubt; that was not why Ole hesitated. But he simply was not able to do it. He explained his circumstances and added that he was afraid to tackle anything more at present. The speculation appealed to him, notwithstanding his inability to participate; his eyes gleamed, and he inquired eagerly into all the details. He took a piece of paper, made estimates, and studied the telegram afresh with a thoughtful air. Finally he declared that he could do nothing.

"Of course I can operate alone," said Tidemand. "I will do it on a smaller scale, that is all. But I should have liked you to be in on this; I would have felt safer. I realise that you cannot go further. However, I'll telegraph myself; have you got a blank?"

Tidemand wrote out his telegram and handed it to Ole.

"I guess that is clear enough?"

Ole stepped back a pace.

"So much?" he exclaimed. "This is a big order, Andreas."

"It is big. But I hope the results will justify it," answered Tidemand quietly. And unable to control a feeling that overwhelmed him at the moment, he looked toward the wall and whispered as if to himself: "I don't care how it turns out or about anything any more."

Ole looked at him and asked:

"Any news?"

"No—"

"Well, we'll see how it turns out."

Tidemand put the telegram in his pocket.

"I should have liked us both to be in this enterprise, Ole. I must confess that I am in deep elsewhere, too, but—I have my ice to realise on. When the warm weather comes I'll make money on that, don't you think?"

"Decidedly! As good as ready money, ice is."

"So I am not altogether on my knees. And may the Lord keep that sad fate from me, both for my own sake and for the sake of mine!"

"But could you not as a matter of safety—Wait a moment. Pardon me for not offering you a cigar; I know how you like to smoke while talking; I forgot. Sit down a moment; I'll be back directly."

Tidemand knew that Ole was on his way to the cellar for the usual bottle of wine, and tried to call him back, but Ole did not hear and returned in a moment with the old, fuzzy bottle. They sat on the sofa as usual and drank to each other.

"I simply wanted to ask," continued Ole, "are you sure you have considered everything in connection with this American affair? I do not flatter myself that I can teach you anything, you know, but—"

"Yes, I fancy I have calculated all contingencies," answered Tidemand. "You notice I am using the term 'Delivery within three days.' Success depends on quick action. I haven't even forgotten to consider the effect of a possible presidential change in America."

"But wouldn't it be safer to place your limit a little closer? Perhaps you ought not to buy over twelve."

"No; that would not be well. For you understand that if Russia closes, then fifteen, or even twenty, is not too much. On the other hand, if she does not close, then a hundred, yes, ninety, is far too much. In that case I am done for."

They both reflected.

"I believe this enterprise is going to be lucky," said Tidemand suddenly. "Really, I feel it. You know what it means when we traders have a premonition of this kind."

"How are things otherwise?" asked Ole.

"Well," Tidemand answered hurriedly, "it does not look so bad just now, not at all. Things are very much as usual at home."

"No change, then?"

"Well, no—I must get back now."

Tidemand got up. Ole followed him to the door and said:

"It wasn't you who didn't care how matters turn out, was it? Well, I am glad you came, anyway."

The awkward fellow! This was Ole Henriksen's way of stiffening a comrade's backbone.

But Tidemand did not go at once; he stood there with his hand on the door-knob and shifted his eyes nervously from place to place.

"It can hardly be thought strange if I get a little downhearted once in a while," he said. "Things do not look very bright for me; I do my best to fix everything up, but I do not make much headway, not very much, no. Well, we'll have to wait and see how matters shape themselves. I think it is getting a little better, thank God."

"Does your wife keep at home more now? It seems to me that—"

"Hanka has been a good mother to the children lately. I have been very happy because of that; it has brought us closer together, as it were. She is busy fitting the children out for the country. It is wonderful the things she gets together; I have never seen anything like it—blue and white and red dresses! They are lying home; I look at them whenever I am home. Perhaps I shouldn't place too much faith in it. She does not consider herself married yet, she continues to call herself Lange. That may be only a whim. She calls herself Tidemand, too; she does not forget that. You yourself heard last night in Tivoli how she asked me for a hundred. I am glad she does that; I don't mind, and shouldn't have mentioned it if you hadn't heard it yourself. But it happened to be the third hundred crowns she had got from me in two days. Don't misunderstand me! But why does she ask me for money before people? Isn't that as if she wanted to give out the impression that that is the only way to take me, otherwise she wouldn't get any? She uses a good deal of money; I hardly think she uses it for herself; I am sure she doesn't, for Hanka was never extravagant. She must be giving it away; it is her affair if she helps somebody. She gets quite a lot of money from me in a week's time; sometimes she gets it when she goes out, and she has nothing left when she returns, although she has bought nothing. Well, that does not matter. As long as I have anything it belongs to her as well as to me; that is only right and natural. I asked her jokingly once if she wanted to ruin me— make a beggar out of me. It was only a joke, and I laughed heartily myself as I said it. But I shouldn't have said it; she offered to leave the house whenever I wanted her to—in short, divorce. She has told me that often enough, but this time simply because of a joke. I said that I was sorry, and I asked her pardon; I had never for a moment thought of such a thing as that she might ruin me. 'Dear Andreas,' she asked me, 'can we never get free from each other?' I do not know what I answered; I guess there was not much sense to it, for she asked immediately for my key, as she had lost her own. I gave it to her, and then she smiled. 'Smile again,' I said, and she did it for my sake, and said smilingly that I was a big baby. Yesterday morning I didn't see her before I got home from the office. She was still working with the children's summer outfit and showed me everything. She took out her handkerchief, and as she pulled it out from her dress a tie fell out, a gentleman's red tie. I made out that I did not see it; but I knew very well that the tie did not belong to me. I knew it only too well. That is—understand me correctly—I did not see it well enough to be sure whom it might belong to. It might even have been one of my own ties, some old rag I have ceased to use. It is a peculiarity of mine never to remember my own ties; I notice them so little, I imagine—So things are coming around, as I said. And if my big trade now succeeds, perhaps that will bring luck for us all. It would be fun to show her that I am not such a dunce, ha, ha!"

The two friends talked a little further, after which Tidemand went to the telegraph office. He was full of hope. His great idea was to discount the crisis, to hold enormous supplies of grain when nobody else should have any. He would succeed! He walked with a springy step, like a youth, and avoided meeting anybody who might detain him.

* * * * *

A telegram to the foreign office announced five days later that the Russian government, owing to the shortage of grain and the dark outlook for the coming harvests, had been obliged to prohibit all exports of rye, wheat, corn, and grist from the harbours of Russia and Finland.

Tidemand's calculations had proven correct.

RIPENING

I

Irgens had published his book. This superior soul, who never took anybody into his confidence, had, to the great surprise of everybody, put out a charming volume of poems just when spring was in full blow. Was that not a surprise? True, it was two years since his drama had appeared; but it was now proven that he had not been idle; he had conceived one poem after another, and quietly put them away, and when the heap had grown big enough he had given it to the printer. It was thus a proud man should act; nobody exceeded Irgens in strong and warm discretion.

His book was exhibited in the bookstore windows; people discussed it and predicted it would attract much attention; the ladies were enraptured with the gently glowing love stanzas scattered through it. There were also many bold and courageous words, full of manliness and will: poems to Justice, to Liberty, to the Kings—God knows he did not spare the kings. But Irgens noticed no more than ever that people admired him when he strolled down the promenade. Gracious! if they enjoyed looking at him, that was their affair. He was frigidly indifferent, as ever.

"I must admit you are a foxy fellow!" exclaimed even Norem, the Actor, when he ran across him on the street. "Here you go along quietly and say nothing, and all of a sudden you set off a rocket right under our very noses. You are unique!"

The Attorney, however, could not help giving him a little dig; he laughed and said: "But you have enemies, Irgens. I was talking to a man today who refused to see anything gigantic in the publishing of a small volume after a lapse of nearly two years and a half!"

Then Irgens flung back the haughty reply: "I take a pride in a limited production. The quantity does not matter."

Later on, however, he inquired concerning the identity of this detractor. He was not tortured by curiosity; people knew fortunately that he was quite indifferent to public opinion. But anyhow—was it Paulsberg?

No, it was not Paulsberg.

Irgens made a few more questions and guesses, but the pretentious Attorney refused to betray his critic. He made a secret out of it, and irritated Irgens as much as he could. "It seems you are not so altogether indifferent," he teased and chuckled gleefully.

Irgens murmured contemptuously: "Nonsense!" But he was evidently considerably bothered by this defamer, this jealous fellow who had criticised him, and tried to belittle his exploit. If not Paulsberg, who then? Who among them had done better during the last two and a half years? Irgens knew nobody; among the younger writers he was absolutely paramount. Suddenly something struck him, and he said indifferently:

"Of course, it is a matter of absolute indifference to me who the person is; but if it is that lout Coldevin—Lord, man! do you really pay any attention to what such a freak says? A man who carries a cigar-holder and a dirty comb in the same pocket! Well, I must be going; so long!"

Irgens walked off. If the enemy was this barbarian from the backwoods, well and good! His mind was again relieved; he nodded to acquaintances and looked quite cheerful. He had for a moment felt aggrieved that anybody should be grumbling behind his back, but that was now forgotten; it would be foolish to take offence at this old bushwhacker.

Irgens intended to take a walk around the harbour so as to be left in peace; this more or less stupid talk about his book had really got on his nerves. Were people now beginning to prate about working hours and quantity in connection with poetry? In that case his book would be found wanting; it was not so very ponderous; it did not outweigh one of Paulsberg's novels, thank God!

When he reached the harbour he suddenly caught a glimpse of Coldevin's head behind a pile of packing-cases. Irgens noticed the direction of his glance, but this told him nothing; the old imbecile was evidently lost in some crazy meditation or other. It was amusing to see him so altogether unconscious of his surroundings, standing there agape with his nose in the air. His eyes were almost in a direct line with the little office window at the end of Henriksen's warehouse; he stared unblinkingly and apparently unseeingly at that particular spot. Irgens was on the point of going over in order to inquire if he perhaps wanted to see Ole Henriksen; he would then be able to turn the conversation to his book and get the old man to express an opinion. It would be quite entertaining; the oaf would be forced to admit that he valued poetry according to weight. But was it worth while? It was really of no account whatever what this person might think. Irgens made a turn across the docks; he looked up—Coldevin had not moved. Irgens sauntered past, crossed the street on his way up-town. Suddenly Ole Henriksen and Aagot came out of the warehouse and caught sight of him.

"Good day, good day, Irgens!" called Ole with outstretched hand. "Glad to see you. I want to thank you for the book you sent us. You are a wonder; you surprise your very best friends even—poet, master!"

Ole talked on, pleased and happy over his friend's accomplishment, admiring now one stanza, now another, and thanking Irgens over and over.

"Aagot and I have read it with beating hearts!" he said. "I really believe Aagot wept a little now and then—Yes; you did; no use denying it, Aagot. You need not feel ashamed of that—What I wanted to say—come along to the telegraph office, Irgens; then we'll drop in at Sara's afterward, if you like. I have a little surprise for you."

Aagot said nothing.

"You can walk up and down a little while I telegraph," said Ole. "But don't get impatient if it takes some time. I have got to catch a ship before it leaves Arendal!"

And Ole ran up the stairs and disappeared; Irgens looked after him.

"Listen—I want to thank you for your book!" said Aagot quickly in a low voice. "You will never know how I have enjoyed it."

"Really? Truly? It is good to hear you say that," he replied, full of gratitude. That she should have waited until Ole had left in order to thank him was a charming and delicate tribute; she had done it now much more genuinely and warmly; her words meant so much more now. She told him what had especially stirred her; it was that wonderful "Song to Life"; never had she read anything so beautiful. Then, as if she feared she had spoken too warmly and laid herself open to misunderstanding, she added in an ordinary tone of voice that Ole had been just as enchanted as she; he had read most of it aloud to her.

Irgens made a wry face. Did she care to have things read to her? Really?

It was intentionally that Aagot had mixed Ole's name into the conversation. This afternoon he had once more asked her about the wedding, and she had left everything to him; there was no reason for delay. It had been decided to have the wedding after Ole had returned from London this coming fall. Ole was as good as the day was long; he never grew impatient with her and was almost absurdly fond of her. He had said that perhaps she had better spend a little time in the house occasionally. She had flushed; she could not help it; it was disgraceful not to have stirred a finger to make herself a little useful instead of hanging around the office early and late. Suppose she began to think a little about their house, said Ole; she might make up her mind about things they wanted, furniture and such. Of course, she should have all the help she needed, but—Yes, it was only too true; she had not given her new home a thought; she had simply hung about the office with him. She had begun to cry, and had told him how silly and useless she really was; she was a goose, a stupid little goose. But Ole had taken her in his arms and had sat down with her on the sofa and told her that she was only a child, a charming, wonderful child, but she was getting older and more sensible right along; time and life were before them. How he loved her! His eyes, too, were wet; he looked like a child himself. Above all, there was no hurry; she had free hands to decide and arrange, just as she pleased. Yes; they were fully agreed....

"I must confess I feared you had lost interest in us poets," said Irgens.
"I was afraid we had forfeited your good-will in some way."

She woke up and looked at him.

"Why do you say that?"

"I had come to that conclusion. You remember that evening at Tivoli when your old tutor was quite severe on us poor scribblers? You looked as if you heartily approved of everything he said."

"No, you are mistaken."

Pause.

"I am very glad that I have met you, anyway," said Irgens as indifferently as he could. "Only to see you is enough to put me in good spirits. It must be wonderful to be able to bring happiness to others simply by appearing."

She had not the heart to show displeasure over that; perhaps he really meant it, strange though it sounded, and she answered smilingly:

"It would be hard on you if you depended on me to bring you good spirits." God knows she had not meant to pain him; she had said it in all innocence, without any veiled thought or ulterior motive; but when Irgens's head drooped and he said quietly, "Yes, I understand!" it occurred to her that several interpretations might be placed upon this sentence, and she added hurriedly: "For you do not see me very often. By the way, I am going to the country this summer; I shall probably be away until fall."

He stopped.

"Are you going to the country?"

"Yes. I am going with Mrs. Tidemand. I shall be with her until fall."

Irgens was silent and thoughtful a few moments.

"Has it been decided that Tidemands are going to the country, then?" he asked. "I understood it was not settled yet."

Aagot nodded and said that it had been decided.

"That pleasure has been denied me," he said with a wistful smile. "No country joys for me."

"Why not?"

She regretted her question immediately; of course, he could not afford it. She was always so indelicate and awkward! She added a few meaningless words to save him the humiliation of a reply.

"When I want to go to the country I hire a boat and row over to the island," he said with his sad smile. "Anyway, it is better than nothing."

The island? She grew 'attentive. "Of course, the island! I haven't been there yet. Is it pretty?"

"Beautiful! There are some wonderful places. I know them all. If I only dared I would ask you to let me row you over some time?"

This was not said in simple courtesy; it was a request. She understood it perfectly. But she said, all the same, that she was not sure she had time; it would be interesting, but—

Pause.

"I wrote many of my poems there," continued Irgens. "I should like to show you the place."

Aagot was silent.

"Come, please!" he exclaimed suddenly, and wanted to take her hand.

Just then Ole Henriksen appeared on the stairs and came toward them. Irgens remained in his pleading attitude; he said with outstretched hand:

"Do, please!"

She glanced at him hurriedly.

"Yes," she whispered.

Ole joined them; he had not been able to get hold of Arendal at once; he could not get a reply until to-morrow. Off to Sara now! He really had a surprise for them—he carried in his pocket Ojen's latest work. They just ought to hear it!

II

Quite a number of the clique were ensconced at Sara's, drinking and gossiping. Tidemand was there, happy and contented with everything. He had been all smiles since his success with that enormous enterprise in rye. The grain had begun to arrive and was being stored in his warehouses, thousands upon thousands of sacks. They grew into mountains; there was no room for anything else; even Ole Henriksen had been obliged to let him have space for storing. Tidemand walked around and viewed this wealth with pride; even he had accomplished something above the ordinary. Never for an instant did he regret that he had given such unlimited orders.

Journalist Gregersen offered Ole one finger and said: "You have something on your conscience, Ole?"

"Oh, nothing sensational, exactly," said Ole. "I had a letter from Ojen; he sends me his latest poem. Do you want to hear it?"

"Does he send you his—Has he sent you a manuscript?" exclaimed Milde in astonishment. "I have never heard anything like it!"

"Now, no personalities!" warned the Journalist.

"Yes, but excuse me—why in the world did he send it to *you*, Ole?" asks Milde again and does not give in.

Irgens glanced at Aagot. She did not appear to be listening, but was talking eagerly with Mrs. Hanka. Irgens turned to Milde and told him curtly that there were certain impertinences which even friends were not supposed to submit to—was that clear enough?

Milde burst out laughing. He had never heard anything funnier. Did they get offended? He had not meant anything of a harmful nature, nothing offensive, mentally or physically! The idea simply had tickled his sense of humour. But if it wasn't funny, all right....

Ole took out his manuscript.

"It is something out of the ordinary," he said. "Ojen calls it 'Memories.'"

"Let me read it," said Norem quickly. "I am, at any rate, supposed to know a little about reading."

Ole handed him the manuscript.

"Jehovah is very busy—" began Norem. "Ojen has expressly stated in a marginal note that it is not to be Jahve; now you know it!"

> Jehovah is very busy; Jehovah has much to attend to. He was with me one night when I wandered in the forest; He descended to me while I lay on my face in prayer.

I lay there praying in the night, and the forest was silent.

> The night oppressed me like an unbending, disjointed absurdity, and the night was like a silence in which something breathing and mute was abroad.

Then Jehovah descended to me.

> When Jehovah came the air rushed away from Him like a wake; birds were blown away like chaff, and I clung to the sod and the trees and the rocks.

"You are calling me?" said Jehovah.

"I call out in my distress!" I answered.

And Jehovah spoke: "You want to know what to choose in life, Beauty or Love or Truth?" And Jehovah said: "You want to know?"

And when He said: "You want to learn that?" I did not answer, but was silent; for He knew my thoughts.

Then Jehovah touched my eyes, and I beheld:

> I saw a tall woman against the skies. She wore no garments, and when she moved her body shimmered like white silk, and she wore no garments; for her body quivered toward me in rapture.

> And she stood against the skies in a sunrise, yes, in a crimson dawn; and the sun shone upon her, and a scarlet light streamed up through the skies, yes, a light of blood surrounded her.

> And she was tall and white, and her eyes were like two blue flowers which brushed my soul when she looked at me; and when she spoke to me she entreated me and urged me toward her, and her voice was like a sweet phosphorescence with a taste of the sea.

> I rose from the earth and stretched forth my arms toward her, and when I stretched both my arms toward her she again implored me, and her body was odorous with rapture. And I was gloriously stirred in my inmost being, and I rose and gave her my lips in the morning glow, and my eyes fell.

> When I looked up again the woman was old. And the woman was old and hoary with years, and her body had shrunk with age, and she had very little life left. But when I looked up the sky was darkling toward

night, yes dark like night, and the woman was without hair. I looked to her and knew her not and knew not the sky, and when I looked toward the woman she was gone.

"This was Beauty!" said Jehovah. "Beauty wanes. I am Jehovah!"

And Jehovah touched my eyes again, and I beheld:

> I saw a terrace, high, beneath a castle. There were two people there, and the two people on the terrace were young and full of joy. And the sun shone on the castle, and on the terrace, and the sun shone on the two people and on the gravel deep, deep down the abyss, on the hard driveway. And the people were two, a man and a woman in the springtide of youth, and both were speaking honeyed words, and both were tender toward each other with desire.
>
> "See the flower on my breast!" he said; "can you hear what it is saying?" And he leaned backward toward the railing on the terrace and said: "This flower which you gave me stands here and murmurs and whispers toward you, and it murmurs: 'Beloved, Queen, Alvilde, Alvilde!' Do you hear it?"
>
> And she smiled and looked down, and she took his hand and placed his hand against her heart and answered: "But do you hear what my heart says to you? My heart throbs toward you and it blushes with emotion for your sake. And my heart babbles in joyful confusion and says: 'Beloved, I pause before you and almost perish when you look at me, Beloved!'"
>
> He leaned toward the terrace-railing and gloriously his breast heaved with love. And deep, deep below was the abyss and the hard driveway. And he pointed his finger down the depths and said: "Throw down your fan, and I will follow it!" And when he had spoken his breast rose and sank, and he placed his hands on the railing and made ready for the leap.

Then I cried out and closed my eyes....

> But when I looked up I saw again the two people, and they were both older and both in their prime. And the two did not speak to each other, but were silent with their thoughts. And when I looked up the sky was grey, and the two walked up the white castle-stairway, and she was full of indifference, yes full of hate in her steely eyes, and when I looked for the third time I saw also anger and hate in his glance, and his hair was grey like the grey skies.
>
> And as they ascended the stairs she dropped her fan, one step down it dropped, and she said with quivering lips and pointed downward: "I dropped my fan—there it lies on the lower step—please hand it to me, dear!"
>
> And he did not answer, but walked on and called a servant to pick up the fan.

"This was Love," said Jehovah. "Love perishes. I am Jehovah!"

And Jehovah touched my eyes for the last time, and I beheld:

> I saw a town and a public square, and I saw a scaffold. And when I listened I heard a seething sound of voices, and when I looked I saw many people who talked and gritted their teeth with joy. And I saw a man who was being bound, a malefactor who was being bound with leather thongs, and the malefactor's countenance was haughty and proud,

and his eyes shone like stars. But his garment was torn and his feet stood naked on the ground, and his clothes were almost gone, yes his cloak was worn to almost nothing.

And I listened and heard a voice, and when I looked I saw that the malefactor was speaking, and the malefactor spoke proudly and gloriously. And they bade him be silent, but he spoke, he testified, he shouted, and when they bade him be silent he did not cease with fear. And when the malefactor spoke the mob ran up and silenced his lips, and when he mutely pointed to the sky and to the sun, and when he pointed to his heart which still beat warmly, the mob ran up and struck him. And when the mob struck him the malefactor fell to his knees, and he knelt and clasped his hands and testified mutely, without words, in spite of the cruel blows.

And I looked at the malefactor and saw his eyes like stars, and I saw the mob throw him down and hold him on the scaffold with their hands. And when once more I looked I saw an axe-blade write in the air, and when I listened I heard the stroke of the axe against the scaffolding and the people joyfully shouting. And while I listened a single-throated cry rose toward heaven from people groaning with ecstasy.

But the malefactor's head rolled in the dirt and the mob ran up and seized it and lifted it high by the hair. And the malefactor's head still spoke, and it testified with unquenchable voice and spoke loudly all the words it uttered. And the malefactor's head was not silent even in death.

But the mob ran up and took hold of the malefactor's head by the tongue and lifted it high by the tongue. And the vanquished tongue was mute, and the tongue spoke no more. But the eyes were like stars, yes, like gleaming stars to be seen by everybody....

Then Jehovah said: "This was Truth. And Truth speaks even after its head is severed. And with its tongue bound its eyes shine like stars. I am Jehovah!"

When Jehovah had spoken I fell on my face and spoke not, but was silent with much thought. And I thought that Beauty was lovely ere it waned and Love was sweet ere it perished, and I thought that Truth endured like stars everlasting. And tremblingly I thought of Truth.

And Jehovah said: "You wanted to know what to choose in life?" And Jehovah said then: "Have you chosen?"

I lay on my face and answered, full of many thoughts:

"Beauty was lovely and Love was very sweet; and if I choose Truth, it is like the stars, eternal."

And Jehovah spake once more and asked me:

"Have you chosen?"

And my thoughts were many, my thoughts warred mightily within me, and I answered:

"Beauty was like a morning glow." And when I had said this I whispered and said: "Love was also sweet and glorious like a little star in my soul."

But then I felt Jehovah's eye on me, and Jehovah's eye read my thoughts. And for the third time Jehovah asked and said:

"Have you chosen?"

And when He said for the third time: "Have you chosen?" my eyes stared with terror, yes, all my strength had left me. And when He said for the last time: "Have you chosen?" I remembered Beauty and Love and remembered them both, and I answered Jehovah:

"I choose Truth!"

* * * * *

But I still remember....

"Well, that's all," concluded Norem.

Everybody was silent for a moment; then the Journalist said:

"I refrain from expressing an opinion; I notice Milde is going to say something."

And Milde did not refrain; far from it; on the contrary, he had a remark to make. Could anybody tell him what it was all about? He admired Ojen as much as anybody, but was there any sense to all this "Jehovah said" and "Jehovah said"? He wanted to be enlightened.

"But why are you always so unkind to Ojen?" asked Mrs. Hanka. "Memories— can't you understand? To me it seemed beautiful and full of feeling; don't spoil it for me now." And she turned to Aagot and said: "Didn't you find it so, too?"

"But, dear Mrs. Hanka," exclaimed Milde, "don't say that I am always unkind to Ojen! Do I not wish him success with his application for the subsidy, contrary to my own interests? But this blessed new 'intention' is beyond me. Memories—all right. But where, in Heaven's name, is the point? Jehovah has never visited him; it is an invention. And, furthermore, why didn't he choose both Youth and Beauty, and Truth as well? That is what I should have done. The point, I say!"

"But that is just it—there is no definite point," replied Ole Henriksen. "So Ojen says in a letter to me. Its effect lies in its euphony, he says."

"He does? No, that fellow is the same wherever he goes. That is the trouble. Not even the mountains can do anything for him. Goats' milk and pine woods and peasant girls have not the slightest effect on him, as it were—I am still at a loss to understand why he sent *you* his manuscript, Ole; but if it is an offence to ask, of course, then—"

"I really don't know why he sent it to me," said Ole quietly. "He tells me that he wanted me to see that he was doing something and not wasting his time altogether. He is anxious to get back, though; he cannot stand Torahus any longer."

Milde whistled.

"I understand! He asked you for carfare!"

"I do not suppose he has much money left. That could hardly be expected," answered Ole, and put the manuscript in his pocket. "As for me, I think it is a remarkable poem, irrespective of your opinion."

"Surely, old fellow; but please don't talk about poetry," interrupted Milde. And as it dawned on him that he had been a little too rude to the poor peddler in Aagot's presence, he added hurriedly: "I mean—Isn't it too much of a bore to talk about poetry and poetry all the time? Give us, for a change, a little fishery talk, a little railway politics—Isn't it a fierce lot of rye you are storing, Tidemand?"

As Tidemand saw many eyes upon him, he could not entirely ignore the Artist's question, and he answered:

"Yes, I have tried to strike a modest blow; I cannot deny it. It all depends now on how things turn out in Russia. If, in spite of everything that had been forecasted, the crops should prove even middling, it does not look any too bright for me and my rye. Rains in Russia now would mean—"

"Rains are falling now," said Gregersen. "The English papers have been informed of a sufficient rainfall in the larger provinces. Are you selling your rye already?"

Of course, Tidemand had bought to sell if he could get his price.

Milde had moved over to Paulsberg, and spoke to him in a low whisper. Ojen's prose poem had caused him some anxiety. Perhaps, after all, there was something to this fellow, this competitor in the matter of the subsidy. What was Paulsberg's opinion?

"You know I don't care to speak for or against in such a matter," said Paulsberg. "But I have called at the ministry a few times and expressed my preference. I hope it may carry some weight."

"Of course, of course, I didn't mean—Well, the Exhibition closes to-morrow. We ought to get busy and finish that picture of yours. Can you sit tomorrow?"

Paulsberg nodded and turned away.

Irgens had gradually lost his good spirits; it irritated him that no one had mentioned his book. It was the latest event; why wasn't it even referred to? Everybody was only too familiar with Ojen's filigree fancies. Irgens shrugged his shoulders. Paulsberg had not indicated approval of his book by a single word. Perhaps he was waiting to be asked? But Irgens could get along without Paulsberg's opinion.

Irgens rose.

"Are you going?" asked Mrs. Hanka.

Irgens said good night to her and to Miss Aagot, nodded to the others, and left Sara's.

He had only gone a few steps when he heard somebody call him. Mrs. Hanka was hurrying after him; she had left her wraps in the cafe and had followed in order to say good night properly. Wasn't that nice of her? She smiled and was very happy.

"I have hardly seen you since I got your book. How I have enjoyed every word!" she exclaimed, and put her hand in his coat pocket in order to be close to him. He felt that she left an envelope in his pocket. "Oh, your verses, your verses!" she said again and again.

He could not remain impassive in the presence of this warm admiration. He wanted to return it, to show her how fond he was of her, and while in this mood he confided to her that he, too, had applied for the subsidy. What did she think of that? He had really applied, briefly and without enclosing any recommendations, simply sending his book. That ought to be sufficient.

Mrs. Hanka did not answer at once.

"You have suffered, then," she said; "you have lacked—I mean, you have had to apply like the others—"

"Well, good Lord," he answered, and laughed, "what are the subsidies for, anyway? I have not suffered want; but why not apply when one can do it without loss of prestige? And I did not humble myself; be sure of that. 'I hereby apply for the subsidy and enclose my last book'—that was all. There was no kowtowing whatever. And when I survey my fellow applicants I hardly think I shall be entirely eclipsed. What is your opinion?"

She smiled and said:

"No, you will not be eclipsed."

He put his arm around her and said:

"Now, Hanka, you must go back—I can endure it all as long as you are in town, but when you go away it will look very dark for me! I shan't know what to do with myself then."

"I am only going to the country," she said.

"Isn't that enough? We shall be separated just the same, for you know I cannot leave the city. When are you going?"

"I imagine in about a week."

"I wish you wouldn't go away, Hanka!" he exclaimed, and stood still.

Mrs. Hanka reflected.

"Would it really please you so much if I stayed?" she asked. "All right; then I'll stay. Yes, I will. It will be hard on the children, but—Anyway, it is enough for me that I make you glad."

They had reached Sara's once more.

"Good night," he said happily. "Thank you, Hanka! When shall I see you again? I am longing—"

III

Three days later Irgens received a note from Mrs. Hanka.

He was down-town; he had met a few acquaintances; he did not say much, but was in a satisfied frame of mind. He had taken a look at Paulsberg's great portrait which was now exhibited in the Arrow, in the large window which everybody had to pass; people crowded in front of it continually. The painting was elegant and obtrusive; Paulsberg's well-groomed form looked very distinguished in the plain cane-bottomed chair, and people wondered if that was the chair in which he had written his books. All the newspapers had mentioned the picture in flattering terms.

Irgens had a glass of wine in front of him and listened abstractedly to the conversation. Tidemand was still optimistic; that bit of rain in Russia had not depressed his hopes. The prices were not soaring as yet, but they surely would. Suddenly Irgens pricked up his ears: Tidemand was talking about their summer plans.

"We are not going to the country after all," he said; "Hanka thought—In fact, I told her plainly that if she wanted to go she would have to go alone; I was too busy to think of getting off. Hanka was very nice about it; she agreed to stay in the city."

The door opened and Milde entered. The corpulent chap beamed happily and shouted, full of the great sensation he was going to spring:

"Congratulate me, good people, I have won the prize! Imagine, in its inscrutable wisdom the ministry has chosen to bestow the subsidy upon me!"

"Have *you* received the subsidy?" asked Irgens slowly.

"Yes, can you understand it? How it happened I am at a loss to know. I got it from under your very noses! I hear that you, too, applied, Irgens?"

Silence fell upon the crowd at the table. Nobody had expected that, and they were all wondering what influence had been brought to bear. Milde had got the subsidy—what next?

"Well, I congratulate you!" said Tidemand, and gave Milde his hand.

"Thank you," Milde replied. "I want you to lend me some money now, so that I can celebrate properly; you'll get it back when I cash in."

Irgens looked at his watch as if he suddenly remembered something and got up.

"I, too, congratulate you," he said. "I am sorry to have to leave at once; I have to—No; my object in applying was an entirely different one; I'll tell you about it later," he added in order to hide his disappointment.

Irgens went home. So Milde had been chosen! That was the way Norway rewarded her talents. Here he had hurled his inspired lyric in their faces, and they did not even know what it was! *Whom* had they preferred? None other than oil-painter Milde, collector of ladies' corsets!

Of course, he knew how it had happened; Paulsberg was behind it. Paulsberg had supported Milde's application, and Milde had painted Paulsberg's picture. A simon-pure advertising conspiracy! And when Irgens passed the Arrow and saw the painting he spat contemptuously on the pavement. He had seen through this hypocritical scurviness. However, he would find means to make himself felt.

But why in the world should Lars Paulsberg be allowed to dispose of these subsidies? True, he had never let slip an opportunity to ingratiate himself with the newspapers; he had his press-agents; he took good care that his name shouldn't be forgotten. But apart from that? Alas, a few novels in the style of the seventies, a popular and amateurish criticism of such a moss-grown dogma as the Atonement! What did it amount to when one looked at it critically? But the fact that he had the press behind him made his words carry weight. Yes, he was certainly a shrewd and thrifty soul, a real backwoods bargain-hunter. He knew what he was doing when he even allowed his wife to accept Journalist Gregersen's beer-perfumed attentions! Faugh, what a sordid mess!

Well, he was not going to gain success by employing such methods; he hoped he would manage to get along without unfairness. He had one weapon—his pen. That was the kind of man *he* was.

He went home and locked his door. There would still be time to regain his composure before Mrs. Hanka's arrival. He tried to write, but found it impossible. He paced back and forth furiously, pale with anger, bitter and vindictive because of this defeat. He would, by Heaven, avenge this wrong; no gentle words were to flow from his pen henceforth!

At last Mrs. Hanka arrived.

No matter how often she had entered this apartment, she always felt a certain embarrassment at first, and she usually said in order to hide it: "Does Mr. Irgens live here?"

But she noticed at once that Irgens was not in a playful mood to-day, and she asked what was the matter. When he had told her of the great calamity she, too, was indignant: "How unjust! What a scandal! Had Milde been selected?"

"In payment for Paulsberg's portrait," said Irgens. "Well, it cannot be helped; don't let it irritate you; I am reconciled."

"You take it beautifully; I don't see how you can."

"The only effect it has on me is to make me a little bitter; it does not break my spirit."

"I simply cannot understand it; no, I can't. Did you send your book with your application?"

"Certainly—Oh, my book! I might as well not have written it; so far nobody seems to have noticed it. There has been no review of it so far in any of the papers." And, angry because of this newspaper neglect of his work, he gritted his teeth and walked up and down.

She looked sadly at him.

"Now, don't allow this to embitter you," she said. "You have great provocation, but all the same—You can live without that miserable subsidy. You know that nobody is your equal!"

"And what good does that do me? Judge for yourself; my book has not been mentioned in a single newspaper!"

Mrs. Hanka had for the first time—yes, for the very first time—a feeling that her hero was not the superior being she had imagined. A shuddering thought pierced her heart: he did not carry his disappointment with more than ordinary pride. She looked at him a little closer. His eyes were not so clear, his mouth was drawn and his nostrils dilated. But it was only a shuddering thought.

Then he added: "You might do me the favour to try to interest Gregersen in my book, and see if he won't review it in the *Gazette*." And as he noticed that she grew more and more thoughtful, that she even looked interrogatingly straight into his eyes, he added: "Of course, you need not ask him directly—only give him a little hint, a reminder."

Could this be Irgens? But she remembered at once his painful position, alone as he was, fighting a conspiracy single-handed; and she excused him. She ought to have thought of giving Gregersen a little hint herself and spared her Poet this humiliation. Yes, she certainly would speak to Gregersen at once.

And Irgens thanked her; his bitterness vanished slowly. They sat silently on the sofa some time; then she said:

"Listen! An awful thing happened with that red tie of yours—you remember the one I took from you once? He saw it!"

"How could you be so careless? What did he say?"

"Nothing; he never says anything. It fell out as I opened my dress. Well, don't let that worry you; it doesn't matter. When can I see you again?"

Ever, *ever* her tenderness was the same! Irgens took her hand and caressed it. How fortunate he was to have her! She was the only one in all the world who understood him, who was good to him—How about that stay in the country? Had she given it up?

Yes; she was not going. She told him frankly that she had had no trouble changing her husband's mind; he had given in at once. But she was sorry for the children.

"Yes," answered Irgens sympathetically. And suddenly he asked in a whisper:

"Did you lock the door as you came in?"

She glanced at him, lowered her eyes and whispered: "Yes."

IV

On the 17th of May, [Footnote: Norway's Independence Day.] in the morning, the birds are singing over the city.

A coal-heaver, tired from a night of toil, wanders up through the docks with his shovel across his shoulder; he is black, weary, and athirst; he is going home. And as he walks along, the city begins to stir; a shade is raised here and there; flags are flung from the windows. It is the 17th of May.

All stores and schools are closed; the roar from the wharves and factories is stilled. Only the winches rattle; they shatter the air with their cheerful noise this bright morning. Departing steamers blow white clouds of steam from their exhausts; the docks are busy, the harbour is alive.

And letter-carriers and telegraph messengers have already commenced their rounds, bringing news, scattering information through the doors, whirling up in the hearts of men emotions and feelings like leaves in an autumn wind.

A stray dog with his nose on the pavement lopes through the streets, hot on a scent and without a thought for anything else. Suddenly he stops, jumps up and whines; he has found a little girl who is leaving on every stoop newspapers full of 17th-of-May freedom and bold, ringing phrases. The little girl jerks her tiny body in all directions, twitches her shoulders, blinks and hurries from door to door. She is pale and emaciated; she has Saint Vitus's dance.

The coal-heaver continues his walk with a heavy, long stride. He has earned a good night's wage; these enormous English coal-steamers and the many merchantmen from all over the world are indeed a blessing to such as he! His shovel is shiny with wear; he shifts it to his other shoulder and it glitters with every step he takes, signals to heaven with gleaming flashes; it cuts the air like a weapon and shines like silver. The coal-heaver runs foul of a gentleman coming out of a gateway; the gentleman smells of liquor and looks a little shaky; his clothes are silk-lined. As soon as he has lit a cigar he saunters down the street and disappears.

The gentleman's face is small and round, like a girl's; he is young and promising; it is Ojen, leader and model for all youthful poets. He has been in the mountains to regain his health, and since his return he has had many glorious nights; his friends have acclaimed him without ceasing.

As he turns toward the fortress he meets a man he seems to know; they both stop.

"Pardon me, but haven't we met before?" asks Ojen politely.

The stranger answers with a smile:

"Yes, on Torahus. We spent an evening together."

"Of course; your name is Coldevin. I thought I knew you. How are you?"

"Oh, so so—But are you abroad so early?"

"Well, to tell the truth, I haven't been to bed yet."

"Oh, I see!"

"The fact of the matter is that I have hardly been in bed a single night since my return. I am in the hands of my friends. And that means that I am in my element once more—It is strange, Mr. Coldevin, how I need the city; I love it! Look at these houses, these straight, pure lines! I only feel at home here. The mountains—Lord preserve us! And yet, I expected much when I went there."

"How did you get on? Did you get rid of your nervousness?"

"Did I? To tell you the truth, my nervousness is part of myself; it belongs to me, as the Doctor says; there is nothing to be done about it."

"So you have been to the mountains and substantiated the fact that your nervousness is chronic? Poor young talent, to be afflicted with such a weakness!"

Ojen looked at him in amazement. But Coldevin smiled and continued to talk innocently. So he did not like the country? But did he not feel that his talent had been benefited by the mountain air?

"Not at all. I have never noticed that my talent stood in need of bracing."

"Of course not."

"I have written a lengthy prose poem while I was away, so you see I have not altogether wasted my time. Well, you will pardon me for renewing our acquaintance so abruptly; but I must get home and get a little sleep now. Very pleased to have met you again."

And Ojen walked off.

Coldevin shouted after him:

"But it is the 17th of May to-day!"

Ojen turned and looked surprised.

"Well, what of it?"

Coldevin shook his head and laughed shortly.

"Nothing. Nothing at all. I only wanted to see if you remembered it. And I see that you remembered it perfectly."

"Yes," said Ojen, "one does not altogether forget the teachings of childhood days."

Coldevin stood there and looked after him. *He* was only waiting for the processions to start. His coat was beginning to be rather shiny; it was carefully brushed, but shabby; in the left lapel was fastened securely a little silk bow in the Norwegian colours.

He shivered, for the air was still chilly; he walked rapidly in order to get down to the harbour whence sounded the energetic rattle of anchor chains. He nodded and glanced at the waving flags, counted them, and followed their graceful billowing against the blue sky. Here and there a few pale theatre bills were posted on pillars; he went from one to another and read great and famous names—masterpieces from earlier periods. He happened to think of Irgens's lyric drama, but he looked for it in vain. And he turned his face toward the sea; the rattle of chains reached his ears refreshingly.

The ships were dressed in bunting; the entire harbour scintillated with these bright colours against the blue. Coldevin breathed deeply and stood still. The odour of coal and tar, of wine and fruit, of fish and oils; the roar from engines and traffic, the shouts, the footfalls on the decks, the song from a young sailor who was shining shoes in his shirtsleeves—it all stirred him with a violent joy which almost made his eyes moisten. What a power was here! What ships! The harbour gleamed; far away he saw Miss Aagot's little yacht with the shining masthead.

He lost himself in this spectacle. Time passed; suddenly he dived into a basement restaurant that had opened up and asked for a sandwich for breakfast. When he emerged a little later there were many people in the streets; it was getting along toward the time for the boys' parade to start. He had to hurry; it would never do to miss the processions.

* * * * *

Along toward three o'clock a few members of the clique had occupied a vantage-point at the corner, in order to see the big procession pass by toward the Royal Castle. None of them marched in the parade. Suddenly one of them called out:

"Look, there is Coldevin!"

They saw him march now under one, now under another banner; it was as if he wanted to belong to them all; he was almost too enthusiastic to keep in step. Attorney Grande crossed over and joined the procession; he caught up with Coldevin and started a conversation.

"And where is the young Norway?" asked Coldevin, "the poets, the artists— why aren't they marching? They ought to; it would not hurt their talent. It might not help it much, either; I don't say that, but I am sure it would never hurt. The trouble is, they don't care! They are indifferent; but it is surely wrong to be so indifferent."

Coldevin had grown still more absurd, although he spoke with his usual calm deliberation. He was obstinate; he talked about the suffrage movement, and even hinted that it would be better if women should be a little more anxious to make their homes attractive. It was wrong, he said, that women should think too little of their home life and prefer a hall-room in order to become what they called "independent." They had to "study" until they, too, could wear glasses; they went to a business school if they could do no better. And they did their things so excellently that they were graduated, and if they were lucky they would finally secure a position at twenty crowns a month. Fine! But they had to pay twenty-seven for the hall-room and meals. Then they were "independent"!

"But you cannot say that it is the fault of the women if their work is paid so poorly," objected the Attorney, whose wife was liberal.

Certainly, these arguments were familiar; they were old and tried. They had been answered, but.... In fact, they had been riddled several thousand times. But the worst of it was that the home was simply destroyed by the corroding influence of these ideas. Coldevin accentuated this. He had noticed that a great many people here in the city mainly lived in the restaurants. He had looked for acquaintances in their homes, but in vain; however, he met them when he occasionally went to a café. He did not want to speak about artists and authors; they simply did not have nor did they want any other home than the cafés, and he did not understand how they could accomplish anything under these circumstances. But women nowadays were lacking in ambition and heart; they were satisfied with the mixed company they found in these hang-outs. They did not extend themselves in any one direction; they were not occupied with any single idea; they became simply roundheaded. God, how rarely one nowadays saw real race!

Somebody in the procession called for cheers and was answered with scattering hurrahs. Coldevin cheered enthusiastically, although he did not hear what the cheers were for. He looked resentfully down the ranks and swung his hat, urging the marchers to shout still louder.

"These people don't know how to cheer!" he said. "They shout in a whisper; nobody can hear them. Help me, Mr. Attorney, and we'll liven them up!"

The Attorney thought it fun and shouted with him until they succeeded in stirring up the dying hurrahs.

"Once again!" shouted Coldevin.

And again the cheers rolled down the ranks.

The Attorney said smilingly:

"That you should *care* to do this!"

Coldevin looked at him. He said seriously:

"You should not say that. We should all care to do this; it would not hurt us. Of course, this parading has not in itself great significance; but there will be opportunities to cheer for Norway, for the flag, and then we ought to be present. Who knows—these booming cheers may have their effect on Parliament; it may be reminded of a few things it has begun to forget— a little loyalty, a little steadfastness. People should not be so unconcerned; now is the time for the young to step forward. Perhaps, if the youth of the country had shown up occasionally and met together and hurrahed at times, Parliament might have settled a few things differently lately. And, if you had cared to take a walk along the docks to-day and witnessed the nation's life throb so mightily, then, by Heaven, you would have felt that the country is worth our cheers—"

The Attorney spied Ojen on the sidewalk; he excused himself and stepped out of the procession. He looked back a moment later and saw that Coldevin had changed places again; he was marching under the business-men's banner, erect, grey-bearded, and shabby, with the glint of the Norwegian colours on his lapel.

V

Aagot was dressed for the excursion; she pulled on her gloves and was ready.

It had not been at all difficult to arrange this little trip; Ole had only requested that she be careful and dress warmly; it was only May.

And they started.

It was calm, warm, and bright; not a cloud in the skies. Irgens had the boat ready; they had only to go aboard. He spoke intentionally about indifferent matters; he wanted to make her forget that she had originally agreed to this island trip with a whispered yes, a sudden submission right before Ole's very eyes. She was reassured. Irgens had not invested her sudden consent with a deeper significance than she had intended; he walked along as unconcernedly as possible and talked about the weather and almost had to be hurried along. Just as they were on the verge of starting she caught a glimpse of Coldevin, who stood on the dock half hidden behind a pile of boxes. She jumped out of the boat and called:

"Coldevin! I want to see you!"

It was impossible to avoid her; he stepped forward and took off his hat.

She gave him her hand. Where in the world had he kept himself all this time? Dear me, why was he never to be seen? It began to look a little strange—really it did.

He stammered an excuse, spoke about library work, a translation from a book, an absolutely necessary bit of work....

But she interrupted and asked where he lived now. She had looked for him at the hotel but was told that he had left; nobody knew where he had gone. She had also had a glimpse of him on the seventeenth; she was in the Grand and saw him march by in the parade.

He repeated his excuses and trotted out the old joke about the impropriety of disturbing sweethearts too much. He smiled good-naturedly as he spoke.

She observed him carefully. His clothes were threadbare, his face had become thinner, and she wondered suddenly if he were in want. Why had he left the hotel, and where did he live? He said something about a friend, a college chum—honest, a teacher, a splendid fellow.

Aagot asked when he was going back to Torahus, but he did not know exactly; he was unable to say. As long as he had this library work and was so busy....

Well, he simply must promise to come before he went away; she insisted. And she asked suddenly: "When I saw you on the seventeenth, didn't you have a bow in your buttonhole?"

Certainly, he had a bow; one had to show the colours on such a day! Didn't she remember that she had given it to him herself? She had wanted him to be decorated last year, when he was going to speak to the peasants at Torahus, and she had given him the bow. Didn't she remember?

Aagot recalled it. She asked:

"Was it really the same bow?"

"Yes; isn't it strange? I happened to come across it; I must have brought it along with some clothes; I found it by accident."

"Imagine! I thought at once it was my bow. It made me glad; I don't know why," she said and bowed her head.

Irgens shouted and asked her if she were coming.

"No!" she called bluntly and without thinking. She did not even turn her head. But when she realised how she had answered she grew confused and cried to Irgens: "Pardon me just a moment!" And she turned to Coldevin again: "I would have loved to stay and talk with you, but I have no time; I am going to the island." She offered Coldevin her hand and said: "Anyway, I hope everything will turn out for the best; don't you think it will, too? I am sorry to have to hurry off. So long; be sure and come up soon!"

She skipped down the steps and into the boat. Again she apologised for keeping Irgens waiting.

And Irgens rowed out. They talked about the sea, the far journeys, the strange countries; he had been abroad only in his dreams, and he supposed that would be the extent of his travellings. He looked sad and listless. Suddenly he said:

"I hear you are not going to the country after all."

"No. The Tidemands have changed their plans."

"So I am told. It is a pity; I am sorry for your sake, in a way." And, resting on his oars, he added bluntly: "But I am glad for my own sake; I admit it frankly."

Aagot skipped up the stone jetty when they landed. The trees delighted her; it was ages since she had seen a real forest—such great big trees, just like home. She sniffed the pungent, pine-laden air, she looked at stones and flowers with a feeling of recognition; memories from home surged through her, and she was for an instant on the verge of tears.

"But here are other people!" she exclaimed suddenly.

Irgens laughed: "What did you expect? This is not a jungle, exactly."

They explored the island thoroughly, saw the changing views, and had refreshments. Aagot beamed. The walk in the bracing air had flushed her cheeks, her lips, her ears, even her nose; her eyes were sparkling gaily. She suddenly remembered that she had almost pouted in disappointment when she saw other people; what must Irgens have thought?

"I was at first a little surprised to find so many people here," she said. "The reason was that you told me you had written some of your poems here, and I did not think you could have done that unless you had been entirely undisturbed."

How she remembered! He gazed at her exultantly and answered that he had his own restful nook where nobody ever came. It was on the other side; should they go over?

They went. It was certainly a restful place, a regular wilderness of rocks and heather and junipers, enclosed on two sides. Far in the distance could be seen a little glade. They sat down.

"So this is where you sit and write!" she exclaimed. "It is strange to think of. Were you sitting here?"

"About here. Do you know, it is refreshing to meet such a spontaneous interest as yours?"

"Tell me, how do you write your things? Do the thoughts come to you without conscious effort?"

"Yes, in a way. Things affect one pleasantly or otherwise, and the mood is there. But the trouble then is to make the words reflect the love or hate one's heart feels at the moment. Often it is useless even to try; one can never find words adequately to express that languid gesture of your hand, to define that evanescent thrill your laughter sends through one—"

Slowly the sun sank; a tremor quivered through the trees, and all was still.

"Listen," he said, "do you hear the noise boiling away yonder in the city?"

He noted how her dress tightened across her knee; he followed the curving outline of her figure, saw how her bosom rose and sank, observed her face with the darling dimple and the somewhat irregular nose; his blood stirred and he moved closer to her. He spoke in fumbling, broken sentences:

"This is now the Isle of the Blest, and its name is Evenrest. The sun is sinking; we are here—the world far off; it is exactly my dream of dreams. Tell me, does my voice disturb you? You seem so far away—Miss Lynum, it is useless to continue the struggle; I surrender to you. I lie at your feet and tell you this, although I have not moved—"

The swift change in his expression, the low, vibrant, fervent voice, his nearness—for a moment she was completely, stupidly stunned. She looked at him for an instant without answering. Then her cheeks began to flame; she started to get up and said quickly:

"But isn't it time to go?"

"No!" he exclaimed. "No, don't go!" He took hold of her dress, flung his arm around her, and held her back. She struggled with face aglow, laughing uncertainly, making vain efforts to free herself.

"You must be crazy," she said again and again; "have you completely forgotten yourself?"

"Please, let me at least tell you something!"

"Well, what is it?" she asked and sat still; she turned her face away, but she listened.

And he began speaking rapidly and incoherently; his heart-beats trembled in his voice, which was persuasive and full of tenderness. She could see that all he wanted was to make her understand how unspeakably he loved her; how he had been conquered, subdued as never before. She must believe him; it had lain dormant and grown in his heart since the very first time he met her. He had fought and struggled to keep his feelings within bounds; but it was true—such a struggle was not very effective. It was too sweet to yield, and so one yielded. One fought on with a steadily slipping grip. And now the end had come; he could not fight any more, he was entirely disarmed.... "I believe my breast will burst asunder."...

Still leaning away from him, she had turned her face and was gazing at him while he spoke. Her hands had ceased their ineffectual efforts and were now resting on his, tightly clasped around her waist; she saw the blood leap through the veins along his throat. She straightened up and sat erect; his hands were still around her, but she did not seem to notice it now. She seized her gloves and said with quivering lips:

"But, Irgens, you should not say such things to me. You know you shouldn't. It is sad, but I cannot help it now."

"No, you are right; I don't suppose I ought to have said it, but—" He gazed at her; his lips were trembling too. "But, Miss Aagot, what would *you* do if your love made you weak and powerless; if it robbed you of your senses and blinded you to everything else? I mean—"

"Yes, but say nothing more!" she interrupted. "I understand you in a way, but—You know, I cannot listen to this." She looked at the arms around her waist, and with a sudden jerk she moved away and got up.

She was still so confused that she remained standing immobile; she did not even brush the heather from her dress. And when he got up she made no effort to go, but remained where she was.

"Listen, I want you to promise not to tell this to anybody. I am afraid— And you must not think of me any more. I had no idea that you really cared; of course, I thought that you liked me very much—I had begun to think that; but I never thought—'How could *he* care for *me?*' I always thought. If you want me to I will go back to Torahus and stay there awhile."

He was deeply moved; he swallowed hard and his eyes grew moist. This delicious simplicity, these candid words, her very attitude, which was free from fear and entirely unaffected—his feelings flared up in him like a consuming flame: No, no, not to Torahus—only stay! He would control himself, would show her that he could control himself; she must not go away. Even should he lose his mind and perish altogether—rather that, if she would only stay!

He continued talking while he was brushing off her dress. She must pardon him; he was not like everybody else, he was a poet; when it came over him he must yield. But he would give her no further cause for complaint if she would only stay.... Wouldn't she mind going away the least little bit, though? No, of course, he had no false illusions.

Pause. He was waiting for her to answer, to contradict him; perhaps she would go to Torahus a little regretfully after all? But she remained silent. Did she, then, hold him in so slight regard? Impossible! Still, the thought began to worry him; he felt aggrieved, hurt, almost slighted. He repeated his question: Did all his love for her not call forth the tiniest responsive spark in her heart?

She answered gently and sorrowfully:

"Please do not ask. What do you think Ole would say if he heard you?"

Ole? He had not given him a thought. Did he really play the role of competitor to Ole Henriksen? It was too ridiculous. He could not believe that she meant what she had said. Ole might be all right as far as that went; he bought and sold, went his peddler rounds through life, paid his bills and added dollars to his hoard. That was all. Did money really matter so much to her? God knows, perhaps even this girlish little head had its concealed nook where thoughts were figuring in crowns and pennies!

Irgens was silent for an instant; he felt the pangs of jealousy. Ole might be able to hold her; he was tall and blue-eyed—perhaps she even preferred him?

"Ole?" he said. "I do not care in the least what he would say. Ole does not exist for me; it is you I love."

She seemed startled for the first time; she frowned a little and began to walk away.

"This is too contemptible!" she said. "I wish you hadn't said that. So it is me you love? Well, don't tell me any more about it."

"Miss Aagot—one word only. Don't you care the least little bit for me?"

He had seized her arm; she had to look at him. He was too violent; he did not control himself as he had promised; he was not very handsome now.

She answered: "I love Ole; I hope you understand that."

The sun sank deeper. People had left the island; only an occasional late straggler was still seen walking along the road toward the city. Irgens did not ask questions any more; he spoke only when necessary. Aagot tried in vain to start a conversation; she had all she could do to keep her heart under control.

When they were in the boat again he said: "Perhaps you would have preferred to drive back alone? I may be able to find a hackman for you, if you like."

"Now don't be angry any more!" she said.

She could hardly keep her eyes from brimming over; she forced herself to think of indifferent matters in order to regain control over herself; she gazed back toward the island, followed the flight of a bird that sailed gracefully above the water. She asked:

"Is that water over there?"

"No," he answered; "it is a meadow; the dew makes it look dark."

"Imagine! To me it looked like water." But as it was impossible to talk further about this green meadow they were both silent.

He was rowing hard; they approached the docks. He landed and jumped out to help her ashore. Neither of them had gloves on; her warm hand rested in his, and she took the opportunity of thanking him for the trip.

"I want to ask you to forget that I have bothered you with my heart troubles," he said.

And he lifted his hat, without waiting for an answer, jumped into the boat, and pushed off.

She had stopped at the head of the steps. She saw that he went back into the boat, and wanted to call to him and ask where he was going; but she gave it up. He saw her fair form disappear across the jetty.

He had in reality not intended to do this; he acted on the spur of the moment, embarrassed as he was, hardly knowing what he was doing. He seized the oars and rowed out again, towards the island. The evening was wondrously calm. Now, when he was alone, he realised how deep was his despair; another disappointment, another fall, the very worst! And not a star in the murky night! He suddenly remembered Hanka, who probably had looked for him to-day; who perhaps was seeking him even now. No; Hanka was not fair; Hanka was dark; she did not radiate, but she allured. But how was it—didn't she walk a little peculiarly? No, Hanka did not have Aagot's carriage. And why was it her laugh no longer made his blood tingle?

He rested on the oars and let the boat drift. It grew darker. Fragmentary thoughts drifted through his brain: a rudderless ship on the buffeting waves, an emperor in defeat, King Lear, thoughts and thoughts. He went aft and began to write on the back of some envelopes, verse upon verse. Thank God, nothing could rob him of his talent! And this thought sent a thrill of warm happiness coursing through his veins.

VI

Tidemand was still optimistic; his ice business in England was very profitable. He did not place much faith in the reports that extensive rains throughout Russia had greatly improved the prospects for a normal harvest. It had rained, of course, but the fact remained that Russia was still closed; not a sack of grain could be smuggled out if one were to offer for it its weight in gold. Tidemand stuck to his price; occasionally he would sell small quantities throughout the country, but his enormous stores were hardly affected by this; he needed a panic, a famine, before he could unload. But there was no hurry; only wait until winter!

As usual, Tidemand was eagerly sought by business solicitors of every description; subscription lists and all kinds of propositions were placed before him; his name was in demand everywhere. Nothing could be started without the support of the business element; and it was especially the younger business men, the energetic and self-made men who conducted the large enterprises, who commanded money and credit and knew and recognised opportunities, whose interest had to be enlisted. There was the electric street-car proposition, the new theatre, the proposed pulp-mills in Vardal, the whale-oil factories in Henningsvaer—everything had to have the business men's stamp of approval. Both Tidemand and Ole Henriksen became share-owners in everything as a matter of course.

"My father should have known this!" Tidemand would often say when he gave his signature. His father had a reputation for miserly thrift which had survived him; he was one of the old-fashioned tradesmen, who went around in his shirt-sleeves and apron, and weighed out soap and flour by the pound. He had no time to dress decently; his shoes were still a byword; the toes were sticking out, and when he walked it looked as if his toes were searching for pennies on the flagstones. The son did not resemble the father much; for him the old horizons had been broken, cracked wide, and opened large views; his optimistic business courage was recognised.

Ole Henriksen had just dropped in on him in his office and was talking about the projected tannery for which an ideal site had been found near Torahus. This enterprise was bound to amount to something in the near future; the great forests were being cut rapidly; the lumber was sold here and abroad. But two and three inch cuttings and the tops were left and went to waste. What a lack of foresight! Pine bark contained nearly twenty per cent tannin; why not utilise it and make money out of it?

"We will see what can be done next spring."

Ole Henriksen looked a little overworked. He had not sufficient help; when he went to England that autumn he would have to give his head assistant power of attorney and leave everything to him. Since Aagot came Ole's work had been only fun; but now she was a little indisposed and had kept up-stairs for a couple of days. Ole missed her. She must have been careless on this excursion day before yesterday and have caught a cold. He had wanted to take her out in the little yacht, but this had now been postponed until Sunday. He asked Tidemand to come along; there would be a few more; they would sail out to some reef and have coffee.

"Are you sure Miss Aagot will be well by Sunday?" asked Tidemand. "These boat-rides are dangerous so early in the year. What I was going to say was: Won't you please ask Hanka yourself? I am not sure I can make her come—In regard to this tannery proposition, I think I shall have to hold the matter in abeyance for the present. It will also depend on the lumber quotations to some extent."

Ole returned after he had looked up Hanka and invited her. He wondered a little over Tidemand's remark about boat-rides being dangerous; Tidemand had given the remark a subtle meaning, and Ole had looked at him interrogatingly.

Ole found Aagot in her own room; she was reading. When he entered she threw down her book and ran to him. She was well again, entirely well— just feel the pulse, not a trace of fever! How she looked forward to Sunday! Ole warned her again about being careful; she would have to dress properly. Even Tidemand had spoken about these risky boat-rides so early in the season.

"And you are going to be the hostess!" he chaffed her. "What a darling little mistress! By the way, what are you reading?"

"Oh, that is only Irgens's poems," she answered.

"Don't say 'only' Irgens's poems," he chided her playfully. "By the way, I ran across Coldevin a moment ago; he said he was looking for somebody. I couldn't get him to come up—he simply wouldn't."

"Did you invite him to our excursion?" asked Aagot quickly. She seemed very much disappointed because Ole had forgotten to ask him. He had to promise her to try his best to find Coldevin before Sunday.

* * * * *

Tidemand rang Henriksen's bell late Saturday evening and asked for Ole. He did not want to come in; it was only a small matter, he would keep Ole only a minute.

When Ole came out he saw at once that something serious had happened. He asked whether they should go down to the office or take a walk; Tidemand did not care which. They went downstairs to the office.

Tidemand took out a telegram and said:

"I fancy my rye speculation isn't going to turn out very well. The prices are normal at present; Russia has lifted the ban."

It was true that Russia had recalled her decree against rye exportations. The favourable prospects had not proved disappointing, and this, in connection with large amounts of grain stored in the elevators from previous years, had made further restrictions superfluous. The famine ghost had been laid; Russian and Finnish harbours were once more open. Such was the purport of the telegraphic message.

Ole sat there silent. This was an awful blow! His brain was awhirl with thoughts: could the telegram be a hoax, a piece of speculative trickery, a bribed betrayal? He glanced at the signature; no, it was out of the question to suspect this reliable agent. But had anything like that ever happened before? A world-power had fooled itself and taken self-destructive measures for no apparent reason! It was even worse than in fifty-nine when a similar edict had been lifted and had caused the world-markets wreck and ruin. But there had been war then.

The clock on the wall ticked and ticked in the unbroken silence.

Finally Ole asked: "Are you sure the wire is authentic?"

"It is authentic enough, I fancy," said Tidemand. "My agent wired me twice yesterday to sell, and I sold what I could, sold even below the day's quotations; but what did that amount to? I lost heavily yesterday, I tell you."

"Well, don't do anything hastily now; let us consider this carefully. But why did you not come to me yesterday? I had a right to expect that from you."

"I ought hardly to have brought you such a piece of news this evening, even, but—"

"Once and for all," Ole interrupted him, "understand that I will help you all I possibly can. With everything I have, you understand. And that is not so very little, either."

Pause.

"I thank you, Ole—for everything. I knew I shouldn't go to you in vain. You could help me a good deal if you would take over some of my obligations—I mean those that are non-speculative, of course."

"Nonsense—anybody will take such things! I am taking rye. We will date the papers day before yesterday—for the sake of the old man."

Tidemand shook his head.

"I am not going to pull you under, too."

Ole looked at him; the veins in his temples were swelling. "You are a damn fool!" he exclaimed angrily.

"Do you for a moment think you can so easily pull me under?" And Ole swore, with blazing eyes, right into Tidemand's face: "By God, I'll show you how easily you can pull *me* under!"

But Tidemand was immovable; not even Ole's anger made him yield. He understood Ole; his means were perhaps not so insignificant, but it was no use making out that he could do everything. Ole boasted only because he wanted to help him, that was all. But from to-morrow on the bottom would simply drop out of the market; it wasn't right to sell rye even to one's enemies at yesterday's prices.

"But what are you going to do? Are you going into a receiver's hands?" asked Ole in a temper.

"No," answered Tidemand, "I think I can skin through without that. The ice in England and Australia is quite a help now; not much, but crowns are money to me now. I shall have to retrench, to sell what I can in order to raise cash. I thought that perhaps you would care to buy—you might use it when you are going to marry, you know, and we don't need it at all; we are never there any more—"

"What are you talking about?"

"Well, I thought that you might want to buy my country estate now—You are going to be married soon, so—" "Your country house? Are you going to sell it?"

"What good is it to us?"

Pause. Ole noticed that Tidemand's composure began to fail him.

"All right. I'll take it. And whenever you want it back it will be for sale. I have a premonition that it will not be mine so very long."

"Well, God only knows. Anyway, I am doing what I can and should. I am glad the place will be yours. It is beautiful; it is not my fault we have not been there this summer. Well, this will help some; as for the rest, we'll see. I trust I can manage without closing up; that would be hard indeed. And worst for the sake of the children!"

Again Ole offered his assistance.

"I appreciate your help, and I will avail myself of it within reasonable limits. But a loss is a loss, and even if I weather the storm without going into bankruptcy I shall be a poor man all the same. I don't know whether I own a penny now or not—I am only glad that you didn't join me in that unhappy speculation, Ole; that is a blessing, anyway. Well, we'll see."

Ole asked:

"Does your wife know about this?"

"No; I'll tell her after the trip to-morrow."

"The trip? I'll cancel that, of course."

"No," said Tidemand, "I will ask you not to do that. Hanka is looking forward to it; she has spoken of it a good deal. No, I would rather ask you to act as if nothing has happened; be as cheerful as you can. I really would appreciate it. Don't mention my misfortune at all, please."

And Tidemand put the fatal wire back in his pocket.

"I am sorry I had to come and bother you with this. But I go home with a lighter heart, now I know you will take the country house."

SIXTYFOLD

I

A party of ladies and gentlemen had gathered on the jetty on the day of the excursion. They were waiting for the Paulsbergs, who were late. Irgens was growing impatient and sarcastic: Would it not be better to send the yacht up for them? When finally Paulsberg and his wife arrived, they all went aboard and were soon tacking out the fiord.

Tidemand held the tiller. A couple of warehousemen from Henriksen's wharf were along as crew. Ole had arranged the trip carefully and had brought along a choice supply of provisions; he had even remembered roasted coffee for Irgens. But he had failed to find Coldevin, and he had purposely avoided asking Gregersen; the Journalist might have heard the news from Russia, and might inadvertently have betrayed the fatal tidings.

Tidemand looked as if he had spent a sleepless night. To Ole's whispered inquiry, he answered smilingly that things might be worse. But he asked to be allowed to keep his place at the tiller.

And the yacht tacked out toward the reefs.

Mrs. Hanka had chosen a place far forward; her face was fresh, and she had thrown her fur coat around her shoulders; Milde said she looked picturesque. He added loudly and gaily:

"And furthermore I wish it were drink time!"

Ole brought out bottles and glasses. He went around and wrapped the ladies in shawls and blankets. Nothing to laugh about; true, the day was bright and warm, but the sea air was treacherous. He repeatedly offered to relieve Tidemand at the tiller, but was not permitted to. No, this was the place for Tidemand; here he would not have to be entertaining, and he was not in a mood for social amenities.

"Don't lose your nerve whatever happens! Have you heard anything further?"

"Only a confirmation. We shall get it officially to-morrow, I guess. But don't worry; I have laid my lines now and shall manage to pull through somehow. I imagine I shall save the ship."

Forward the spirits of the company rose rapidly. Ojen began to get a little seasick, and drank steadily in order to subdue his qualms.

"It seems good to see you again," said Mrs. Hanka, prompted by a desire to enliven him. "You still have your delicate face, but it is not quite as pale as before you went away."

"But what is the matter with your eyes?" cried Mrs. Paulsberg mercilessly. "I have never seen him as pallid as at this very moment."

This reference to his seasickness caused general merriment. Mrs. Hanka continued to speak: She had heard his latest poem, that exquisite gem, "Memories." His excursion had certainly been fruitful in results.

"You haven't heard my very latest poem, though," said Ojen in a weak voice; "it has an Egyptian subject; the action takes place in an ancient tomb—" And, sick and miserable as he was, he looked through all his pockets for this poem. What could have become of it? He had taken it out that morning with the intention of bringing it along; he had thought that perhaps somebody would care to listen to it. He was not afraid of saying that it really was a little out of the ordinary. He sincerely hoped he hadn't lost it; in that case the trip would have proved most unfortunate for him. Never had he produced anything so remarkable; it was only a couple of pages, but....

"No," said Mrs. Hanka, "you must surely have left it behind." And she did her best to make the poor poet forget his groundless fears. She had been told that he preferred the city to the country?

He did, most assuredly. No sooner had his eyes beheld the straight lines of streets and houses than his brain was aquiver, and he had conceived that Egyptian prose poem. If that had been lost, now....

Milde had lately begun to appreciate Ojen; at last his eyes had been opened to his poetry's delicate uniqueness. Irgens, who sat close enough to hear this unusual praise, leaned over to Mrs. Hanka and said in a low voice:

"You understand? Milde knows he has nothing to fear from his competitor any more—hence his change of attitude." And Irgens pressed his lips together and smiled venomously.

Mrs. Hanka glanced at him. How he persisted in his bitterness; how unbecoming it was in him! He did not realise it, or he would not have thus compressed his lips and continually shot baleful glances at his fellow applicants. Otherwise Irgens was silent; he ignored Aagot entirely. She thought: What have I done to him? Could I possibly have acted in any other way?

The coffee was made on board, but out of regard for Ojen, who still felt badly, it was decided to drink it on the very first reef they should reach. They camped on the rocks, flung themselves on the ground, and threw dignity to the winds. It was great fun; Ojen looked with big, astonished eyes at everything—the sea, the waves which filled the air with a continuous roar, the barren reef where not a tree grew and where the grass was yellow from sun and spray. Aagot skipped round with cups and glasses; she walked in a constant fear of dropping anything and stuck the tip of her tongue out like a rope-walker.

Milde proposed that they drink her health. "Haven't you got champagne, Ole?" he asked.

The champagne was produced, the glasses filled, and the toast drunk amid cheers. Milde was in high spirits; he proposed that they throw the bottle in the sea with a note enclosed which they all were to sign.

They all put their names down except Paulsberg, who curtly refused. A man who wrote as much as he did could not sign his name to nonsensical notes, he said. And he rose and walked away in dignified aloofness.

"Then I'll sign for him," said Milde, and seized a pencil.

But Mrs. Paulsberg cried indignantly:

"You will do nothing of the kind! Paulsberg has said that he does not want his name on the note, and that ought to be sufficient for all of us." She looked quite offended as she crossed her legs and held her cup in her usual masculine fashion.

Milde apologised instantly; his proposition was meant as a harmless joke; however, after considering the matter he admitted that perhaps it was a little foolish and that it would not do for Paulsberg to have anything to do with it. Perhaps they had better drop the whole thing; what did they think? If Paulsberg wasn't going to be in it, then....

Irgens could not control himself any longer; he sneered openly and almost hissed:

"Mr. Subsidist! You are divine!"

That subsidy was never out of his thoughts.

"And as for you," answered Milde scathingly, glaring at him with angry eyes, "it is getting so that it is impossible to be near you."

Irgens feigned surprise.

"What is that? It would appear from your tone that I have offended you."

Mrs. Hanka had to intervene. Couldn't they stop quarrelling even on a pleasure trip? They ought to be ducked if they couldn't behave!

And Irgens was silent at once; he did not even mumble maliciously between his teeth. Mrs. Hanka grew thoughtful. How her poet and hero had changed in a few brief weeks! What had really happened? How dull and lustreless his dark eyes had become! Even his moustache seemed to be drooping; he had lost his fresh immaculateness; he was not nearly as alluring as before. But then she reminded herself of his disappointments, of that miserable subsidy, and of his book, his beautiful lyric creation which they were conspiring to kill by their studied silence. She leaned toward Aagot and said:

"It is sad to observe how bitter Irgens has grown; have you noticed it? I hope he will get over it soon." And Mrs. Hanka, who wanted to save him from making too unfavourable an impression, added in the goodness of her heart what she had heard Irgens himself say so often: It was not so strange, after all; bitterness of that character could only arouse respect. Here he had toiled and worked for years, had given freely of his treasures, and the country, the government, had refused to offer him a helping hand.

"Can you understand it?" said Aagot also. And she realised instantly that she had not treated this man with the consideration due him; she had been tactless; she had rebuffed him with unnecessary harshness. She wished her conduct had been different; however, it was too late now.

Paulsberg returned from his solitary walk and suggested that it was time to think of the return. The clouds held a menace of rain, he said; the sun was sinking and it was blowing up a little.

Aagot went around again and poured coffee. She bent over Irgens, bent deeper than necessary, and said:

"May I pour you some, Mr. Irgens?"

The almost supplicating note in her voice made him glance at her in surprise. He did not want any coffee, thanks; but he smiled at her. She was happy at once; she hardly knew what she was carrying, but she stammered:

"Just a little, please."

He looked at her again and said: "No, thanks."

On the return trip Irgens seemed a different person. He chatted, entertained the ladies, helped even poor Ojen, who suffered greatly. Milde had captured a bottle on the pretext that it was drink time again, and Irgens drank with him simply to be accommodating. Mrs. Hanka's spirits also rose; she was lively and cheerful, and a strange association of ideas made her suddenly decide to ask her husband for a couple of hundred crowns this very evening.

Tidemand was at the tiller and could not be dislodged; he sailed the boat and did not utter a syllable. He looked well as he stood high in the stern, rising and falling against the blue background of sea and sky. His wife called to him once and asked him if he were cold, an attention he could hardly believe and therefore pretended not to hear.

"He is deaf," she said smilingly. "Are you cold Andreas?"

"Cold? Not at all," he called back.

And by and by the party reached the jetty.

Hardly had Ojen stepped ashore before he called a cab. He was in a hurry to get home and find his manuscript or learn the worst. He could not rest until he knew his fate. But perhaps he would meet the company later on. Would they be at Sara's?

They looked at each other uncertainly and did not know what to say. But Ole Henriksen declared that he was going home; he was thinking of Tidemand, who was in need of rest and quiet. They parted outside Tidemand's house.

Mrs. Hanka asked abruptly, before even the door was opened:

"Will you please let me have a hundred or so?"

"A hundred? Hm. Certainly. But you will have to come with me to the office; I haven't got the money here."

In the office he handed her the bill; his hand was trembling violently.

"Here is the money," he said.

"Thanks—Why are you trembling?" she asked.

"Oh—I suppose because I have held the tiller so long—Hm. Listen, Hanka, I have a pleasant surprise for you! You have asked me a number of times to consent to a divorce; I have decided in God's name to do what you ask—You understand, I am not going to oppose you any more."

She could hardly believe her ears. Did he agree to a divorce? She gazed at him; he was deathly pale, his eyes were lowered. They were standing opposite each other, the large desk between them.

He continued:

"Circumstances are different now—My big speculation has failed; even if I am not a bankrupt this moment, I am a poor man. I may avoid closing up shop, but that will be all. Anyway, I shall not be able to keep up this mode of life. And, this being so, I feel that I have no right to interfere with your plans and desires any longer."

His words reached her as from afar. For a moment she felt a vague sensation of happiness—she was free; she would escape the yoke that had become oppressive; she would be a girl once more! Hanka Lange—imagine, only Hanka Lange! And when she realised that her husband was almost a bankrupt it did not greatly upset her; he had said he might not be forced to shut down. Of course, he was not wealthy, but neither was he a beggar; it might have been a great deal worse.

"Is that so?" she said simply; "is that so?"

Pause. Tidemand had regained his composure; he stood again as he had stood aboard the yacht; one could almost see the tiller in his hand. His eyes were on her. She had not said no; her intentions were evidently not shaken. Well, he had hardly expected that they would be.

He said:

"Well, that was all I wanted to tell you."

His voice was remarkably even, almost commanding; she thought: "He has not spoken to me like that in three years." His strength was marvellous to behold.

"Well, do you really want to?" she asked. "You think, then, that we ought to separate? Of course, but—I hope you have thought it over—that you are not doing this simply to please me?"

"It goes without saying that I do it to please you," he answered. "You have requested it often enough, and I sincerely regret that I have opposed you until now." And he added without a trace of malice: "You must forgive me for having interfered with your wishes so long."

She grew attentive at once.

"I don't know what you mean," she said a trifle haughtily.

He did not care about that and did not answer. Hadn't she spoken about a divorce time and time again? Hadn't he put her off? Perfectly composed, he opened his coat and took out his pocket calendar, in which he proceeded to make an entry.

She could not help being impressed by this quiet superiority, which she never before had noticed in him; she happened to say:

"I think you have changed greatly."

"Oh, well, one gets a little grey, but—"

"No, you misunderstand me!" she interrupted.

Tidemand said slowly and looked straight into her eyes:

"I wish to God you had understood me as well as I have you, Hanka! Perhaps, then, this would not have become necessary." He buttoned his coat as if preparing to leave, and added: "Now, in regard to the money—"

"Yes, dear, here is the money!" she said, and wanted to give him back the bill.

For the first time since their interview he tossed his head impatiently and said:

"I am not talking about *that* money now! Kindly make at least an effort to understand me—Whatever money you need shall be sent you as soon as you inform me where to send it."

"But, dear me," she said in confusion, "do I have to go away? I thought I could stay in the city. What do you want me to do?"

"Whatever is agreeable to you. You will let the children remain here, won't you? I shall take good care of them; you need not worry about that. As for yourself, I suppose you will want to take an apartment somewhere. You know it takes three years, don't you?"

She was standing with the bill in her hand, gazing at it abstractedly. She was unable to think clearly; her mind was whirling; but deep down she had a vague feeling of relief—she was free at last! She said nothing; he felt his self-control give way and wanted to get it over with quickly so as not to break down.

"Good-bye, then—" He could say no more, but offered her his hand; she took it. "I hope we shall see each other occasionally; but I want to thank you now for everything; this may be the last chance I shall have—I shall send you the money every month." And he put on his hat and went to the door.

She followed him with her eyes. Was this Andreas?

"Well, I suppose you want to go," she said, bewildered, "and I am standing here delaying you. I suppose we shall have to do as you say—I don't know what I am saying—" Her voice broke suddenly.

Tidemand opened the door with trembling hands and let her out. At the foot of the stairs she stopped and let him walk ahead. When he reached the landing he waited for her; then he opened the door with his key and held it for her. When she was inside he said:

"Good night, then!"

And again Tidemand walked down-stairs, down to his office, where he shut himself in. He went over to the window and stood there, his hands clasped behind him, staring out into the street with unseeing eyes. No, she had not changed her mind in the least, that was not to be expected. She had not hesitated. There she had stood, with her elbow on the desk; she had heard what he said and she had replied; "Well, I suppose we shall have to do as you say." There had been no hesitation, no, none at all.... But she had not exulted, either; she had spared him from witnessing any outburst of joy. She had been considerate—he had to admit that. Oh, Hanka was always considerate; God bless her wherever she went! She had stood there. Hanka, Hanka!... But probably she was rejoicing now; why shouldn't she be? She had had her way.... And the children were asleep now, both Ida and Johanna. Poor little things; they did not even reach up to their pillows! Well, they would be provided for. One might be getting a little grey, but there was still a fight or two left....

And Tidemand went back to his desk. He worked over his books and papers until daylight.

II

Mrs. Hanka looked in vain for Irgens for several days. She had hurried to him to bring him the joyful news; she was free at last! But he was never at home. His door was locked, and it was not opened when she knocked; consequently he must be out. She did not meet him in his usual haunts, either. Finally she had to write to him and make an appointment; she wrote that she had excellent news for him.

But during these two days, these long hours of waiting in which she could do nothing, it seemed as if her joy over the coming divorce had begun to wane. She had dwelt on her happiness so long that she had grown accustomed to it; it did not make her heart beat faster any more. She was going to be free from her husband—true, but she had not been so entirely shackled before. The difference was not so pronounced that she could steadily continue to revel in it.

And to this was added an indefinable fear, now when the irrevocable separation confronted her; the thought that she was to leave her home was tinged with a vague sense of regretfulness, of impalpable foreboding. Sometimes a quivering pang would pierce her heart when the children put out their little arms to her; why that pain? She had got out of her bed last night and looked at them in their sleep. There they were lying, each in her little bed; they had kicked the blankets off and were uncovered up to their very arms, but they slept soundly and moved, now and then, a rosy finger or a dimpled toe in their sleep. Such children! To lie there unblushingly naked, with arms and legs pointing in all directions! She tucked them carefully in and left them with bowed head, her shoulders shaken by inaudible sobs.

How was she going to arrange her future? She was free, but in reality she was married still; for three years she would have to live somewhere, pay rent, keep house for herself. She had worried and fretted about this for two long days without anyone to help her; what could have happened to Irgens? God only knew where he kept himself. She had not once seen her former husband.

She started for Irgens's rooms. Surely he would help her find a place and get settled! Oh, it was fine to have an end to this daily galling restraint; here she had been tortured by dissatisfaction and restlessness for months and years, ever since she had been introduced to the clique and had acquired a taste for their irresponsible mode of living. She was free, free and young! She would overwhelm Irgens with this joyful news, he who had so often sighed for that divorce during their most intimate hours—

Irgens was at home at last.

She told him the great news at once. She recounted how it had happened, repeated Tidemand's words, and praised his superiority. She gazed into Irgens's eyes; her own were sparkling. Irgens, however, did not show any great exultation; he smiled, said yes and no, asked her if she were satisfied now. So she was really going to get a divorce? He was glad to hear it; it was foolish to go through life in this heart-breaking manner.... But he sat there very quietly and discussed the great news in an every-day voice.

Gradually, very gradually, she came to earth; her heart began to flutter wildly.

"It seems as if the news does not make you so very happy, Irgens," she said.

"Happy? Of course I am. Why shouldn't I be happy? You have sighed for this for a long time; why shouldn't I rejoice with you now? I do, most assuredly."

Words only, without fire, without warmth even! What could have happened? Did he not love her any more? She sat there, her heart heavy within her; she wanted to gain time, to hush the wakening terror in her breast. She said:

"But, dear, where have you been all this time? I have called on you three times without finding you in."

He answered, choosing his words carefully, that she must have missed him because of an unfortunate series of accidents. He went out occasionally, of course; but he spent most of his time at home. Where in the world could he go? He went nowhere.

Pause. Finally she yielded abjectly to her fears and stammered:

"Well, Irgens, I am yours now, entirely yours! I am going to leave the house—You will thank me, won't you? It will take three years, of course, but then—"

She stopped suddenly; she felt that he was squirming, that he was bracing himself against the inevitable; her terror increased as he remained silent. A few anguished moments went by.

"Well, Hanka, this is rather unfortunate, in a way," he began finally. "You have evidently understood me to mean that when you got your divorce— that if you only were free—Of course, I may have said something to that effect; I admit that if you have interpreted my words literally such a supposition is probably justified. I have most likely said things more than once—"

"Yes, of course," she interrupted; "we have never meant anything else, have we? For you love me, don't you? What is the matter? You are so strange to-day!"

"I am awfully sorry, but really—things are not as they used to be." He looked away sadly and searched for words. "I cannot lie to you, Hanka, and the plain truth is that I am not enraptured by you as much as I used to be. It would hardly be right to deceive you; anyway, I couldn't do it—it is beyond me."

At last she understood; these were plain words. And quietly bending her head, yielding to the inevitable, letting go of the last lingering hope, she whispered in a dull and broken voice:

"Couldn't do it; no—It is all over, irrevocably over—"

He sat there silent.

Suddenly she turned and looked at him. Her white teeth showed beneath the slightly raised upper lip as she endeavoured to force a smile. She said slowly:

"But surely it cannot all be over, Irgens? Remember, I have sacrificed a great deal—"

But he shook his head.

"Yes, I am awfully sorry, but—Do you know what I was thinking of just now when I didn't answer you? You said 'irrevocably over.' I was wondering if that was proper grammar, if it sounded right. That shows how little this scene really affects me; you can see for yourself that I am not beside myself with grief—not even deeply stirred. That ought to show you—" And as if he wanted to utilise the opportunity to the utmost and leave no room for doubt, he continued: "Did you say that you have been here three times, looking for me? I know that you have been here twice. I think I ought to tell you, so that you can see how impossible it is for me to pretend: I sat here and heard you knock, but I didn't open. That surely proves the matter is serious—Dearest Hanka, I cannot help it; really, you mustn't be unhappy. But you surely will admit that our relationship must have been a little galling, a little humiliating, to me as well? It is true; it has not been easy for me to accept money from you continually; I have said to myself: 'This degrades you!' You understand, don't you—a man with a nature like mine; unhappily, I am proud, whether it is a virtue or a vice in me—"

Pause.

"All right," she said mechanically, "all right." And she rose in order to go. Her eyes were wide and staring, but she saw nothing.

However, he wanted to explain himself thoroughly; she must not leave with a wrong impression of him. He called her back; he wanted to prove why it could not have been otherwise, why his conduct was beyond reproach. He spoke at length and cleared up the matter perfectly; it seemed as if he had expected this and had prepared himself thoroughly. There were a number of bagatelles; but it was just the little things that counted with a man like him, and these little things had gradually made it so clear to him that they were not compatible. Of course, she was fond of him, a great deal more so than he deserved; but all the same he was not sure that she understood and appreciated him fully. This was not said reproachfully, but—She had said that she was proud of him, and that she enjoyed seeing the ladies turn and look after him when they walked down the street together. All right! But that did not prove that she valued his individuality. She took no pride in the fact that he was, above all, a somewhat different individuality. Of course, he did not blame her; but, unfortunately, it proved that her understanding of him was not deep enough. She was not proud of him for what he had thought or written; not primarily, at any rate; she loved to see the ladies look after him on the street. But ladies might turn and look after anybody, even after an officer or a tradesman. She had once given him a cane so that he might look well on the street....

"No, Irgens, I had no such thought, not at all," she interrupted.

All right, he might have been mistaken; if she said so, of course.... Nevertheless, he had the impression that such was her reason. He had thought that if he couldn't pass muster without a cane, then.... For even those two sheared sheep of Ojen's used a cane.

In brief, he gave the cane away to the first comer.... But there were other little things, other bagatelles: She liked to go to the opera; he didn't. She went without him, and he was very much pleased, of course; still.... She wore a light woollen dress, and when he was with her his clothes got full of fuzz from her dress, but she never noticed it. He had to brush and pick fuzz unceasingly to avoid looking as if he had been in bed fully dressed; but did she notice? Never. And in this manner one thing after another had come between them and had affected his feelings for her. There were hundreds of little things! A little while ago her lips had been so badly cracked that she couldn't even smile naturally; and just think, an insignificant thing like that had repulsed him, absolutely spoiled her for him! Dear me, she must not think that he found fault with her because of a cracked lip; he knew very well that she could not help such a thing; he was not stupid.... But the truth of the matter was that it had reached a point where he was beginning to dread her visits. He had to admit it; he had sat on this very chair and suffered, suffered tortures, when he heard her knock on the door. However, no sooner had she gone away than he felt relieved; he got ready and went out, too. He went to some restaurant and dined, dined unfeelingly and with a good appetite, not at all deploring what he had done. He wanted her to know these things so that she would understand him.... "But, dearest Hanka, I have told you all this and perhaps added to your sorrow instead of alleviating it. I wanted you to see how necessary has become our parting—that there are deep and weighty reasons for it—that it is not merely a whim. Unfortunately, these things are deeply rooted in my nature—But don't take it so to heart! You know I am fond of you and appreciate all you have done for me; and I shall never be able to forget you; I feel that only too well. Tell me that you will take it calmly—that is all I ask—"

She sat there, dull and immobile. Her premonition had not deceived her; it was all over. There he sat; he had spoken about this and that and remembered this and that—everything that could possibly explain and justify his actions. He had said a great deal, he had even bared himself in spots; yes, how penuriously hadn't he scraped up the least little thing that might vindicate him in the slightest degree! How could she ask him to advise her? He would simply refer her to the newspaper advertisements: "Flats and Apartments to Let." How insignificant he suddenly appeared! Slowly he blurred before her eyes; he was blotted out; he became lost in the dim distance; she saw him as through a haze; she barely discerned his mother-of-pearl buttons and his sleek and shiny hair. She realised how her eyes had been opened during his long speech; there he sat.... She felt languidly that she ought to go, but she lacked the energy to get up. She felt hollow and empty; the last little illusion to which she had clung so tenaciously had collapsed miserably. Somebody's step sounded on the stairs; she did not remember whether or no the door was locked, but she did not go and make sure. The steps died down again; nobody knocked.

"Dearest Hanka," he said in an effort to console her as best he might, "you ought to start in in earnest and write that novel we have talked about. I am sure you could do it, and I will gladly go over the manuscript for you. The effort, the concentration would do you good; you know I want to see you content and satisfied."

Yes, once upon a time, she had really thought she would write a novel. Why not? *Here* one miss bobbed up, and *there* another madam bobbed up, and they all did write so cutely! Yes, she had really thought that it was her turn next. And how they all had encouraged her! Thank God, she had forgotten about it until now!

"You do not answer, Hanka?"

"Yes," she said absently, "there is something in what you say."

She got up suddenly and stood erect staring straight ahead. If she only knew what to do now! Go home? That would probably be the best. Had she had parents she would most likely have gone to them; however, she had never had any parents, practically. She had better go home to Tidemand, where she still lived....

And with a desolate smile she gave Irgens her hand and said farewell.

He felt so relieved because of her calmness that he pressed her hand warmly. What a sensible woman she was, after all! No hysterics, no heartrending reproaches; she said farewell with a smile! He wanted to brace her still more and talked on in order to divert her mind; he mentioned his work and plans; he would surely send her his next book; she would find him again in that. And, really, she ought to get busy on that novel.... To show her that their friendship was still unbroken he even asked her to speak to Gregersen about that review of his book. It was most extraordinary that his verses had attracted so little attention. If she would only do him this favour. He himself would never be able to approach Gregersen; he was too proud; he could never stoop to that....

She went over to the mirror and began arranging her hair. He could not help watching her; she really surprised him a little. It was of course admirable in her to keep her feelings in leash; still, this unruffled composure was not altogether *au fait*. He had really credited her with a little more depth; he had ventured to think that a settlement with him would affect her somewhat. And there she stood tranquilly and arranged her hair with apparent unconcern! He could not appreciate such a display of *sang-froid*. To tell the truth, he felt snubbed; and he made the remark that he was still present; it seemed peculiar that she had already so completely forgotten him....

She did not answer. But when she left the mirror she paused for a moment in the middle of the room, and with her eyes somewhere in the vicinity of his shoes, she said wearily and indifferently:

"Don't you understand that I am entirely through with you?"

But in the street, bathed in the bright sunshine, surrounded by people and carriages—there her strength gave way entirely and she began to sob wildly. She covered her face with her veil, and sought the least-frequented side-streets in order to avoid meeting anybody; she walked hurriedly, stooping, shaken by convulsive sobs. How densely dark the outlook whichever way she turned her eyes! She hurried on, walking in the middle of the street, talking to herself in a choked voice. Could she return to Andreas and the children? What if the door should be closed against her? She had wasted two days; perhaps Andreas now had grown impatient. Still, the door might be open if she only hurried....

Every time she took out her handkerchief she felt the crinkle of an envelope. That was the envelope with the hundred-crown bill; she still had that! Oh—if she only had somebody to go to now, a friend—not any of her "friends" from the clique; she was through with them! She had been one of them a year and a day; she had listened to their words and she had seen their deeds. How had she been able to endure them? Thank God, she was done with them forever. Could she go to Ole Henriksen and ask help from him? No, no; she couldn't do that.

Andreas would probably be busy in his office. She had not seen him for two days; very likely it was an accident, but it was so. And she had accepted a hundred crowns from him, although he was ruined! Dear me, that she hadn't thought of this before now! She had asked him for that money. "Yes," he had said; "will you please come into the office? I have not so much with me." And he had opened his safe and given her the hundred; perhaps it was all the money he had! He had proffered the bill in such a gentle and unobtrusive manner, although, perhaps, it was all the money he owned! His hair had turned a little grey and he looked as if he hadn't had much sleep lately; but he had not complained; his words were spoken in proud and simple dignity. It had seemed as if she saw him then for the first time.... Oh, would that she never had asked him for this money! Perhaps he might forgive her if she brought it back. Would she bother him very much if she stopped at his office a moment? She would not stay long....

Mrs. Hanka dried her eyes beneath her veil and walked on. When at last she stood outside Tidemand's office she hesitated. Suppose he turned her out? Perhaps he even knew where she had been?

A clerk told her that Tidemand was in.

She knocked and listened. He called: "Come in." She entered quietly. He was standing at his desk; he put down his pen when he saw her.

"Pardon me if I disturb you," she said hurriedly.

"Not at all," he said, and waited. A pile of letters was before him; he stood there, tall and straight; he did not look so very grey, and his eyes were not so listless.

She took the bill out and held it toward him.

"I only wanted to return this; and please forgive me for asking for money when I might have known that you must need it so badly. I never thought of it until now; I am extremely sorry."

He looked at her in surprise and said:

"Not at all—you just keep that! A hundred more or less means nothing to the business—nothing at all."

"Yes, but—please take it! I ask you to take it."

"All right, if you don't need it. I thank you, but it is not necessary."

He had thanked her! What a fortunate thing that she had the money and could give it back to him! But she suppressed her agitation and said "Thank you" herself as she shoved the bill over toward him. When she saw him reach for his pen again, she said with a wan smile:

"You must not be impatient because of this long delay—I have made very little progress in the matter of taking an apartment, but—"

She could control herself no longer; her voice broke entirely and she turned away from him, fumbling for her handkerchief with trembling fingers.

"There is no great hurry about that," he said. "Take all the time you want."

"I thank you."

"You thank me? I don't quite understand. It isn't I who—I am simply trying to make it easy for you to have your own way."

She was afraid she had irritated him, and she said hastily:

"Of course, yes! Oh, I didn't mean—Pardon me for disturbing you."

And she turned and fled out of the office.

III

Tidemand had not been idle a moment since the blow struck him. He was at his desk early and late; papers, bills, notes, and certificates fluttered around him, and his energy and skill brought order out of confusion as the days went by. Ole Henriksen had supported him on demand; he had paid cash for the country estate and had relieved him of several outstanding obligations.

It was made clear that the firm did not have an impregnable fortune to throw into the breach, even though it carried on such a far-reaching business and although its transactions were enormous. And who had even heard of such a crazily hazardous speculation as Tidemand's fatal plunge in rye! Everybody could see that now, and everybody pitied or scorned him according to his individual disposition. Tidemand let them talk; he worked, calculated, made arrangements, and kept things going. True, he held in storage an enormous supply of rye which he had bought too high: but rye was rye, after all; it did not deteriorate or shrink into nothingness; he sold it steadily at prevailing prices and took his losses like a man. His misfortunes had not broken his spirits.

He now had to weather the last turn—a demand note from the American brokers—and for this he required Ole Henriksen's assistance; after that he hoped to be able to manage unaided. It was his intention to simplify his business, to reduce it to original dimensions and then gradually extend it as it should show healthy growth. He would succeed; his head was still full of plans and he was resourceful as ever.

Tidemand gathered his papers together and went over to Ole's office. It was Monday. They had both finished their mail and were momentarily disengaged, but Tidemand had to make a call at the bank; he had arranged an appointment at five.

As soon as Ole saw him he laid down his pen and arose to meet him. They still celebrated their meetings in the usual manner; the wine and the cigars appeared as before; nothing had changed. Tidemand did not want to disturb; he would rather lend a hand if he could, but Ole refused smilingly; he had absolutely nothing to do.

Well, Tidemand had brought his usual tale of woe. He was beginning to be a good deal of a nuisance; he simply came to see Ole whenever there was anything the matter....

Ole interrupted him with a merry laugh.

"Whatever you do, don't forget to apologise every time!"

Ole signed the papers and said:

"How are things coming out?"

"Oh, about as usual. One day at a time, you know."

"Your wife hasn't moved as yet?"

"Not yet—no. I imagine she has a hard time finding a suitable apartment. Well, that is her lookout. What I want to say—how is Miss Aagot?"

"All right, I guess; she is out walking. Irgens called for her."

Pause.

Ole said: "You still have all your help?"

"Well, you see, I couldn't fire them all in a minute; they have to have time to look around for something else. But they are leaving soon; I am only going to keep one man in the office."

They discussed business matters for a while. Tidemand had ground up a large quantity of his grain in order to accelerate the sales; he sold and lost, but he raised money. There was no longer any danger of a receivership. He had also a little idea, a plan which had begun to ferment in his brain; but he would rather not mention it until it had been developed a little more fully. One did not stand knee-deep in schemes day in and day out without occasionally stumbling over an idea. Suddenly he said:

"If I could be sure of not offending you I should like to speak to you about something that concerns yourself only—I don't want to hurt your feelings, but I have thought a good deal about it. Hm; it is about Irgens—You should not allow Aagot to go out so much. Miss Aagot walks a good deal with him lately. It would be all right if you were along; of course, it is perfectly right as it is—that she should take a walk occasionally, but—Well, don't be angry because I mention this."

Ole looked at him with open mouth, then he burst out laughing.

"But, friend Andreas, what do you mean? Since when did *you* begin to look at people distrustfully?"

Tidemand interrupted him brusquely.

"I only want to tell you that I have never been in the habit of carrying gossip."

Ole looked at him steadily. What could be the matter with Tidemand? His eyes had become cold and steely; he put down his glass hard. Gossip? Of course not. Tidemand did not carry gossip, but his mind must have become affected.

"Well, you may be right if you mean that this kind of thing may lead to unpleasant comment, to gossip," Ole said finally. "I really have not given it a thought, but now you mention it—I will give Aagot a hint the first opportunity I have."

Nothing further was said on the subject; the conversation swung back to Tidemand's affairs.

How was it—did he still take his meals in restaurants?

He did for the present. What else could he do? He would have to stick to the restaurants for a while, otherwise the gossips would finish poor Hanka altogether. People would simply say that she was to blame if he hadn't kept house the last few years; no sooner had she departed than Tidemand again went to housekeeping and stayed at home. Nobody knew what construction might be put on such things; Hanka did not have too many friends. Tidemand laughed at the thought that he was fooling the slanderous tongues so capitally. "She came to see me a couple of days ago; I was in my office. I thought at first it was some bill-collector, some dun or other, who knocked at my door; but it was Hanka. Can you guess what she wanted? She came to give me a hundred crowns! She had probably saved the money. Of course, you might say that it really was my own money; you *might* say that. Still, she could have kept it; but she knew I was a little pinched—She hasn't gone out at all the last few days; I am at a loss to know how she is keeping alive. I don't see her, but the maid says she eats in her room sometimes. She is working, too; she is busy all the time."

"It wouldn't surprise me at all to see her stay with you. Things may turn out all right yet."

Tidemand glanced at his friend sharply.

"You believe that? Wasn't it you who once said that I was no glove to be picked up or thrown away according to some one's fancy? Well, she has probably no more thought of coming back than I have of accepting her."

And Tidemand rose quickly and said good-bye; he was going to the bank and had to hurry.

Ole remained lost in contemplation; Tidemand's fate had made him thoughtful. What had become of Aagot? She had promised to be back in an hour, and it was much more than two hours since she had left. Of course, it was all right to take a walk, but.... Tidemand was right. Tidemand had his own thoughts, he had said; what could he have meant? Suddenly a thought struck Ole—perhaps Irgens was the destroyer of Tidemand's home, the slayer of his happiness? A red tie? Didn't Irgens use a red tie once?

Suddenly Ole understood Tidemand's previous significant remark about the danger of boat-rides in May. Well, well! Come to think of it, Aagot *had* really seemed to lose the desire to be with him in the office early and late; instead, she took a good many walks in good company; she wanted to view things and places in this good company.... Hadn't she once expressed a regret that he was not a poet? Still, she had apologised for that remark with such sweet and regretful eagerness; it was a thoughtless jest. No; Aagot was innocent as a child; still, for his sake, she might refuse an occasional invitation from Irgens....

Another long hour went by before Aagot returned. Her face was fresh and rosy, her eyes sparkling. She threw her arms around Ole's neck; she always did that when she had been with Irgens. Ole's misgivings dissolved and vanished in this warm embrace; how could he reproach her now? He only asked her to stay around the house a little more—for his sake. It was simply unbearable to be without her so long; he could do nothing but think of her all the time.

Aagot listened quietly to him; he was perfectly right; she would remember.

"And perhaps I might as well ask another favour of you: please try to avoid Irgens's company a little more, just a little more. I don't mean anything, you know; but it would be better not to give people the least cause for talk. Irgens is my friend, and I am his, but——Now, don't mind what I have said—"

She took his head in both her hands and turned his face toward her. She looked straight into his eyes and said:

"Do you doubt that I love you, Ole?"

He grew confused; he was too close to her. He stammered and took a step backward.

"Love me? Ha, ha, you silly girl! Did you think I was chiding you? You misunderstood me; I thought only of what people might say; I want to protect you from gossip. But it is silly of me; I should have said nothing—you might even take it into your head to avoid going out with Irgens in the future! And that would never do; then people would surely begin to wonder. No; forget this and act as if nothing had been said; really, Irgens is a rare and a remarkable man."

However, she felt the need of explaining matters: she went just as gladly with anybody else as with Irgens; it had only happened that he had asked her. She admired him; she would not deny that, and she was not alone in that; she pitied him a little, too; imagine, he had applied for a subsidy and had been refused! She felt sorry for him, but that was all....

"Say no more about it!" cried Ole. "Let everything remain as it is—" It was high time to think a little of the wedding; it was not too early to make definite arrangements. As soon as he returned from that trip to England he would be ready. And he thought it would be best for her to go home to Torahus while he was away; when everything was in order he would come up for her. Their wedding trip would have to be postponed until spring; he would be too busy until then.

Aagot smiled happily and agreed to everything. A vague, inexplicable wish had sprung up within her: she would have liked to remain in the city until he should return from England; then they could have gone to Torahus together. She did not know when or where this strange desire had been born in her, and it was, for that matter, not sufficiently clear or definite to be put in words; she would do as Ole wished. She told Ole to make haste and return; her eyes were open and candid; she spoke to him with one arm on his shoulder and the other resting on the desk.

And he had presumed to give *her* a hint!

IV

Over a week went by before Irgens turned up again. Had he become suspicious? Or had he simply tired of Aagot? However, he entered Ole's office one afternoon; the weather was clear and sunny, but it was blowing hard and the dust whirled through the streets in clouds and eddies. He was in doubt whether Miss Aagot would want to go out on such a day, and for this reason he said at once:

"It is a gloriously windy day, Miss Aagot; I should like to take you up on the hills, up to the high places! You have never seen anything like it; the town is shrouded in dust and smoke."

At any other time Ole would have said no; it was neither healthy nor enjoyable to be blown full of dust. But now he wanted to show Aagot that he was not thinking of their recent conversation.... Certainly; run along! Really, she ought to take this walk.

And Aagot went.

"It is an age since I have seen you," said Irgens.

"Yes," she said, "I am busy nowadays. I am going home soon."

"You are?" he asked quickly and stopped.

"Yes. I am coming back, though."

Irgens had become thoughtful.

"I am afraid it is blowing a little too hard, after all," he said. "We can hardly hear ourselves think. Suppose we go to the Castle Park? I know a certain place—"

"As you like," she said.

They found the place; it was sheltered and isolated. Irgens said:

"To be entirely candid, it was not my intention to drag you up into the hills to-day. The truth of the matter is that I was afraid you would not care to come; that is the reason I said what I said. For I *had* to see you once more."

Pause.

"Really—I have ceased to wonder at anything you say."

"But think—it is ten days since I have seen you! That is a long, a very long time."

"Well—that is not altogether my fault—But don't let us talk about it any more," she added quickly. "Rather tell me—why do you still act toward me in this manner? It is wrong of you. I have told you that before. I should like to be friends with you, but—"

"But no more. I understand. However, that is hardly sufficient for one who is distracted with suffering, you know. No, you do not know; you have never known. Ever and ever one must circle around the forbidden; it becomes a necessity continually to face one's fate. If, for instance, I had to pay for a moment like this with age-long wreck and ruin, why, I would gladly pay the price. I would rather be with you here one brief moment, Miss Aagot, than live on for years without you."

"Oh, but—It is too late now, you know. Why talk about it, then? You only make it so much harder for us both."

He said, slowly and emphatically:

"No, it is not too late."

She looked at him steadily and rose to her feet; he, too, got up; they walked on. Immersed in their own thoughts, without conscious realisation of what they were doing, walking slowly, they made the circuit of the park and returned to their sheltered nook. They sat down on the same bench.

"We are walking in a circle," he said. "That is the way I am circling around you."

"Listen," she said, and her eyes were moist, "this is the last time I shall be with you, probably. Won't you be nice? I am going home, you know, very soon now."

But just as he was preparing to answer her out of the fullness of his heart somebody had to pass their seat. It was a lady. In one hand she carried a twig with which she struck her skirt smartly for every step she took. She approached them slowly; they saw that she was young. Irgens knew her; he got up from his seat, took off his hat, and bowed deeply.

And the lady passed blushingly by.

Aagot asked:

"Who was that?"

"Only my landlady's daughter," he said. "You told me to be nice. Yes, dearest—"

But Aagot wanted further information concerning this lady. So they lived in the same house? What was she doing? What kind of a person was his landlady?

And Irgens answered her fully. Just as if she were a child whose curiosity had been aroused by the merest chance occurrence, Aagot made him tell her everything he knew concerning these strange people in Thranes Road No. 5. She wondered why the lady had blushed; why Irgens had greeted her so obsequiously. She did not know that this was the way Irgens always paid his rent—by being particularly gracious to his landlady's family on the street.

The young lady was good-looking, although she had a few freckles. She was really pretty when she blushed; didn't he think so?

And Irgens agreed; she was pretty. But she didn't have one only dimple; there was only one who had that....

Aagot glanced at him quickly; his voice thrilled her; she closed her eyes. The next instant she felt that she was bending toward him, that he kissed her. Neither spoke; all her fears were lulled; she ceased to struggle and rested deliciously in his arms.

And nobody disturbed them. The wind soughed through the trees; it hushed and soothed.... Somebody came along; they rushed apart and kept their eyes on the gravelled walk while he passed. Aagot was quite equal to the occasion; she did not show the slightest trace of confusion. She got up and began to walk away. And now she began to think; the tears were dripping from her long lashes, and she whispered, dully, despairingly:

"God forgive me! What have I done?"

Irgens wanted to speak, to say something that would soften her despair. It had happened because it had to happen. He was so unspeakably fond of her; she surely knew he was in earnest.... And he really looked as if he were greatly in earnest.

But Aagot heard nothing; she walked on, repeating these desperate words. Instinctively she took the way down toward the city. It seemed as if she were hurrying home.

"Dearest Aagot, listen a moment—"

She interrupted violently:

"Be quiet, will you!"

And he was silent.

Just as they emerged from the park a violent gust tore her hat from her hair. She made an effort to recover it, but too late; it was blown back into the park. Irgens caught up with it as it was flattened against a tree.

She stood still for a moment; then she, too, began to run in pursuit, and when at last they met by the tree her despair was less poignant. Irgens handed her the hat, and she thanked him. She looked embarrassed.

As they were walking down the sloping driveway toward the street the wind made Aagot turn and walk backward a few steps. Suddenly she stopped. She had discovered Coldevin; he was walking through the park in the direction of Tivoli. He walked hurriedly, furtively, and as if he did not want to be seen. So he was still in the city!

And Aagot thought in sudden terror: What if he has seen us! As in a flash she understood. He was coming from the park; he had wanted to wait until they should have had time to reach the street; then the accident with her hat had spoiled his calculations and made him show himself too soon. How he stooped and squirmed! But he could find no hiding-place on this open driveway.

Aagot called to him, but the wind drowned her voice. She waved her hand, but he pretended not to see it; he did not bow. And without another word to Irgens she ran after him, down the slope. The wind blew her skirts to her knees; she grabbed her hat with one hand and ran. She caught up with him by the first cross-street.

He stopped and greeted her as usual—awkwardly, with an expression of melancholy gladness, moved in every fibre of his being. He was miserably dressed.

"You—You must not come here and spy on me," she said hoarsely, all out of breath. She stood before him, breathing hard, angry, with flashing eyes.

His lips parted but he could not speak; he did not know which way to turn.

"Do you hear me?"

"Yes—Have you been sick, perhaps? You haven't been out for two weeks now; of course, I don't *know* that you haven't, but—"

His helpless words, his wretched embarrassment, moved her; her anger died down, she was again on the verge of tears, and, deeply humiliated, she said:

"Dear Coldevin, forgive me!"

She asked him to forgive her! He did not know what to say to this, but answered abstractedly:

"Forgive you? We won't speak about that—But why are you crying? I wish I hadn't met you—"

"But I am glad I met you," she said. "I wanted to meet you; I think of you always, but I never see you—I long for you often."

"Well, we won't speak about that, Miss Aagot. You know we have settled our affair. I can only wish you every happiness, every possible happiness."

Coldevin had apparently regained his self-control; he commenced even to speak about indifferent matters: Was not this a fearful storm? God knew how the ships on the high seas were faring!

She listened and answered. His composure had its effect on her, and she said quietly:

"So you are still in the city. I shall not ask you to come and see me; that would be useless. Ole and I both wanted to ask you to come with us on a little excursion, but you could not be found."

"I have seen Mr. Henriksen since then. I explained that I was engaged that Sunday anyway. I was at a party, a little dinner—So everything is well with you?"

"Yes, thanks."

Again she was seized with fear. What if he had been in the park and seen everything? She said as indifferently as she could: "See how the trees are swaying in the park! I suppose, though, there must be sheltered places inside."

"In the park? I don't know. I haven't been there—But your escort is waiting for you; isn't it Irgens?"

Thank God, she was saved! He had not been in the park. She heard nothing else. Irgens was getting tired of this waiting, but she did not care. She turned again to Coldevin.

"So you have seen Ole since the excursion? I wonder why he hasn't mentioned it to me."

"Oh, he cannot remember everything. He has a lot to think of, Miss Aagot; a great deal. He is at the head of a big business; I was really surprised when I saw how big it is. Wonderful! A man like him must be excused if he forgets a little thing like that. If you would permit me to say a word, he loves you better than anybody else! He—Please remember that! I wanted so much to say this to you!"

These few words flew straight to her heart. In a flash she saw the image of Ole, and she exclaimed joyously:

"Yes, it is true! Oh, when I think of everything—I am coming!" she called to Irgens and waved her hand at him.

She said good-bye to Coldevin and left him.

She seemed to be in a great hurry; she asked Irgens to pardon her for having kept him waiting, but she walked on rapidly.

"Why this sudden haste?" he asked.

"Oh, I must get home. What a nasty wind!"

"Aagot!"

She shot him a swift glance; his voice had trembled; she felt a warm glow throughout her being. No, she couldn't make herself colder than she was; her eyes drooped again and she leaned toward him; her arm brushed his sleeve.

He spoke her name again with infinite tenderness, and she yielded.

"Give me a little time, please! Whatever shall I do? I will love you if you will only let me alone now."

He was silent.

Finally they reached the last crossing. Ole Henriksen's house could be seen in the distance. The sight of that house seemed to bring her to her senses. Whatever could she have said? Had she promised anything? No, no, nothing! And she said with averted eyes:

"That which has happened to-day—your having kissed me—I regret it; God knows I do! I grieve over it—"

"Then pronounce the sentence!" he answered briskly.

"No, I cannot punish you, but I give you my hand in promise that I will tell Ole if you ever dare do that again."

And she gave him her hand.

He took it, pressed it; he bent over it, and kissed it repeatedly, defiantly, right below her own windows. Covered with confusion, she finally succeeded in opening the door and escaping up the stairs.

V

Ole Henriksen received a telegram which hastened his departure for London. For twenty-four hours he worked like a slave to get through—wrote and arranged, called at the banks, instructed his clerks, gave orders to his chief assistant, who was to be in charge during his absence. The Hull steamer was loading; it was to sail in a couple of hours. Ole Henriksen did not have any too much time.

Aagot went with him from place to place, sad and faithful. She was labouring under suppressed emotion. She did not say a word so as not to disturb him, but she looked at him all the time with moist eyes. They had arranged that she should go home the next morning on the first train.

Old Henriksen shuffled back and forth, quiet and silent; he knew that his son needed to hurry. Every once in a while a man would come up from the dock with reports from the steamer; now there was only a shipment of whale-oil to load, then she would start. It would take about three-quarters of an hour. At last Ole was ready to say farewell. Aagot only had to put on her wraps; she would stay with him to the last.

"What are you thinking of, Aagot?"

"Oh, nothing. But I wish you were well back again, Ole."

"Silly little girl! I am only going to London," he said, forcing a gaiety he did not feel. "Don't you worry! I shall be back in no time." He put his arm around her waist and caressed her; he gave her the usual pet names: Little Mistress, dear little Mistress! A whistle sounded; Ole glanced at his watch; he had fifteen minutes left. He had to see Tidemand a moment.

As soon as he entered Tidemand's office he said: "I am going to London. I want you to come over occasionally and give the old man a lift. Won't you?"

"Certainly," said Tidemand. "Are you not going to sit down, Miss Aagot? For you are not departing, I hope?"

"Yes, to-morrow," answered Aagot.

Ole happened to think of the last quotations. Rye was going up again. He congratulated his friend warmly.

Yes, prices were better; the Russian crops hadn't quite come up to expectations; the rise was not large, but it meant a great deal to Tidemand with his enormous stores.

"Yes, I am keeping afloat," he said happily, "and I can thank you for that. Yes, I can—" And he told them that he was busy with a turn in tar. He had contracts from a house in Bilbao. "But we will talk about this when you get back. *Bon voyage!*"

"If anything happens, wire me," said Ole.

Tidemand followed the couple to his door. Both Ole and Aagot were moved. He went to the window and waved to them as they passed; then he went back to his desk and worked away with books and papers. A quarter of an hour passed. He saw Aagot return alone; Ole had gone.

Tidemand paced back and forth, mumbling, figuring, calculating every contingency regarding this business in tar. He happened to see a long entry in the ledger which was lying open on his desk. It was Irgens's account. Tidemand glanced at it indifferently; old loans, bad debts, wine and loans, wine and cash. The entries were dated several years back; there were none during the last year. Irgens had never made any payments; the credit column was clean. Tidemand still remembered how Irgens used to joke about his debts. He did not conceal that he owed him twenty thousand; he admitted it with open and smiling face. What could he do? He had to live. It was deplorable that circumstances forced him into such a position. He wished it were different and he would have been sincerely grateful if anybody had come along and paid his debts, but so far nobody had offered to do that. Well, he would say, that could not be helped; he would have to carry his own burdens. Fortunately, most of his creditors were people with sufficient culture and delicacy to appreciate his position; they did not like to dun him; they respected his talent. But occasionally it would happen that a tailor or a wine-dealer would send him a bill and as like as not spoil an exquisite mood. He simply must open his door whenever anybody knocked, even if he were just composing some rare poem. He had to answer, to expostulate: What, another bill? Well, put it there, and I will look at it some time when I need a piece of paper. Oh, it is receipted? Well, then I will have to refuse to accept it; I never have receipted bills lying round. Take it back with my compliments....

Tidemand walked back and forth. An association of ideas made him think of Hanka and the divorce. God knows what she was waiting for; she kept to herself and spent all her time with the children, sewing slips and dresses all day long. He had met her on the stairs once; she was carrying some groceries in a bundle; she had stepped aside and muttered an excuse. They had not spoken to each other.

What could she be thinking of? He did not want to drive her away, but this could not continue. He was at a loss to understand why she took her meals at home; she never went to a restaurant. Dear me, perhaps she had no more money! He had sent the maid to her once with a couple of hundred crowns— they could not last for ever! He glanced in his calendar and noticed that it was nearly a month since he had had that settlement with Hanka; her money must have been used up long ago. She had probably even bought things for the children with that money.

Tidemand grew hot all of a sudden. At least *she* should never lack anything; thank God, one wasn't a pauper exactly! He took out all the money he could spare, left the office, and went up-stairs. The maid told him that Hanka was in her own little room, the middle room facing the street. It was four o'clock.

He knocked and entered.

Hanka sat at the table, eating. She rose quickly.

"Oh—I thought it was the maid," she stammered. Her face coloured and she glanced uneasily at the table. She began to clear away, to place napkins over the dishes. She moved the chairs and said again and again: "I did not know—everything is so upset—"

But he asked her to excuse his abrupt entrance. He only wanted to—she must have been in need of money, of course she must; it couldn't be otherwise; he wouldn't hear any more about it. Here—he had brought a little for her present needs. And he placed the envelope on the table.

She refused to accept it. She had plenty of money left. She took out the last two hundred crowns he had sent her and showed him the bills. She even wanted to return them.

He looked at her in amazement. He noticed that her left hand was without the ring. He frowned and asked:

"What has become of your ring, Hanka?"

"It isn't the one you gave me," she answered quickly. "It is the other one. That doesn't matter."

"I did not know you had been obliged to do that, or I would long ago—"

"But I was not obliged to do it; I wanted to. You see I have plenty of money. But it does not matter in the least, for I still have *your* ring."

"Well, whether it is my ring or not, you have not done me a favour by this. I want you to keep your things. I am not so altogether down and out, even if I have had to let some of my help go."

She bowed her head. He walked over to the window; when he turned back he noticed that she was looking at him; her eyes were candid and open. He grew confused and turned his back to her again. No, he could not speak to her of moving now; let her stay on awhile if she wanted to. But he would at least try to persuade her to cease this strange manner of living; there was no sense in that; besides, she was getting thin and pale.

"Don't be offended, but ought you not—Not for my sake, of course, but for your own—"

"Yes, I know," she interrupted, afraid of letting him finish; "time passes, and I haven't moved yet."

He forgot what he intended to say about her housekeeping eccentricities; he caught only her last words.

"I cannot understand you. You have had your way; nothing binds you any more. You can be Hanka Lange now as much as you like; you surely know that I am not holding you back."

"No," she answered. She rose and took a step toward him. She held out her hand to him in a meaningless way, and when he did not take it, she dropped it to her side limply, with burning cheeks. She sank into her chair again.

"No, you are not holding me back—I wanted to ask you—Of course, I have no right to expect that you will let me, but if you would—if I could remain here awhile yet? I would not be as I was before—I have changed a good deal, and so have you. I cannot say what I want to—"

His eyes blurred suddenly. What did she mean? For a moment he faltered; then he buttoned his coat and straightened his shoulders. Had he, then, suffered in vain during all these weary days and nights? Hardly! He would prove it now. Hanka was sitting there, but evidently she was beside herself; he had excited her by calling on her so "unexpectedly".

"Don't excite yourself, Hanka. Perhaps you are saying what you do not mean."

A bright, irrepressible hope flamed up within her.

"Yes," she exclaimed, "I mean every word! Oh, if you could forget what I have been, Andreas? If you would only have pity on me! Take me back; be merciful! I have wanted to come back for more than a month now, come back to you and to the children; I have stood here behind the curtains and watched you when you went out! The first time I really saw you was that night on the yacht—do you remember? I had never seen you until then. You stood by the tiller. I saw you against the sky; your hair was a little grey around the temples. I was so surprised when I saw you. I asked you if you were cold. I did it so you would speak to me! I know—time passed, but during all these weeks I have seen nobody but you—nobody! I am four and twenty years old, and have never felt like this before. Everything you do, everything you say—And everything the little ones do and say. We play and laugh, they cling to my neck…. I follow you with my eyes. See, I have cut a little hole in the curtain so that I can see you better. I can see you all the way to the end of the street. I can tell your steps whenever you walk down-stairs. Punish me, make me suffer, but do not cast me off! Simply to be here gives me a thousand joys, and I am altogether different now—"

She could hardly stop; she continued to speak hysterically; at times her voice was choked with emotion. She rose from the chair. She smiled while the tears rained down her face. Her voice trailed off into inarticulate sounds.

"For Heaven's sake, be calm!" he exclaimed abruptly, and his own tears were falling as he spoke. His face twitched. He was furious because he could not control himself better. He stood there and snapped out his words. He could not find the ones he sought. "You could always make me do whatever you wanted. I am not very clever when it comes to bandying words, no, indeed! The clique knows how to talk, but I haven't learned the art—Forgive me, I did not mean to hurt you. But if you mean that you want me to take somebody else's place now—If you want me as a successor—Of course, I do not know, but I ask. You say you want to come back now. But *how* do you come back? Oh, I don't want to know; go in God's name!"

"No, you are right. I simply wanted to ask you—I had to. I have been unfaithful to you, yes. I have done everything I shouldn't do, everything—"

"Well, let us end this scene. You need rest more than anything else."

Tidemand walked to the door. She followed him with wide-open eyes.

"Punish me!" she cried. "I ask you to—have pity! I should be grateful to you. Don't leave me, I cannot bear to have you go! Do not cast me off; I have been unfaithful and—But try me once more; try me only a little! Do you think I might remain here? I don't know—"

He opened the door. She stood still, her eyes dilated. From them shone the great question.

"Why do you look at me like that? What do you want me to do?" he asked. "Come to your senses. Do not brood over the past. I will do all I can for the children. I think that is all you can reasonably ask."

Then she gave up. She stretched her arms out after him as the door closed. She heard his steps down the stairs. He paused a moment as if uncertain which way to take. Hanka ran to the window, but she heard his office door open. Then all was quiet.

Too late! How could she have expected otherwise? Good God, how could she have expected otherwise! How she had nourished that vain hope night and day for a whole month! He had gone; he said no, and he went away. Most likely he even objected to her staying with the children!

Mrs. Hanka moved the following day. She took a room she saw advertised in the paper, the first room she came across; it was near the Fortress. She left home in the morning while Tidemand was out. She kissed the children and wept. She put her keys in an envelope and wrote a line to her husband. Tidemand found it upon his return; found the keys and this farewell, which was only a line or two.

Tidemand went out again. He sauntered through the streets, down toward the harbour. He followed the docks far out. A couple of hours went by, then he returned the same way. He looked at his watch; it was one o'clock. Suddenly he ran across Coldevin.

Coldevin stood immovable behind a corner and showed only his head. When he saw Tidemand coming straight toward him he stepped out in the street and bowed.

Tidemand looked up abstractedly.

And Coldevin asked:

"Pardon me, isn't this Mr. Irgens I see down there—that gentleman in grey?"

"Where? Oh, yes, it looks like him," answered Tidemand indifferently.

"And the lady who is with him, isn't that Miss Lynum?"

"Perhaps it is. Yes, I fancy that is she."

"But wasn't she going away to-day? It seems to me I heard—Perhaps she has changed her mind?"

"I suppose she has."

Coldevin glanced swiftly at him. Tidemand looked as if he did not want to be disturbed. He excused himself politely and walked off, lost in thought.

VI

No, Aagot did not go away as had been arranged. It occurred to her that she ought to buy a few things for her smaller sisters and brothers. It was quite amusing to go around and look at the store windows all alone; she did that all the afternoon, and it was six when at last she was through and happened to meet Irgens on the street. He relieved her of her parcels and went with her. Finally they hailed a carriage and took a ride out in the country. It was a mild and quiet evening.

No, she must not go away to-morrow. What good would that do? One day more or less didn't matter. And Irgens confessed frankly that he was not very flush at present, or he would have accompanied her.... If not in the same compartment, at least on the same train. He wanted to be near her to the very last. But he was too poor, alas!

Wasn't it a crying shame that a man like him should be so hard up? Not that she would have allowed him to come, but.... How it impressed her that he so frankly told her of his poverty!

"Besides, I am not sure that my life is safe here any more," he said smilingly. "Did you tell my friend Ole how I acted?"

"It is never too late to do that," she said.

They told the driver to stop. They walked ahead, talking gaily and happily. He asked her to forgive him his rashness—not that he wanted her to think that he had forgotten her, or could forget her.

"I love you," he confessed, "but I know it is useless. I have now one thing left—my pen. I may write a verse or two to you; you must not be angry if I do. Well, time will tell. In a hundred years everything will be forgotten."

"I am powerless to change anything," she said.

"No, you are not. It depends, of course—At least, there is nobody else who can." And he added quickly: "You told me to give you a little time, you asked me to wait—what did you mean by that?"

"Nothing," she answered.

They walked on. They came into a field. Irgens spoke entertainingly about the far, blue, pine-clad ridges, about a tethered horse, a workingman who was making a fence. Aagot was grateful; she knew he did this in order to maintain his self-control; she appreciated it. He even said with a shy smile that if she would not think him affected he would like to jot down a couple of stanzas which just now occurred to him. And he jotted down the couple of stanzas.

She wanted to see what he wrote. She bent toward him and asked him laughingly to let her see.

If she really wanted to! It was nothing much, though.

"Do you know," he said, "when you bent toward me and your head was so close to me, I prayed in my heart that you would remain like that! That is the reason I first refused to let you see what I had written."

"Irgens," she said suddenly, in a tender voice, "what would happen if I said yes to you?"

Pause. They looked at each other.

"Then it would happen, of course, that—that you would say no to another."

"Yes—but it is too late now, too late! It is not to be considered—But if it is any comfort to you to know it, then I can say that you are not the only one to grieve—"

He took this beautifully. He seized her hand and pressed it silently, with a happy glance, and he let it go at once.

They walked along the road. They had never been closer to each other. When they reached the new fence the workman took off his cap. They stopped before a gate; they looked at each other a moment and turned back. They did not speak.

They came back to the carriage. During the drive Irgens held all Aagot's bundles in his arms. He did not move and was not in the least insistent.

She was really touched by his tactful behaviour, and when he finally asked her to stay another day she consented.

But when the carriage had to be paid for he searched his pockets in vain; at last he had to ask her to pay the driver herself. She was pleased to be able to do that; she only wished she had thought of it at once. He had looked quite crestfallen.

They met each other early the next day. They walked along the docks, talking together in low voices, trembling with suppressed feeling. Their eyes were full of caresses; they walked close to each other. When, finally, Irgens caught sight of Coldevin standing half hidden behind a corner, he did not mention his discovery with a single syllable in order not to distress her. He said simply:

"What a pity you and I are not ordinary working people now! We seem to attract attention; people are for ever staring at us. It would be preferable to be less prominent."

They spoke about seeing each other at the Grand in the evening. It was quite a while since she had been there; she had really had few pleasures of late. Suddenly he said:

"Come and go up to my place. There we can sit and talk in peace and quiet."

"But would that do?"

Why not? In broad daylight? There was absolutely no reason why she shouldn't. And he would always, always have the memory of her visit to treasure.

And she went with him, timid, fearful, but happy.

FINALE

I

Milde and Gregersen walked down the street together. They talked about Milde's portrait of Paulsberg which had been bought by the National Galleries; about the Actor Norem, who, together with a comrade, had been found drunk in a gutter and had been arrested; about Mrs. Hanka, who was said at last to have left her husband. Was anything else to be expected? Hadn't she endured it for four long years down in that shop? They asked each other for her address; they wanted to congratulate her; she must know that they fully sympathised with her. But none of them knew her address.

They were deeply interested in the situation. It had come to this that Parliament had been dissolved without having said the deciding word, without having said anything, in fact. The *Gazette* had advised against radical action at the last moment. The paper had talked about the seriousness of assuming responsibilities, about the unwisdom of a straightforward challenge.

"What the devil can we do—with our army and navy?" said Gregersen with deep conviction. "We shall simply have to wait."

They went into the Grand. Ojen was there with his two close-cropped poets. He was speaking about his latest prose poems: "A Sleeping City," "Poppies," "The Tower of Babel." Imagine the Tower of Babel—its architecture! And with a nervous gesture he drew a spiral in the air.

Paulsberg and his wife arrived; they moved the tables together and formed a circle. Milde stood treat; he still had money left from the first half of the subsidy. Paulsberg attacked Gregersen at once because of the *Gazette's* change of front. Hadn't he himself, a short time ago, written a rather pointed article in the paper? Had they entirely forgotten that? How could he reconcile this with their present attitude? It would soon be a disgrace for an honest man to see his name in that sheet. Paulsberg was indignant and said so without mincing words.

Gregersen had no defence. He simply answered that the *Gazette* had fully explained its position, had given reasons....

"What kind of reasons?" Paulsberg would show them how shallow they were. "Waiter, the *Gazette* for to-day!"

While they waited for the paper even Milde ventured to say that the reasons were anything but convincing. They consisted of vague vapourings about the easterly boundary, the unpreparedness of the army, even mentioning foreign intervention....

"And fifteen minutes ago you yourself agreed with the *Gazette* unqualifiedly," said Gregersen.

Paulsberg commenced reading from the *Gazette*, paragraph after paragraph. He laughed maliciously. Wasn't it great to hear a paper like the *Gazette* mention the word responsibility? And Paulsberg threw the paper aside in disgust. No; there ought to be at least a trace of honesty in our national life! This sacrifice of principle for the sake of expediency was degrading, to say the least.

Grande and Norem entered, with Coldevin between them. Coldevin was talking. He nodded to the others and finished what he was saying before he paused. The Attorney, this peculiar nonentity, who neither said nor did anything himself, took a wicked pleasure in listening to this uncouth person from the backwoods. He had happened upon Coldevin far up in Thranes Road; he had spoken to him, and Coldevin had said that he was going away soon, perhaps to-morrow. He was going back to Torahus; he was mainly going in order to resign his position; he had accepted a situation farther north. But in that case Grande had insisted that they empty a glass together, and Coldevin had finally come along. They had met Norem outside.

Coldevin, too, spoke about the situation; he accused the young because they had remained silent and accepted this last indignity without a protest. God help us, what kind of a youth was that? Was our youth, then, *entirely* decadent?

"It looks bad for us again," said Milde in a stage whisper.

Paulsberg smiled.

"You will have to grin and bear it—Let us get toward home, Nikoline. I am not equal to this."

And Paulsberg and his wife left.

II

Coldevin looked very shabby indeed. He was in the same suit he wore when he came to town; his hair and beard were shaggy and unkempt.

The Journalist brought him over to the table. What did he want? Only a glass of beer?

Coldevin glanced around him indifferently. It would seem that he had had a hard time. He was thin to emaciation and his eyes shone through dark, shadowy rings. He drank his beer greedily. He even said it was a long time since a glass of beer had tasted better. Perhaps he was hungry, too.

"To return to the matter under discussion," said the Attorney. "One cannot affirm offhand that we are floating on the battered hull. One must not forget to take the young Norway into consideration."

"No," answered Coldevin, "one should never affirm anything offhand. One must try to reach the basic reason for every condition. And this basic reason might just be—as I have said—our superstitious faith in a power which we do not possess. We have grown so terribly modest in our demands; why is it? Might this not lie at the very root of our predicament? Our power is theoretical; we talk, we intoxicate ourselves in words, but we do not act. The fancy of our youth turns to literature and clothes; its ambition goes no further, and it is not interested in other things. It might, for instance, profitably take an interest in our business life."

"Dear me, how you know everything!" sneered the Journalist.

But Milde nudged him secretly and whispered: "Leave him alone! Let him talk. He, he! He really believes what he says; he trembles with eagerness and conviction. He is a sight in our day and generation!"

The Attorney asked him:

"Have you read Irgens's latest book?"

"Yes, I have read it. Why do you ask?"

"Oh, simply because I am at a loss to understand how you can have such a poor opinion of our youth when you know its production. We have writers of rank—"

"Yes—but, on the other hand, there is in your circle a young man who has lost heavily in rye," answered Coldevin. "I am more interested in him. Do you know what this man is doing? He is not crushed or broken by his loss. He is just now creating a new article of export; he has undertaken to supply a foreign enterprise with tar, Norwegian tar. But you do not mention his name."

"No; I must confess that my knowledge of Norwegian tar is limited, but—"

"There may be nothing lacking in your knowledge, Mr. Attorney, but you have possibly too little sympathy for commerce and the creation of values. On the other hand, you are thoroughly up to date as far as the aesthetic occurrences are concerned; you have heard the latest prose poem. We have so many young writers; we have Ojen, and we have Irgens, and we have Paulsberg, and we have many more. That is the young Norway. I see them on the streets occasionally. They stalk past me as poets should stalk past ordinary people. They are brimful of new intentions, new fashions. They are fragrant with perfume—in brief, there is nothing lacking. When they show up everybody else is mute: 'Silence! The poet speaks.' The papers are able to inform their readers that Paulsberg is on a trip to Honefos. In a word—"

But this was too much for Gregersen. He himself had written the news notes about Paulsberg's trip to Honefos. He shouted:

"But you have the most infernal way of saying insolent things! You look as if you were saying nothing of consequence—"

"I simply cannot understand why you lose your temper," said Milde tranquilly, "when Paulsberg himself told us to grin and bear it!"

Pause.

"In a word," resumed Coldevin, "the people do their duty, the papers do their duty. Our authors are not ordinary, readable talents; no, they are flaming pillars of fire; they are being translated into German! They assume dimensions. This, of course, can be repeated so often that people at last believe it; but such a self-delusion is very harmful. It makes us complacent, it perpetuates our insignificance."

Gregersen plays a trump card:

"But tell me, you—I don't remember your name:—do you know the story of Vinje and the potato? I always think of that when I hear you speak. You are so immensely unsophisticated; you are from the country, and you think you can amaze us. You have not the slightest suspicion that your opinions are somewhat antiquated. Your opinions are those of the self-taught man. Once Vinje began to ponder over the ring in a newly cut, raw potato; being from the country, you, at least, must know that there in springtime, often, is a purple figure in a potato. And Vinje was so interested in this purple outline that he sat down and wrote a mathematical thesis about it. He took this to Fearnley in the fond belief that he had made a great discovery. 'This is very fine,' said Fearnley; 'it is perfectly correct. You have solved the problem. But the Egyptians knew this two thousand years ago—' They knew it ages ago, ha, ha, ha! And I am always reminded of this story when I hear you speak! Don't be offended, now!"

Pause.

"No, I am not offended in the least," said Coldevin. "But if I understand you correctly, then we agree. I am only saying what you already know?"

But Gregersen shook his head in despair and turned to Milde.

"He is impossible," he said. He emptied his glass and spoke again to Coldevin, spoke in a louder voice than necessary; he bent toward him and shouted: "For Heaven's sake, man, don't you understand that your opinions are too absurd—the opinions of the self-taught man? You think that what you say is news to us. We have heard it for ages; we know it, and we think it ridiculous. Isch! I don't want to talk to you!"

And Gregersen got up and walked unsteadily away. It was six o'clock. The three men who remained at the table sat silently a few moments. At last Coldevin said:

"There goes Journalist Gregersen. That man has my unqualified pity and sympathy."

"He would hardly accept it," said Milde with a laugh.

"But he cannot avoid it. I think often of these writers for the daily press, these faithful workers who accomplish more in a month than the poets wring from themselves during a year. They are often married men in poor circumstances; their fate is not too pleasant at best. They have probably dreamed about a freer and richer life than this slavery in an office where their best efforts are swallowed up in anonymity, and where they often have to repress themselves and their convictions in order to keep their jobs. It might be well if these men were given the approbation they deserved; it might even be profitable; it might bear fruit in a free and honest newspaper literature. What have we at present? An irresponsible press, lacking convictions and clearly defined principles, its policy dictated by personal preferences—by even worse motives. No; a truly great journalist ranks far higher than a poet."

Just then the door opened and Irgens and Miss Aagot entered. They stopped by the door and looked around; Aagot showed no sign of embarrassment, but when she caught sight of Coldevin, she stepped forward quickly, with a smile on lips that were already opened as if to speak. Suddenly she stopped. Coldevin stared at her and fumbled mechanically at his buttons.

This lasted a few moments. Irgens and Aagot went over to the table, shook hands, and sat down. Aagot gave Coldevin her hand. Milde wanted to know what they would have. He happened to be flush. "Order anything you like—"

"You come too late," he said smilingly. "Coldevin has entertained us splendidly."

Irgens looked up. He shot a swift glance at Coldevin and said, while he lit a cigar:

"I have enjoyed Mr. Coldevin's entertainment once before in Tivoli, I believe. This will have to satisfy me for the present."

It was only with difficulty that Irgens succeeded in hiding his displeasure. This was the second time to-day he had seen Coldevin; he had observed him outside his lodgings in Thranes Road No. 5. He had not been able to get Aagot out until this infernal fellow had disappeared. By a happy chance Grande had passed by; otherwise he would probably have been there still. And how had he acted? He had stood like a guard, immovable; Irgens had been furious. He had had the greatest difficulty in keeping Aagot from the windows. If she had happened to glance out she must have discovered him. He had made no effort to conceal himself. One would think he had stood there with the avowed intention of being seen, in order to keep the couple in a state of siege.

Now he appeared slightly embarrassed. He fingered his glass nervously and looked down. But suddenly it seemed as if Irgens's insolence had roused him; he said bluntly and without connection with what had been discussed before:

"Tell me one thing—Or, let me rather say it myself: These poets are turning everything upside down; nobody dares to grumble. An author might owe in unsecured debts his twenty thousand—what of it? He is unable to pay, that is all. What if a business man should act in this manner? What if he were to obtain wine or clothes on false promises of payment? He would simply be arrested for fraud and declared bankrupt. But the authors, the artists, these talented superbeings who suck the country's blood like vampires to the nation's acclaim—who would dare take such measures with them? People simply discuss the scandal privately and laugh and think it infernally smart that a man can owe his twenty thousand—"

Milde put his glass down hard and said:

"My good man, this has gone far enough!"

That splendid fellow Milde seemed all at once to have lost his patience. While he was sitting alone with the Attorney and the Actor he had found the miserable Tutor's bitter sarcasms amusing, but no sooner had one of the Authors appeared than he felt outraged and struck his fist on the table. It was Milde's excellent habit always to await reinforcements.

Coldevin looked at him.

"Do you think so?" he said.

"I'll be damned if I don't."

Coldevin had undoubtedly spoken intentionally. He had even addressed his remarks very plainly. Irgens bit his moustache occasionally.

But now Norem woke up. He understood that something was happening before his dull eyes, and he began to mix in, to declaim about business morals. It was the rottenest morality on earth, usury—a morality for Jews! Was it right to demand usurious interest? Don't argue with him. He knew what he was talking about. Ho! business morals! The rottenest morals on earth....

Meanwhile the Attorney was talking across the table to Irgens and Miss Aagot. He told them how he had come across Coldevin.

"I ran across him a moment ago up your way, Irgens, in Thranes Road, right below your windows. I brought him along. I couldn't let the fellow stand there alone—"

Aagot asked quickly, with big, bewildered eyes:

"Thranes Road, did you say? Irgens, he was standing below your windows!"

Her heart was fluttering with fear. Coldevin observed her fixedly; he made sure that she should notice he was staring straight at her.

Meanwhile Norem continued his impossible tirade. So it was charged that the people as a whole was corrupt, that its men and women were debased because they honoured literature and art. "Ho! you leave art alone, my good man, and don't you bother about that! Men and women corrupt!—"

Coldevin seized this chance remark by the hair and replied. He did not address Norem; he looked away from him. He spoke about something that evidently was vitally important in his eyes. He addressed himself to nobody in particular, and yet his words were meant for some one. It was hardly correct to say that men and women were corrupt; they had simply reached a certain degree of hollowness; they had degenerated and grown small. Shallow soil, anaemic soil, without growth, without fertility! The women carried on their surface existence. They were not tired of life, but they did not venture much either. How could they put up any stakes? They had none to put up. They darted around like blue, heatless flames; they nibbled at everything, joys and sorrows, and they did not realise that they had grown insignificant. Their ambitions did not soar; their hearts did not suffer greatly; they beat quite regularly, but they did not swell more for one thing than for another, more for one person than for another. What had our young women done with their proud eyes? Nowadays they looked on mediocrity as willingly as on superiority. They lost themselves in admiration over rather every-day poetry, over common fiction. Some time ago greater and prouder things were needed to conquer them. There was a page here and there in Norway's history to prove that. Our young women had modified their demands considerably; they couldn't help it; their pride was gone, their strength sapped. The young woman had lost her power, her glorious and priceless simplicity, her unbridled passion, her brand of breed. She had lost her pride in the only man, her hero, her god. She had acquired a sweet tooth. She sniffed at everything and gave everybody the willing glance. Love to her was simply the name for an extinct feeling; she had read about it and at times she had been entertained by it, but it had never sweetly overpowered her and forced her to her knees; it had simply fluttered past her like an outworn sound. "But the young woman of our day does not pretend to all this; alas, no! She is honestly shorn. There is nothing to do about it; the only thing is to keep the loss within limits. In a few generations we shall probably experience a renaissance; everything comes in cycles. But for the present we are sadly denuded. Only our business life beats with a healthy, strong pulse. Only our commerce lives its deed-filled life. Let us place our faith in that! From it will the newer Norway spring!"

These last words seemed to irritate Milde; he took out of his pocketbook a ten-crown bill which he threw across the table to Coldevin. He said furiously:

"There—take your money! I had almost forgotten that I owed you this money, but I trust you understand that you can go now!"

Coldevin coloured deeply. He took the bill slowly.

"You do not thank me very politely for the loan," he said.

"And who has told you that I am a polite man? The main thing is that you have got your money and that we hope now to be rid of you."

"Well, I thank you; I need it," said Coldevin. The very way in which he picked up the bill showed plainly that he was not used to handling money. Suddenly he looked straight at Milde and added:

"I must confess I had not expected you ever to repay this loan."

Milde blazed up, but only for a moment. Even this direct insult did not make him lose his temper. He swallowed it, mumbled a reply, said finally that he had not intended to be rude; he would apologise....

But Norem, who sat there drunk and dull, could no longer repress his amusement. He only saw the comical side of the incident and cried laughingly:

"Have you touched this fellow, too, Milde? So help me, you can borrow money from anybody! You are inimitable. Ha, ha! from him, too!"

Coldevin rose.

Aagot got up simultaneously and ran over to him. She took his hand, a prey to the greatest excitement. She began whispering to him. She led him over to a window and continued speaking earnestly, in a low voice. They sat down. There was nobody else around, and she said:

"Yes, yes, you are right; it is true. You were speaking to me; I understood it only too well; you are right, right, right! Oh, but it is going to be different! You said that I couldn't, that it was not within my power; but I can; I will show you! I understand it all now; you have opened my eyes. Dear, do not be angry with me. I have done a great wrong, but—"

She wept with dry eyes. She swallowed hard. She sat on the very edge of the chair in her excitement. He injected a word now and then, nodded, shook his head when she appeared too disconsolate, and in his confusion he called her "Aagot, dearest Aagot." She must not apply everything he had said to herself, not at all. Of course, he had thought of her, too, that was true; but then he had been mistaken—thank God for that! He had simply wanted to warn her. She was so young; he, who was older, knew better from where danger threatened. But now she must forget it and be cheerful.

They continued to speak. Irgens grew impatient and rose. He stretched himself and yawned as if to indicate that he was going. Suddenly he remembered something he had forgotten. He walked quickly over to the bar and got some roasted coffee which he put in his vest pocket.

Milde settled the checks. He flung money around with the greatest unconcern; then he said good-bye and left. A moment afterward they saw him bow to a lady outside. He spoke a few words and they walked away through a side-street. The lady wore a long boa which billowed behind her in the breeze.

And still Aagot and Coldevin sat there.

"Won't you take me home? Excuse me a moment, I want to—"

She ran over to Irgens's table and took her coat from the chair.

"Are you going?" he asked her in amazement.

"Yes. Ugh—I won't do this any more. Goodbye!"

"What won't you do any more? Don't you want me to take you home?"

"No. And not later either; not to-morrow. No, I am through for good." She gave Irgens her hand and said good-bye quickly. All the time she looked at Coldevin and seemed impatient to be off.

"Remember our engagement for to-morrow," Irgens said.

III

Aagot and Coldevin walked together down the street. He said nothing about his going away, and she didn't know of his intention. She was happy to be with Coldevin, this phenomenon who irritated everybody with his impossible harangues. She walked close beside him; her heart was fluttering.

"Forgive me!" she pleaded. "Yes, you must forgive me everything, both that which has happened before and to-day. A while ago I should have been afraid to ask you, but no sooner am I with you than I become bold again. You never reprove me, never. But I haven't done anything wrong to-day—I mean to-day when I was far up-town; you understand what I mean." And she looked at him with an open, straightforward glance.

"Are you going back home soon, Miss Aagot?"

"Yes, I am going back at once—Forgive me, Coldevin, and believe me, believe me—I have done nothing wrong to-day; but I am so sorry, I repent everything—Blue, heatless flames, without much pride—I am not so stupid that I do not know whom you had in mind when you said this."

"But, dearest Aagot," he exclaimed in his perplexity, "it was not meant for you—I didn't mean it at all! And besides, I was mistaken, greatly mistaken; thank God, *you* are entirely different. But promise me one thing, Aagot; promise that you will be a little careful, do! It is none of my business, of course; but you have fallen in with a crowd—believe me, they are not your kind of people. Mrs. Tidemand has gained bitter experience through them."

She glanced at him inquiringly.

"I thought it best to tell you. Mrs. Tidemand, one of the few sterling personalities in the clique, even she! One from that crowd has destroyed her, too."

"Is that true?" said Aagot. "Well, I don't care in the least for them; alas, no! I don't want to remember any of them." And she seized Coldevin's arm and pressed close to him as if in fear.

This embarrassed him still more. He slowed up a little, and she said with a smile as she let go his arm:

"I suppose I mustn't do that?"

"H'm. What are you going to do when you get back home? By the way, have you heard from your fiancé?"

"No, not yet. But I suppose it is too early. Are you afraid of anything happening to him? Dear me, tell me if you are!"

"No; don't worry! He will get back safe enough."

They stopped at her door and said good-bye. She ascended the few steps hesitatingly, without even lifting her dress; suddenly she turned, ran downstairs again, and seized Coldevin's hand.

Without another word she hurried up-stairs and through the door.

He stood still a moment. He heard her steps from inside, then they died down. And he turned and drifted down the street. He saw and heard nothing of what happened around him.

Instinctively he walked toward the basement restaurant where he usually took his meals. He went down and ordered something. Hurriedly he ate everything that was placed before him; apparently he had not eaten for a long while. And when he was through he took out the ten-crown bill and paid his check from that. At the same time he felt in his waistcoat pocket for a little package, a few crowns in silver—the small amount he had put aside for his railway ticket, and which he had not dared to touch.

* * * * *

The following day, around five, Aagot was walking down toward the docks, toward the same place where she had walked the day before. Irgens was already waiting for her.

She hurried toward him and said:

"I came after all, but only to tell you—I won't meet you any more. I haven't time to talk to you now, but I did not want you to come here and wait for me."

"Listen, Miss Aagot," he said boldly, "you can't back out now, you know."

"I am not going home with you any more, never. I have learned something. Why don't you get Mrs. Tidemand to go with you? Why don't you?" Aagot was pale and excited.

"Mrs. Tidemand?" he asked, startled.

"Yes, I know everything. I have asked questions—Yes, I have thought of it all night long. Go to Mrs. Tidemand, why don't you?"

He stepped close to her.

"Mrs. Tidemand has not existed for me since I saw you. I haven't seen her for weeks. I don't even know where she lives."

"Well, it doesn't matter," she said. "I suppose you can look her up. I won't go home with you, but I can walk with you a few moments."

They walked on. Aagot was quiet now.

"I said I have thought of it all night," she continued. "Of course, not all night. All day, I meant. Not all the time, I mean—You ought to be ashamed of yourself! Married ladies! You don't defend yourself very warmly, Irgens."

"What is the use?"

"No, I suppose you love her." And when he was silent she grew violently jealous. "You might at least tell me if you love her!"

"I love you," he answered, "I do not lie; it is you and nobody else I love, Aagot. You can do with me what you like, but it is you." He did not look at her. He gazed down on the pavement and he wrung his hands repeatedly.

She felt that his emotion was genuine and she said gently:

"All right, Irgens, I'll believe you. But I won't go home with you."

Pause.

"What has made you so hostile toward me all of a sudden?" he asked. "Is it this—? He has been your tutor, but I must frankly say that he disgusts me, dirty and unkempt as he is."

"You will be good enough to speak civilly of Coldevin," she said coldly.

"Well, he is going away to-night, so we shall be rid of him," he said.

She stopped.

"Is he going this evening?"

"So I heard. On the night train."

Was he going? He hadn't mentioned that to her. Irgens had to tell her how he knew. She was so taken up with this news about Coldevin that she forgot everything else; perhaps she even felt a sense of relief at the thought that henceforth she would be free from his espionage. When Irgens touched her arm lightly she walked mechanically ahead. They went straight to his rooms. When they stood by the entrance she suddenly recoiled. She said "No!" repeatedly while she looked at him with staring, bewildered eyes. But he pleaded with her. Finally he took her arm and led her firmly inside.

The door slammed behind them....

On the corner Coldevin stood and watched. When the couple disappeared he stepped forward and walked over to the entrance. He stood there awhile. He bent forward stiffly as if he were listening. He was much changed. His face was fearfully drawn and his lips were frozen in a ghastly smile. Then he sat down on the steps, close by the wall, waiting.

An hour passed by. A tower-clock boomed. His train was not due to leave for another hour. Half an hour went by. He heard somebody on the stairs. Irgens came first. Coldevin did not stir; he sat motionless with his back to the door. Then Aagot appeared. Suddenly she cried out loudly. Coldevin arose and walked away. He had not looked at her nor had he said a word; he had simply shown himself—he had been on the spot. He swayed like a man in a stupor. He turned the very first corner, the frozen smile still on his lips.

Coldevin walked straight down to the railway station. He bought his ticket and was ready. The doors were thrown open. He walked out to the train-shed; a porter came after him with his trunk. His trunk? All right; he had almost forgotten it. Put it in there, in this empty compartment! He entered after it had been stowed away; then he collapsed utterly. He sat in the corner; his gaunt, emaciated body shivered convulsively. In a few moments he took from his pocketbook a tiny silken bow in the Norwegian colours and began to tear it to pieces. He sat there quietly and plucked the threads apart. When he had finished he stared at the shreds with a fixed, vacant stare. The engine gave a hoarse blast; the train started. Coldevin opened the window slowly and emptied his hand. And the tiny bits of red and blue whirled away behind the train, fluttered and sank to the gravel, to be ground in the dust beneath every man's foot.

IV

It was several days later before Aagot went home. Irgens had not persisted in vain. He had succeeded, and now he reaped the reward of all his labour. Aagot was with him continually. She was as much in love with him as she could be. She clung to his neck.

The days passed by.

Finally a telegram arrived from Ole, and Aagot woke from her trance. The wire had been sent to Torahus. It reached her after much delay. Ole was in London.

Well, what was to be done? Ole was in London, but he was not here yet. She did not remember clearly how he looked. Dark, with blue eyes; tall, with a stray wisp of hair which always fell across his forehead. Whenever she thought of him he seemed to belong to an age long past. How long, long it was since he went away!

The telegram stirred to life again her dormant feelings for the absent one. She trembled with the old sense of possession. She whispered his name and blessed him for his goodness. She called him to her, blushing breathlessly. No, nobody was like him! He did not wrong anybody. He walked his straightforward way, guileless and upright. How he loved her! Little mistress, little mistress! His breast was so warm! She grew warm herself when she nestled close to him. How he could look up from a row of figures and smile!... Oh, she had not forgotten!...

She packed her belongings resolutely and wanted to go home in spite of everything. The evening before she left she said good-bye to Irgens, a protracted good-bye which rent her heart. She was his now, and Ole would probably get over it. She made up her mind. She would go home and she would cancel her engagement as soon as Ole returned. What would he say when he read her letter with the ring enclosed? She writhed at the thought that she wouldn't be near him to comfort him. She had to strike him from afar! And thus it had to end!

Irgens was full of tenderness and cheered her as much as he could. They should not be separated for long. If nothing else turned up he would walk up to her on his feet! Besides, she could get back to town; she wasn't a pauper exactly; she even owned a yacht, a real yacht—what more did she want? And Aagot smiled at this jest and felt relieved.

The door was locked; they were alone. Everything was quiet; they heard their hearts beat. And they said farewell to each other.

Irgens would not take her to the train. It might give rise to too much gossip; the town was so small and he was, unfortunately, so well known. But they would write, write every day; otherwise she would never be able to endure the separation....

Tidemand was the only one who knew of Aagot's departure and who followed her to the train. He was paying his usual call to Henriksen's office during the afternoon and was having his daily chat with the old man. As he left he met Aagot outside: she was ready to go. Tidemand accompanied her and carried her valise; her trunk had been sent ahead.

It had rained and the streets were muddy. Aagot said several times:

"What a disagreeable, mournful day!"

They hardly spoke. Aagot simply said:

"It was very kind of you to come with me; otherwise I should have been altogether alone." And Tidemand noticed that she tried to appear unconcerned. She smiled, but her eyes were moist.

He, too, smiled and said comfortingly that he was glad she was going to leave all this mud and filth; now she was going to the country, to cleaner roads, to purer air. These few words were all they spoke. They stood in the train-shed beneath the glass vault. It had begun to rain, and they heard the drops beating on the roof while the engine stood wheezing on the track. Aagot entered her compartment and gave Tidemand her hand. And in a sudden desire to be forgiven, to be judged charitably, she said to this stranger, whom she knew so slightly:

"Good-bye—And do not judge me too harshly!" and she coloured deeply.

"But, child!" he said amazed. He had no time to say more.

She put her fair little face out of the window and nodded as the train moved along. Her eyes were wet, and she struggled not to break down. She looked at Tidemand as long as she could see him, then she waved a tiny handkerchief.

The strange girl! Her unaffected simplicity moved him. He did not stop waving until the train was out of sight. Not judge her too harshly? He certainly wouldn't! And if he ever had been tempted to, he would know better in the future. She had waved to him—almost a stranger! He would be sure and tell Ole—how that would please him!...

* * * * *

Tidemand walked toward his own wharf. He was very busy. He was altogether taken up with his affairs. His business was steadily growing. He had been forced to take on several of his old employees. At present he was shipping tar.

When he had given his orders in the warehouse, he walked over to the restaurant where he usually took his meals. It was late. He ate hurriedly and spoke to no one. He was engrossed in thought about a new enterprise he had in mind. His tar was going to Spain. The rye held firm, with good prices; he sold steadily, his business began to stretch forth new arms. There was that new tannery near Torahus. How would it do if one gave a little thought to a tar-manufacturing plant alongside? He really was going to speak to Ole about that. He had had it in mind several weeks. He had even consulted an engineer about it. There were the cuttings and the tops. If the tannery took the bark, why shouldn't the tar plant take the wood?

Tidemand walked home. It rained steadily.

A few steps from his office entrance he stopped abruptly; then he sidled quietly into an area-way. He stared straight ahead. His wife was standing out there in the rain, outside his office. She was gazing, now at his office windows, now up to the second story. There she stood. He could not be mistaken, and his breath came in gasps. Once before he had seen her there. She had circled around in the shadows beneath the street lamps, just as now. He had called her name in a low voice, and she had immediately hurried around the street corner without looking back. This happened a Sunday evening three weeks ago. And now she was here again.

He wanted to step forward. He made a movement and his raincoat rustled. She glanced around quickly and hurried away. He stood immovable where he was until she had disappeared.

V

Ole Henriksen returned a week later. He had become uneasy. He had telegraphed to Aagot again and again, but could get no reply. He finished up his business in a hurry and returned. But so far was he from suspecting the true condition of affairs that on the very last afternoon in London he bought her a little present, a carriage for her fiord pony on Torahus.

And on his desk he found Aagot's letter with her ring enclosed.

Ole Henriksen read the letter almost without grasping its meaning. His hands commenced to tremble, and his eyes were staring. He went over and locked the office door, and read the letter once more. It was brief and to the point; it could not be misunderstood; she gave him back his "freedom." And there was the ring, wrapped in tissue-paper. No, he could hardly be uncertain as to the meaning of that letter.

And Ole Henriksen drifted back and forth in his office for several hours. He placed the letter on his desk and walked with hands tightly clasped behind him. He took the letter again and read it once more. He was "free"!

He must not think that she did not love him, she had written. She thought of him as much as ever; yes, more even. She begged his forgiveness a hundred times every day. But what good was it if she thought of him ever so much? she continued. She was his no more, it had come to that. But she had not surrendered at once, nor without a struggle; God knows that she had loved him so dearly, and that she did not want to belong to anybody but to him. However, it had gone entirely too far now; she would only ask him to judge her kindly, though she did not deserve it, and not to grieve over her.

The letter was dated twice. She had not noticed that. It was written in Aagot's large, childish hand, and was touching in its simplicity; she had made several corrections.

Yes, he had understood it clearly; and, besides, there was the ring. After all, what did *he* amount to? He was no prominent man, known all over the country; he was no genius who could interest a girl greatly; he was just an ordinary toiler, a business man—that was all. He should have known better than imagine he would be allowed to keep Aagot's heart for himself. Just see how he had fooled himself! Of course, he attended to his business and worked conscientiously early and late, but that could not make people fond of him. There was nothing to say to that. Anyhow, he knew now why his telegrams had remained unanswered. He ought to have understood it at once, but he hadn't.... She had gone entirely too far. She said goodbye and loved somebody else. Nothing could be done about that. If she loved somebody else, then.... It was probably Irgens—he would get her after all. Tidemand had been right. It was dangerous with these many boat-rides and walks; Tidemand had had experience. Well, it was too late to think of that now. However, one's love could not have been so very firmly rooted if a walk or two had been enough to break it down....

And suddenly the anger blazed up in the poor fellow. He walked more rapidly and his forehead flamed. She had gone entirely too far. That was his reward for the love he had lavished on her! He had knelt before a hussy. He had let that miserable lover of hers cheat him openly for years! He could prove it by the ledger—look here—now Aagot's fine friend had been hard up for ten, now for fifty crowns! And he, Ole Henriksen, had even been afraid that Aagot some day might chance to see the poet's account in his books. He had finally put away the ledger, entirely out of regard for the great man's feelings. It was a most suitable partnership; they were worthy of each other. The poet had something to write about now, a splendid subject! Ha, he must not grieve too much over her; she could not stand that; she might even lose sleep over it! Think of that! But who had said that he would grieve? She was mistaken. He might have knelt before her, but he hadn't licked her boots; no, he would hardly be compelled to take to his bed on account of this. She need not worry; she need not weep scalding tears on his account. So she had jilted him; she returned his ring. What of it? But why had she dragged the ring all the way up to Torahus? Why hadn't she simply left it on his desk and saved the postage? Good-bye; good riddance! Go to the devil with your silk-lined deceiver, and never let me hear of you again!...

He wrung his hands in anguish and paced back and forth with long, furious strides. He would take it like a man. He would fling his own ring in her face and end the comedy quickly. He stopped at the desk and tore the ring off his finger, wrapped it up, and put it in an envelope. He wrote the address in large, brutal letters; his hand trembled violently. Somebody knocked. He flung the letter into a drawer and closed it hastily.

It was one of his clerks who came to remind him that it was late. Should he close up?

"Yes, close up. But wait; I am through now; I am going, too. Bring me the keys."

Nobody should be able to say that he broke down because of a shabby trick like this. He would show people that he could keep his composure. He might go to the Grand and celebrate his return with a plain glass of beer! That would be just the thing. He had no intention of avoiding people. He had a revolver lying in a desk drawer; but had he wanted to use that, even for the briefest moment? Had he *thought* of it even? Not at all. It just occurred to him now that it might be getting rusty. No, thank God! one was not exactly weary of life....

Ole Henriksen went to the Grand.

He sat down at a table and ordered his glass of beer. A moment later he felt somebody slap him on the shoulder. He looked up; it was Milde.

"Good old boy!" shouted Milde. "Are you sitting here without saying a word? Welcome back! Come over to the window; you will find a couple of the fellows there."

Ole went over to the window. There were Ojen, Norem, and Gregersen, all of them with half-empty wine-glasses in front of them. Ojen jumped up and said pleasantly:

"Welcome home, old man! I am glad to see you again. I have missed you a good deal. I am coming down to-morrow to see you. There is something I want to see you about."

Gregersen gave him a finger. Ole took it, sat down, and told the waiter to bring him his beer.

"What! are you drinking beer? No, beer will never do on this occasion; it must be wine!"

"Well, drink what you want to. I am drinking beer."

Just then Irgens arrived, and Milde called to him: "Ole is drinking beer, but we are not going to do that. What do you say?"

Irgens did not show the least sign of embarrassment when he faced Ole; he barely nodded and said indifferently: "Welcome home!" And Ole looked at him and noticed that his cuffs were not entirely clean; as a matter of fact, his dress was not quite up to his usual standard.

But Milde repeated his question: wasn't it a little too commonplace to drink beer at a double celebration?

"A double celebration?" asked Gregersen.

"Exactly—yes. In the first place, Ole has returned, and that is of the greatest importance to us at present; I frankly admit that. But I have, in the second place, just been dispossessed from my studio, and that has also a certain solemn significance. What do you think? The landlady came and wanted money. 'Money?' I asked in amazement, and so on and so on. But the outcome was that I was put out, without notice—only a couple of hours'. Ha, ha! I have never heard of such a notice. Of course, she had already given me her ultimatum a month ago; still—I had to leave a couple of finished canvases. But I think this ought to be celebrated in wine, for Ole does not care what we drink."

"Of course not; why should I care?" asked Ole.

And the gentlemen drank industriously. They grew well disposed and cheerful before they took their departure. Irgens was first to leave; then Ojen followed. Ole remained until they had all gone, all except Norem, who sat there as usual and slumbered. He had listened to the talk. Occasionally he had injected a word. He had grown weary and subdued; a bitter disgust had taken possession of him and made him dully indifferent to everything.

At last he got up and paid his check.

The waiter halted him.

"Pardon me," he said, "but the wine—"

"The wine?" asked Ole. "I have only had a couple of glasses of beer."

"Yes, but the wine isn't paid for."

So the gentlemen hadn't paid their checks? For a moment the hot anger blazed up in him again; he was on the point of saying that if they would send the bill to Torahus it would be paid instantly. But he said: "All right; I can pay it, I suppose."

But what should he do at home? Go to bed and sleep? If he only could! He turned into the darkest streets in order to be alone. He was going homeward, but he swung aside and walked toward the Fortress.

Here he suddenly came across Tidemand. He was standing in front of a dark gateway gazing at the house opposite. What could Tidemand be doing there?

Ole walked over to him. They looked at each other in surprise.

"I am taking a walk, a little walk," said Tidemand somewhat sheepishly. "I came by here by accident—Thank goodness, you are back, Ole! Welcome home! Let us get away from here!"

Tidemand could not get over his surprise. He had not known that Ole was back. Everything was all right at the office; he had called on the old man regularly, as he had promised.

"And your sweetheart has gone away," he continued. "I went with her to the train. She is a darling girl! She was a little upset because she was going away; she stood there and looked at me with real shining eyes; you know how she is. And as the train went off she took out her handkerchief and waved to me—waved so sweetly, just because I had come with her. You ought to have seen her; she was lovely."

"Well, I am not engaged any more," said Ole in a hollow voice.

* * * * *

Ole went into his office. It was late at night. He had walked with Tidemand a long time and told him everything. He was going to write a letter to Aagot's parents, respectful and dignified, without reproaches. He felt he ought to do that.

When he had finished this letter he read Aagot's once more. He wanted to tear it to pieces and burn it up, but he paused and placed it in front of him on the desk. It was at least a letter from her, the last. She had sat there and written to him and thought of him while she wrote. She had held the paper with her tiny hands, and there her pen had scratched. She had probably wiped it on something and dipped it and written on. That letter was for him, for no one else. Everybody had probably been in bed while she wrote.

He took the ring out of its wrapping and looked at it for a long time. He was sorry that he had lost his temper and said words which he now regretted. He took them back, every one. Good-bye, then, Aagot....

And he placed Aagot's last letter with the others.

VI

Ole began to work hard again; he spent practically all his time in his office. He lost flesh; he did not get out enough; his eyes became absent and flickering. He was hardly off the wharves or outside the warehouses for several weeks. Nobody should say that he pined and drooped because his engagement was cancelled! He worked and minded his own business and was getting on nicely.

He was getting thin; that was simply because he worked too hard. He hoped nobody would think it might be due to other causes. There were so many things to be done since his return from England; he had explained it all to Tidemand. But he was going to take it a little easier now. He wanted to get out a little, observe what was doing, amuse himself.

And he dragged Tidemand to theatres and to Tivoli. They took long walks in the evenings. They arranged to start the tannery and the tar works this coming spring. Ole was even more enthusiastic than Tidemand; he threw himself so eagerly into the project that nobody could for a moment harbour any mistaken notions about his being grief-stricken. He never mentioned Aagot; she was dead and forgotten.

And Tidemand, too, was getting along comfortably. He had lately re-engaged his old cook and he took his meals at home now. It was a little lonely. The dining-room was too large, and there was an empty chair; but the children carried on and made the most glorious noise throughout the house; he heard them sometimes clear down in his office. They disturbed him often, took him away from his work at times; for whenever he heard their little feet patter on the floors up-stairs and their merry shouts echo through the rooms he simply had to put down his pen and run up for a moment. In a few minutes he would come back and throw himself into his work like an energetic youth.... Yes, Tidemand was getting along famously; he couldn't deny it. Everything had begun to turn out well for him.

On his way home one evening Tidemand happened to drop in at a grocery store he supplied with goods. It was entirely by accident. He entered the store and walked over to the owner who stood behind the counter. Suddenly he saw his wife at the counter; in front of her he noticed some parcels.

Tidemand had not seen her since that evening outside his office. He had fortunately caught sight of her ring in a jewellery window as he passed by one day and had immediately bought it and sent it to her. On a card she had written a few words of thanks. She had not missed the ring, but it was another matter now; she would keep it always.

She stood there at the counter in a black dress; it was a little threadbare. For a moment he wondered if perhaps she was in need, if he did not give her enough money? Why did she wear such old dresses? But he had sent her a good deal of money. Thank God, he was able to do that. In the beginning, when he was still struggling, he hadn't sent her such large amounts, it was true. He had grieved over it and written to her not to be impatient; it would be better soon. And she had thanked him and answered that he was sending her altogether too much; how was she going to use it all? She had lots and lots of money left.

But why did she dress so shabbily, then?

She had turned around; she recognised his voice when he spoke to the owner. He grew confused; he bowed smilingly to her as he had to the grocer, and she blushed deeply as she returned his bow.

"Never mind about the rest," she said to the clerk in a low voice. "I'll get that some other time." And she paid hurriedly and gathered up her bundles. Tidemand followed her with his eyes. She stooped as she walked and looked abashed until she disappeared.

VII

And the days passed by. The town was quiet; everything was quiet.

Irgens was still capable of surprising people and attracting everybody's attention. He had looked a little careworn and depressed for some time; his debts bothered him; he earned no money and nobody gave him any. Fall and winter were coming; it did not look any too bright for him. He had even been obliged to make use of a couple of last year's suits.

Then all of a sudden he amazed everybody by appearing on the promenade, rehabilitated from top to toe in an elegant fall suit, with tan gloves and money in his pockets, distinguished and elegant as the old and only Irgens. People looked at him admiringly. Devil of a chap—he was unique! What kind of a diamond mine had he discovered? Oh, there was a head on these shoulders, a superior talent! He had been obliged to move from his former apartments on Thranes Road. Certainly; but what of it? He had taken other apartments in the residential district—elegant apartments, fine view, furniture upholstered in leather! He simply couldn't have stood it much longer in the old lodgings; his best moods were constantly being spoiled; he suffered. It was necessary to pay a little attention to one's surroundings if one cared to produce good work. Miss Lynum had come to town a week ago and was going to remain awhile; she made him feel like a new man. How the whole town burst into bloom and colour when Aagot returned!

It had all been decided: they were going to get married next spring and pin their faith to next year's subsidy. It would seem that he must be recognised sometime, especially now when he was going to found a family and was publishing a new collection of poems. They couldn't starve him to death entirely; hardly that! And Irgens had approached Attorney Grande, who had approached the Minister personally in regard to next year's subsidy. "You know my circumstances," he had said to Grande. "I am not well off, but if you will speak to the Minister I shall be much obliged to you. Personally, I will do nothing. I cannot stoop to that!" Grande was a man whom Irgens otherwise honoured with his contempt. But it could not be helped; this brainless Attorney began to have influence; he had been appointed on a royal commission and had even been interviewed by the *Gazette*.

When Tidemand told Ole that he had seen Aagot on the street it gave him a fearful shock. But he recovered himself quickly and said with a smile:

"Well, how does that concern me? Let her be here as much as she likes; I have no objections. I have other things to worry about." He forced himself to renewed interest in the conversation, talked about Tidemand's new orders for tar, and said repeatedly: "Be sure to have the cargo well insured; it never hurts!" He was a little nervous but otherwise normal.

They drank a glass of wine as of old. A couple of hours went by while they chatted cosily, and when Tidemand left Ole said, full of gratitude:

"I am awfully glad that you came to see me. I know you have enough to do besides this—Listen," he continued; "let us go to the farewell performance of the opera this evening; I want you to come!" And the serious young man with the hollow eyes looked as if he were exceedingly anxious to attend that performance. He even said he had looked forward to it for several days.

Tidemand promised to come; Ole said that he would get the tickets.

No sooner had Tidemand left the office than Ole telephoned for the tickets he wanted—three tickets together, 11, 12, and 13. He was going to take No. 12 to Mrs. Hanka, to her room near the Fortress. She would surely want to come, for nobody could be fonder of the opera than she used to be. He rubbed his hands in satisfaction as he walked along—No. 12; she should sit between them. He would keep No. 13 for himself; that was a proper number for him, a most unlucky number.

He walked faster and faster and forgot his own misery. He was done and through with it all; his sufferings lay behind; he had recovered fully. Had he been so very much shaken because Aagot had come to town? Not at all; it had not affected him in the least.

And Ole walked on. He knew Mrs. Hanka's address well; more than once had he taken her home when she had called on him secretly, asking for news about the children. And had he not found Tidemand outside her windows that night he returned from England? How their thoughts were ever busy with each other! With him it was different; he had forgotten his experience and did not think of such things any more.

But when he inquired for Mrs. Hanka he was told that she had gone away for a couple of days; she had gone to the country house. She would be back to-morrow.

He listened and did not understand at once. The country house? Which country house?

Of course, yes; Tidemand's country house. Ole glanced at his watch. No; it was too late to try and get Mrs. Hanka back to-day. What reason could he have given, anyway? He had wanted to surprise them both with his little scheme, but now it had become impossible. Alas, how everything turned out badly for him of late!

Ole turned back.

To the country house! How she haunted the old places! She had been unable to resist; she had to see once more that house and these grounds, although the leaves were almost gone and the garden was desolate. Oh! Aagot had intended to spend the summer there if everything had turned out all right. Well, that was another matter, something that did not concern him in the least.

Ole was weary and disappointed. He decided to go to Tidemand at once and tell him everything. He had meant it for the best.

"We shall have to go alone after all," he said. "I really have a ticket for your wife, though."

Tidemand changed colour.

"You have?" he simply said.

"Yes, I had planned to have her sit between us; perhaps I ought to have told you beforehand; but any way, she has gone away and won't be back till to-morrow."

"Is that so?" said Tidemand as before.

"Listen, you mustn't be angry with me because of this! If you only knew— Your wife has called on me quite frequently of late; she asks about you and the children—"

"That is all right."

"What?"

"I say, that is all right. But why do you tell me this?"

Then Ole's anger blazed forth; he stuck his face close up to Tidemand's and shouted furiously, in a shrill voice:

"I want to tell you something, damn you—you don't understand your own welfare! You are a fool, you are killing her—that will be the end of it. And you are doing your very best to go the same way yourself—don't you think I see it? 'That is all right'—so it is all right for her to steal down to me when darkness falls and ask about you and the children with the tears dripping from her eyes? Do you for a moment imagine it is for *your* sake I have been inquiring about your health these last months? Why should I ask if not for her? You personally can go to the devil as far as I am concerned. You say nothing; you cannot understand that she is wearing her heart away for you. I saw her outside your office once at midnight, saying good night to you and to the children. She wept and blew kisses to Johanna and Ida; she tiptoed up-stairs and caressed the door-knob because your hand had held it a moment before. I have seen this several times from the corner. I suppose you will say that 'that is all right,' too; for your heart must be petrified—Well, perhaps I shouldn't say that your heart is exactly petrified," added Ole repentantly when at last he noticed Tidemand's terrible face. "But you need not expect any apology from me, either. You are hardened; that's what you are! I tell you, Hanka wants to come back!"

Pause.

"I wish to God she wanted to come back—I mean—Back, you say? But how? Do you know what has happened? I do. I have wanted to go to Hanka and beg her to come back—beg her on my knees, if necessary; but how would she come back—how would she come back? She told me herself—Of course, it is nothing much; you mustn't think it is anything bad, anything very bad; don't think that of Hanka. But, anyway, I am not so sure that she wants to come back. From where have you got that idea?"

"Well, perhaps I ought not to have tried to interfere," said Ole. "But think of it anyway, Andreas; and pardon my violence; I take it all back. I don't know how it is; I am getting to be so hot-tempered lately. But think it over. And let us be ready in an hour or so."

"So she still asks for the children," said Tidemand. "Think of that!"

VIII

Ole Henriksen stood in his office a few days later. It was in the afternoon, about three; the weather was clear and calm; the docks were busy as ever.

Ole walked over to the window and looked out. An enormous coal-steamer was gliding in from the fiord; masts and rigging pointed skyward everywhere; cargoes were being unloaded along the wharves. Suddenly he started; the yacht was gone! He opened his eyes wide. Among all the hundreds of mastheads none were golden.

He wanted to go out and look into this, but paused at the door. He went back to his desk again, leaned his head on his hands, and reflected. In reality the yacht did not belong to him any more; it was hers, Miss Lynum's; he had given it to her, and the papers were in her keeping. She had not returned these papers together with the ring; she might have forgotten it—how could he know? Anyway, the yacht was hers; he had nothing to do with it. But if it had been stolen? Well, even that was no affair of his.

Ole took up his pen again, but only for a few moments. Dear me, she used to sit there on the sofa and sew so busily on the little cushions! They had been so cute and tiny that it was almost absurd. There she used to sit; he could see her still....

And Ole wrote again.

Then he opened the door and called out to the clerks that the yacht had disappeared; what had happened?

One of the clerks informed him that the yacht had been removed this morning by two men from a lawyer's office; she was anchored outside the Fortress now.

"Which lawyer?" asked Ole.

The clerk didn't know.

Ole grew curious. The yacht was not his any more, of course; but Miss Lynum had no business with a lawyer either; there must be a misunderstanding somewhere. And straightway he went down to the Fortress landing and made inquiries for a couple of hours. Finally he learned the name of the lawyer and went to his office.

He saw a man of his own age and asked a few guarded questions.

Yes, it was quite true; he had orders to sell the yacht; as a matter of fact, he had already advanced a thousand crowns on it. Here were the papers; Irgens had left them with him, the poet Irgens. He hoped there were no objections?

None at all.

The lawyer grew more and more polite and cordial; he probably knew everything about the whole matter, but he did not betray his knowledge. How much was the yacht worth, did Mr. Henriksen think? Irgens had come to him with a request that he take charge of this transaction; he had said that he needed some money at once, and of course one had to stretch a point where a man like Irgens was concerned. Unfortunately, our men of talent were not rewarded any too liberally, as a rule; but if there was the least objection to this sale he would try his best to arrange everything satisfactorily.

And Ole said again that there was none; he had simply missed the yacht and wondered what had become of it. And he left.

Now it had become clear why Irgens suddenly had blossomed forth in gay plumage, rejuvenated from top to toe! The whole town was talking about it; however, nobody knew the real source of his affluence. That *she* should do such a thing! Didn't she understand that this was dishonourable, disgraceful? On the other hand, why was it so disgraceful? Her possessions were his; they shared lovingly; there was nothing to say to that. In God's name, let her act as she thought right and proper. She was in town now; she was going to take a course in the School of Industries. It was quite natural that she should realise on that bit of a yacht. Could anybody blame her because she helped her fiancé? On the contrary, it reflected credit on her.... But she might not even know that the yacht had been put on the market. Perhaps she had forgotten both yacht and documents and did not care what became of them. At any rate, she had not wanted to sell the yacht simply to raise money on her own account—never; he knew her too well. She had done it for somebody else's sake; that was she. And that was the important point.

He remembered her so distinctly: her fair curls, her nose, her dimple; she would be nineteen on the seventh of December. Never mind the yacht; that didn't matter. He might have wished to save the cushions, but it would probably be too late for that.

He returned to his office, but could only concentrate his attention on what was absolutely necessary. He paused frequently and gazed straight ahead, lost in reflection. What if he should buy back the yacht? Would she mind, perhaps? God knows; she might think it was done spitefully, with malice aforethought. It might be better to remain neutral. Yes, that would be best; what was the use of making a fool of himself?—Miss Lynum and he were through with each other for ever. Nobody should say that he collected souvenirs of her.

He closed the office as usual and went out. The street lamps were burning brightly; the evening was calm. He saw a light in Tidemand's office and started to go in; but he paused on the stairs and reflected. Tidemand might be busy; he had better go on.

Hour after hour passed by; he wandered around as in a stupor. How tired and weary he was! His eyes were half-closed. He found himself in the vicinity of the park. He turned and strode toward the hills behind the city. He sat down on a stoop to rest. By and by he looked at his watch; it was half past eleven. And he sauntered down toward the city again. His mind was almost a blank.

He turned aside and passed by Tivoli and Sara. What a walk this had been! To-night he was going to sleep—at last! Outside Sara he stopped abruptly. He drew back in the shadows slowly, four, six steps; his eyes were staring fixedly toward the entrance to the cafe. A cab was standing outside.

He had heard Aagot's voice; she came out with Irgens. Irgens appeared first. Aagot had been delayed by something on the stairs.

"Hurry up, now!" called Irgens.

"Just a moment, Mr. Irgens," said the driver; "the lady is not quite ready."

"Do you know me?" asked Irgens in surprise.

"I certainly do," said the cabman.

"He knows you! he knows you!" cried Aagot as she stumbled down the steps. She had not put on her wrap yet; it was dragging after her and she tripped in it. Her eyes were expressionless and staring. Suddenly she laughed. "That nasty fellow, Gregersen; he was kicking me on the leg all the time! I am sure I am black and blue! Imagine, Irgens, the cabby knows you!"

"You are drunk," said Irgens brutally, and helped her into the carriage.

Her hat was awry, she tried to get into her coat and she babbled incoherently.

"No, I am not drunk; I am only a little cheerful—Won't you see if my leg is bruised? I am sure I am dripping blood! It hurts, too; but that doesn't matter; nothing matters now. Drunk, you say? What if I am? It is your fault. I do everything for your sake—do it gladly—Ha, ha, ha! I have to laugh when I think of that wretched Gregersen. He told me he would write the most beautiful article about me if I would only let him see where he had kicked me. It is different if you see it—That was an awful strong wine; it makes my head swim—And all those cigarettes!"

"Drive on, damn you!" cried Irgens.

And the carriage rolled off.

Ole stood there and stared after the carriage; his knees shook under him. He fumbled convulsively with his hands up and down his clothes, around his chest. So that was Aagot! How they had corrupted her! how they had spoiled her! Aagot—his Aagot....

Ole sat down on a stoop. A long time passed by.

The lamps outside Sara were extinguished; it grew very dark. An officer tapped him on the shoulder and said that he could not sit there and sleep. Ole looked up bewildered. Of course not; he was going now. Thanks! And he swayed down the street as if he were intoxicated.

He reached home about two o'clock and entered his office. He lit the lamp and hung his hat mechanically on the rack; his face was drawn and void of expression. A long hour went by while he strode up and down. Then he walked over to his desk and commenced to write—letters, documents, brief lines on various papers which he sealed and filed away. He looked at his watch; it was half past three. He wound it up mechanically while he held it. He went out and mailed a letter to Tidemand which he had just written. Upon his return he took Aagot's letters from the safe and loosened the string that bound them together.

He did not read any of these letters; he carried them over to the fireplace and burned them one by one. The last, the very last one, he pulled halfway-out of its envelope and looked at it a moment; then he burned also that, without taking out the ring.

The little clock on the wall struck four. A steamer's whistle sounded. Ole went away from the fireplace. His face was full of anguish; every feature was distorted; the veins around his temples were swollen. And slowly he pulled out a little drawer in his desk.

* * * * *

They found Ole Henriksen dead in the morning; he had shot himself. The lamp was burning on the desk; a few sealed letters were lying on the blotter; he himself lay stretched on the floor.

In the letter to Tidemand he had asked to be forgiven because he could not come for the last time and thank him for his friendship. He had to finish it all now; he could not live another day; he was sick unto death. The country house he gave to Tidemand in memory of everything. "It will probably bring you more pleasure than it brought me," he wrote; "it is yours, my friend; accept it from me. Mrs. Hanka will be glad to have it; remember me to her. And if you ever should find Miss Lynum in need of help, be good to her; I saw her this evening, but she did not see me. I cannot collect my thoughts and write to you as I would like to. One thing only is clear to me, and that thing I will have to do in half an hour."

A picture of Aagot was still in his pocketbook; he had probably forgotten to burn it. He had also forgotten to send the two or three telegrams he had carried in his pocket since the previous afternoon; they were found on him. He had spoken truly: to him only one thing was clear!

IX

Part of September had passed; the weather was cool, the sky clear and high; the city was free from dust and dirt; the city was beautiful. As yet no snow had fallen on the mountains.

Event had followed event; Ole Henriksen's suicide had only caused a passing sensation. The shot down there in the young business man's office had not been followed by a very loud or reverberating echo; days and weeks had come and gone, and nobody mentioned it any more. Only Tidemand could not forget.

Tidemand was busier than ever. He had to assist Ole's father for a while; the old man did not want to retire, but he made the chief assistant his partner and carried on the business as before; he did not allow his sorrow to break him down. Old man Henriksen proved that he was not too old to work when circumstances required it.

And Tidemand was unceasing in his efforts. His rye was at last dwindling; he sold heavily at advancing prices now winter was approaching; his losses were diminishing. He had to take back still more of his old employees; he was shipping tar; to-morrow a new cargo was to sail.

He had finished the preparations, made out the papers, taken out his insurance; it was all done. Before he turned to something else he lit a cigar and reflected. It was about four in the afternoon. He went over to the window and looked out. While he stood there a gentle knock was heard; his wife entered. She asked if she disturbed him; it was only a small matter of business....

She wore a heavy veil.

Tidemand threw away his cigar. He had not seen her for weeks, long, weary weeks; one evening he had thought he recognised her in a lady whose walk was somewhat similar to hers; he had followed this lady a long time before he discovered that he was mistaken. He had never objected to her coming, and she knew it; still, she did not come. She had probably forgotten both him and the children; it looked that way. And, although he had strolled around the streets near the Fortress many a night when it was too lonely at home and at times seen a light in her window, her he had never seen. What could she be doing? He had sent her money occasionally in order to hear from her.

Now she stood there before him, only a few steps away.

"So you have come?" he said at last.

"Yes, I have come," she answered. "I had—I wanted to—" And suddenly she commenced to fumble with her hand-bag; she brought forth a package of money which she placed before him on the desk. Her hands trembled so violently that she disarranged the bills, she even dropped a few; she stooped down and picked them up and stammered: "Take it, please; don't say no! It is money which I have used for—which I have put to unworthy uses. Spare me from saying what I have used it for; it is too degrading. There ought to be much more, but I couldn't delay any longer; there ought to be twice as much, but I was too impatient to wait until I could bring it all. Take it, please! I shall bring you the rest later; but I simply had to come to-day!"

He interrupted her, much annoyed:

"But will you never understand? You bring up this subject of money for ever! Why are you saving money for me? I have all I need; the business is very profitable, increasingly so; I don't need it, I tell you—"

"But this money is altogether a different matter," she said timidly. "It is for my own sake I give it to you. If I hadn't been able to think that I might repay it I never could have endured life. I have counted and counted every day and waited until I should have enough. I was wrong in saying that it was only half; it is at least three-fourths—Oh, how I have suffered under the disgrace—"

And suddenly he understood why she had wanted to bring him this money. He took it and thanked her. He did not know what to say except that it was a lot of money, quite a lot. But could she spare it? Surely? For he really would be glad if she would let him have it for the present; he could use it in the business. As a matter of fact, it was most fortunate that she had come just now; he needed some money, he was not ashamed to confess it....

He watched her closely and saw the joy well up in her; her eyes sparkled beneath her veil, and she said:

"God, how happy I am that I came to-day, after all!"

This voice! Oh, this voice! He remembered it so well from their first delightful days. He had walked around the edge of the desk; now he stepped back again, bewildered by her proximity, her lovely form, her radiant eyes beneath the veil. He dropped his own.

"And how are you?" she asked, "and the children?"

"Fine, thank you. The children are growing out of their clothes. We are all well. And you?"

"I have heard nothing from you for so long. I had intended to wait until I could bring it all to you, but it was beyond my strength. While Ole lived he told me about you; but since I cannot go to him any more I have been very impatient. I was here yesterday, but I didn't come in; I turned back—"

Should he ask her to go up to the children a moment?

"Perhaps you would like to go up-stairs a moment?" he asked. "The children will be delighted. I don't know how the house looks, but if you don't mind—"

"I thank you!"

He saw how deeply she was moved, although she said nothing more. She gave him her hand in farewell. "I hope they will know me," she said.

"I'll be up in a moment," he remarked. "I haven't much to do just now. Perhaps you would like to stay awhile? Here is the key; you need not ring. But be careful of their shoes if you take them on your lap. Well, don't laugh; God knows if their shoes aren't muddy!"

Hanka went. He opened the door for her and followed her to the foot of the stairs; then he returned to his office.

He walked over to the desk, but he did not work. There she had stood! She wore her black velvet dress to-day; she was up-stairs. Could he go up now? He did not hear the children; they were probably in her lap. He hoped they had on their red dresses.

He walked up-stairs, a prey to the strangest emotions. He knocked on the door as if it were somebody else's home he was entering. Hanka got up at once when she saw him.

She had taken off her veil; she flushed deeply. He could see now why she used a veil. The joyless days in her solitary room had not left her unmarked; her face spoke plainly of her sufferings. Johanna and Ida stood beside her and clung to her dress; they did not remember her clearly; they looked at her questioningly and were silent.

"They don't know me," said Mrs. Hanka, and sat down again. "I have asked them."

"Yes, I know you," said Johanna, and crawled up into her lap. Ida did the same.

Tidemand looked at them unsteadily.

"You mustn't crawl all over mamma, children," he said. "Don't bother mamma now."

They didn't hear him; they wanted to bother mamma. She had rings on her fingers and she had the strangest buttons on her dress; that was something to interest them! They began to chatter about these buttons; they caught sight of the mother's brooch and had many remarks to make about that.

"Put them down when you are tired of them," said Tidemand.

Tired? She? Let them be, let them be!

They spoke about Ole; they mentioned Aagot. Tidemand wanted to look her up some day. Ole had asked him to do it; he felt, in a way, responsible for her. But the nurse came and wanted to put the children to bed.

However, the children had no idea of going to bed; they refused pointblank. And Hanka had to come along, follow them into their bed-room, and get them settled for the night. She looked around. Everything was as it used to be. There were the two little beds, the coverlets, the tiny pillows, the picture-books, the toys. And when they were in bed she had to sing to them; they simply wouldn't keep still but crawled out of bed continually and chattered on.

Tidemand watched this awhile with blinking eyes; then he turned quickly away and went out.

In half an hour or so Hanka came back.

"They are asleep now," she said.

"I was wondering if I might ask you to stay," said Tidemand. "We live rather informally here; we keep house in a way, but nothing seems to go right for us. If you would like to have dinner with us—I don't know what they are going to give us to eat, but if you will take things as they are?"

She looked at him shyly, like a young girl; she said: "Thank you."

After dinner, when they had returned to the drawing-room, Hanka said suddenly:

"Andreas, you mustn't think I came here to-day thinking that everything could be well again with us. Don't think that. I simply came because I couldn't wait any longer; I had to see you again."

"I have not thought of that at all," he said. "But it seems the children don't want to let you go."

"I have no thought of asking you again what I asked you for once," she said. "That would be impossible; I know it too well. But perhaps you would allow me to come and visit you at times?"

Tidemand bowed his head. She had no thought of coming back; it was all over.

"Come whenever you like; come every day," he said. "You are not coming to see me."

"Oh, yes, to see you also. I think of you with every breath. Ever since that sail last summer; it began then. You have changed and so have I. But that is neither here nor there. I have seen you on the streets oftener than you know; I have followed you at times."

He rose and went in his confusion over to the barometer on the wall; he examined it carefully and tapped the tube.

"But in that case—I don't understand why it is necessary to live apart. I mean—Things are in a sad state of disorder here; and then there are the children—"

"I didn't come for that!" she exclaimed. "Yes, I did, in a way; of course I did; but—I am afraid you will never be able to forget—Oh, no. I cannot expect that—"

She took her wraps.

"Don't go!" he called. "You have never been out of my thoughts, either. As far as that goes, I am as much to blame as you, and it is true that I have changed. I am, perhaps, a little different now. But here is your room just as before. Come and see! We haven't touched a single thing. And if you would stay—By the way, I am afraid I shall have to stay in the office all night. I am almost sure there is a lot of mail to attend to. But your room is just as when you left it. Come and see!"

He had opened the door. She came over and peeped in. The lamp was lit. She looked at everything and entered. He really wanted to, after all, after all! She could stay; he had said so; he took her back! She stood there timidly and said nothing; then their eyes met. He flung his arms around her and kissed her, as he had kissed her the first time, all these many years ago. Her eyes closed and he felt suddenly the pressure of her arms around his neck.

X

And morning came.

The city woke up and the hammers danced their ringing dance along the shipyards. Through the streets the farmers' wagons rolled in a slow procession. It is the same story. The squares are filling with people and supplies, stores are opened, the roar increases, and up and down the stairs skips a slip of a girl with her papers and her dog.

It is the same story.

It is twelve before people begin to group themselves on the "corner," young and carefree gentlemen who can afford to sleep late and do what they feel like. There are a few from the well-known clique, Milde and Norem and Ojen. It is cold, and they are shivering. The conversation is not very lively. Even when Irgens appears, in high spirits and elegant attire, as befits the best-dressed man in town, nobody grows very enthusiastic. It is too early and too chilly; in a few hours it will be different. Ojen had said something about his latest prose poem; he had half-finished it last night. It was called "A Sleeping City." He had begun to write on coloured paper; he had found this very soothing. Imagine, he says, the heavy, ponderous quiet over a city asleep; only its breathing is heard like an open sluice miles away. It takes time; hours elapse, a seeming eternity; then the brute begins to stir, to wake up. Wasn't this rather promising?

And Milde thinks it very promising; he has made his peace with Ojen long ago. Milde is busy on his caricatures to "Norway's Dawn." He had really drawn a few very funny caricatures and made ruinous fun of the impossible poem.

Norem said nothing.

Suddenly Lars Paulsberg bobs up; with him is Gregersen. The group is growing; everybody takes notice; so much is gathered here in a very small space. Literature is in the ascendant; literature dominates the entire sidewalk. People turn back in order to get a good look at these six gentlemen in ulsters and great-coats. Milde also attracts attention; he has been able to afford an entirely new outfit. He says nothing about Australia now.

At two the life and traffic has risen to its high-water mark; movement everywhere, people promenade, drive in carriages, gossip; engines are breathing stertorously in the far distance. A steamer whistles in the harbour, another steamer answers with a hoarse blast; flags flutter, barges swim back and forth; sails rattle aloft and sails are furled. Here and there an anchor splashes; the anchor-chains tear out of the hawse-holes in a cloud of rust. The sounds mingle in a ponderous harmony which rolls in over the city like a jubilant chorus.

Tidemand's tar steamer was ready to weigh anchor. He had come down himself to see it off. Hanka was with him; they stood there quietly arm in arm. They glanced at each other every few moments with eyes that were filled with youth and happiness; the harbour saluted them with a swirl of flags. When the steamer at last was under way, Tidemand swung his hat in the air and Hanka waved with her handkerchief. Somebody on the ship waved back a greeting. The steamer slid quietly out into the fiord.

"Shall we go?" he asked.

And she clung to him closer, and said: "As you will."

Just then another steamer entered the harbour, an enormous leviathan from whose funnels smoke poured in billowy masses. Tidemand had goods aboard; he had been waiting for this steamer the last two days, and he said in great good humour:

"She is also bringing us goods!"

"Yes?" she answered quietly. But he felt, as she looked into his face, that a quivering joy shot through her being; her arm trembled in his.

And they went home.

Made in the USA
Columbia, SC
17 September 2024